BA'IR

Nikki Clarke

Cover Art: Alex Campbell

@alexdrawl

Follow and Get More Nikki

Lyqa Planet Lovers and Soulmates of Somii (in reading order):

 Kwarq: Lyqa Planet Lovers Series 1

 Bati: Lyqa Planet Lovers Series 2

 My Lyqa Valentine: Lyqa Planet Lovers Series 2.5

 Sol: Lyqa Planet Lovers Series 3

 My Alien Captor, Nyo: Soulmates of Somii Prequel 0.5

 Kyr: Soulmates of Somii 1

 Ah'dan: Lyqa Planet Lovers Series 4

 Qim: Lyqa Planet Lovers Series 5

 Something Lyqa Christmas

 Malcolm and Dinar: A Hosa Empire Love Story

Black Valley Wolves:

 Nothing but the Wolf in Me

 For My Wolves

 A Wolf Is a Wolf

* * *

Third Street Conjure Boys:
   Jinx: Third Street Conjure Boys
   Lure: Third Street Conjure Boys
   Abra: Third Street Conjure Boys

Black Girls Off World:
   My Alien Threshers
   My Alien Invader, Fi'r
   My Alien Thresher, Nial

Monarchs of Midaan:
   Gaad's Plan: Monarchs of Midaan Quickie
   My's Way: Monarchs of Midaan Quickie

Speculative Quickies:
   The Battle Prince's Prize Bride
   The Girl: Wake the Girl

Blooded and Bound:
   Taste: A Vampire Quickie
   Lick: A Vampire Quickie

Contemporary:
   If There's Still Time
   Tempting Mr. Reality
   Noora and Bilal Do (each other for) Christmas

Visit my website and join my mailing list for exclusive updates!
   www.nikkiclarkeromance.com

* * *

Join my Facebook Readers Group to chat with me and other Nikki Clarke readers!

To everyone who's been rocking with these
Legroes.

Content Warnings

Ba'ir is a second-chance, fated-mates alien romance with themes and references that may disturb some readers. Please review the content warnings below to decide whether to continue reading. This is not an exhaustive list.

- Kidnapping and enslavement
- Reference to violence against the FMC (no details)
- Scene leading to violence against the FMC (no details)
- References to the results of physical violence, including disfigurement
- Physical and mental trauma
- On-page graphic violence and murder
- References to gun violence
- Explicit, on-page sex
- Explicit human/non-human sex
- Aggression from the MMC toward the FMC

Fein Colony Twenty Rotations Ago

IVY

"Are you sure?"

Something shaky and foreboding fills my middle as I look over the large clay mountain. It's a behemoth of a hill, the sides caked with red mud that sags down like melted wax. Smoke billows from the cavernous mouth in thick golden spirals. It could be a path to the heavens if it weren't so scary.

"You are my *lehti.* I want to make you happy. If this will make you happy, let me do it." Ba'ir's deep brown eyes soften. Like the smoke, the honey center of his eyes draws me in, easing my tension but not dispelling it.

There are too many dark shadows lurking like spirits around the rocks and clay piled high across the planet's surface. It doesn't help that I keep imagining movement out of the corners of my eyes, only for there to be nothing but dust and crimson when I look.

Actually, fuck this place. I want to go home, but I hold my tongue because if being away from Earth has taught me anything, it's that I know nothing of the Universe.

Like every experience since Ba'ir brought me off-world, my first view of the mineral planet as we hovered in space above it was fascinating.

The surface seemed to crest and roll. The atmosphere swirled with thick, violet clouds. As we got closer, however, the jagged mountains became more ominous.

"Ba'ir, when I said my people usually give rings, I didn't mean we had to go to another planet to get one. We could just go to JCPenney or something."

"This is special, and you should have something special. I will let nothing happen to you. You should know this." He cradles my face with his big hand, and I'm reminded of how gently he made love to me earlier in the day.

He is the only person I've ever been with. We'd waded through the fumbling initial experience together, and after the intensity and fear lessened, I'd experienced a pleasure I didn't know was possible.

After our night together, he asked me to stay with him forever. That led me to joke that he was asking me to marry him, which in turn sparked a conversation about human mating customs and diamond rings, which ultimately led us to a far-off planet where Ba'ir claims the rarest stones in the Universe exist.

"I don't need special, and this looks dangerous. Are we supposed to go in there? What if it's occupied?"

He chuckles as he does every time I'm nervous about something too alien. Like when we walked to his home on Lyqa from the transport station the first night I arrived, and an animal—small, face like a weasel, covered in wiry fur that stuck in spirals from its dog-like body—had scampered across our path, stopping briefly to hiss at us. I'd screamed, my hands clawing at Ba'ir's shirt as I tried to climb his towering body to get away. He'd merely chuckled and picked me up, tucking my butt beneath his massive arm.

"I've got you, *lehti*." He'd side-stepped the little beast, which hissed again, making me flinch. "It is nothing, just a scavenger species. If it bites you, however, you will die unless we can get you to the healers in time."

I'd reared back, nearly tipping from his arms, only for him to catch me around the back with his other arm, another light chuckle escaping him.

"Are you serious?"

"Very much so," he'd hummed. "They are quite venomous, but it takes much to make them attack. Instances are extremely rare." And then he'd carried on like rabid, venomous dog-rodents roaming unchecked in the streets was nothing to worry about at all.

One thing I've realized about the big, beautiful Lyqa, who saved me from being trampled when some redneck let off shots into the air at a food festival in my hometown, is that he doesn't really take too much seriously.

Me?

I like to take it easy, but I'm not causing problems where there aren't none.

This place feels like a problem.

"If any are here, I am sure they are harmless. Lehti, it is not like on your world. No one owns this planet. No one owns any planet, and there are no customs that I must be mindful of. I checked." He hits me with his cockiest grin, one that flashes the top row of straight, white teeth, a little bigger than a human's. "There is nothing here to harm you; if there is, I will protect you. I promise."

The confidence of his declaration filters through the translation device he stuck behind my ear when he first took me to Lyqa. At first, watching his mouth move out of sync with the words I was hearing was a little weird, but I'm used to it now.

I'm also hopelessly in love with Ba'ir, and everything says to trust him.

"Okay, but if some wild animal comes crawling out of the darkness like before, I'm running. You're just gonna have to keep up."

He smirks and leans in to give me a hard kiss. "I love you, *lehti*. Everything will be fine..."

"GO!" Ba'ir's strangled shout makes my heart double beat in my chest.

I scream and duck when one of the tall, scaly monsters that flooded the tunnel where Ba'ir was attempting to dig out what was probably the largest stone I've ever seen in my life launches itself through the air toward us.

The diamond-like rock was lavender and sparkled like a million stars. In the cave's dark, it seemed to have trapped the only light, casting it across the red clay and illuminating the blank, waxen faces of the beings now trying to claw us to death.

The thing flying toward me has claws that shimmer with a metallic gleam, and for a split second, it occurs to me that women on Earth pay hundreds of dollars for a full set that nice. Unfortunately, the eyes that flash in glowing red slits reflect a sinister intent.

"Ivy, run! *Lehti*, please hurry!" Ba'ir shoves me from behind again, lifting me off my feet and pushing me several feet ahead.

I stumble but manage to keep my balance and continue running. I can hear the things scrambling behind us, their frantic pace triggering an answering rush of adrenaline throughout my body. Their screeches are as sharp as claws along my skin, and I flinch, my hands coming up to cover my ears as I cry out and force my legs to move faster.

I have to move faster.

My heart thumps hard behind my breastbone, a bass drum in my ears. I stare ahead to the pod in the distance and focus on putting one foot in front of the other, my arms pumping. My chest burns so severely that I worry I'm going to throw up again.

That would have been a perfect excuse not to come here. Why didn't I think to use being sick to stop Ba'ir from wanting to make this trip? It's not like I would have been exaggerating. I had vomited so long and so violently that I thought I was going to pass out, only for it to end as quickly as it started. I'd chalked it up to the alien feast they'd fed me the night before, but it felt like an omen of some kind. I should have listened to my gut.

And now we're going to die. The beautiful alien behind me is going to die.

The entrance to the ship is so close and yet so far. I run faster, even though I'm getting light-headed and my heart is about to explode.

Ba'ir is at my back; his feet catch my heels, and he grunts in fearful frustration.

I'm a track star. My coaches all say I have Olympic potential, but I know I'm slowing Ba'ir down. I've seen how fast he can move.

My feet leave the ground, and I'm launched forward, my

arms flailing a wild windmill as I hit the wall inside the ship. My head smacks into the metal; light dances before my eyes.

The door starts to close as I stumble toward the sound of Ba'ir's screams. Before I can reach it, the entrance seals shut, and the ship launches into the air.

Thresher Mission to Save A Lyqa Trapped by Fein Colony

FOLA BUSHIR (FORMER POP STAR AND MATE TO THE BUSHIR TRIPLETS)

"What is this place?"

I lean forward in the command deck like I'm actually looking out of the window, even though the screen is a projection of the ground below and not a visual of the space around us.

We're still in orbit above the smoldering red planet where our rescue, Ba'ir, is captive. Movement along the surface makes it appear to bubble and shift beneath the plumes of deep-ochre smoke rising from the volcanic mountains scattered across the landscape.

"Don't worry, Fola. That's only clay. This is a mineral planet. Planets like these sit mostly on the edge of the galaxies, where it's harder to access, and the miners can retain forced labor without repercussion." Syree moves his

7

hand, expanding the display so I can see the towering piles of sand.

It looks like a mine. Small figures move up and through the dunes.

"Are those people?"

"They are beings of various races, yes." Nial's voice is stern, and I know this is difficult for him.

"They couldn't just build machines to do the work? I thought you all were beyond manual labor."

Syree shakes his head. "This is a living planet. It would react to inorganic machinery, even nanos. But living beings would only be felt as symbiotic."

"So all those folks down there are captives?"

He nods, and I sigh. "I guess we're not just here to save Ba'ir, then. It's so weird that you have all of this technology, and you still feel compelled to follow the rules when it comes to stopping bad guys. I would have bum-rushed the hell out of this place."

"If there were no rules, then there would be more bad guys. We do what we can." Hail doesn't sound offended. It's clear he has accepted the way things are.

"Yeah, but twenty years? You're telling me no one could have rescued this guy in twenty years?"

"I'm telling you that Thresh acts on high-level diplomacy issues, and this one wasn't brought to our attention. This would have been considered a private matter for Lyqa or even his family. Often, these beings go missing without a record of their capture, so no one knows where to rescue them. According to the intel, they have tried numerous times to get this male out but have been unsuccessful, which makes me wonder how this has finally come to be assigned to us."

I look away, pretending to check something on the

display.

"Fola?"

Rolling my eyes, I turn back with a sigh. "Okay, so, maybe I was talking to one of my Lyqa friends the other day, and he mentioned this case and how they were going to appeal to the new Council to get a special assignment for it, and I might have volunteered."

They sigh in unison.

"Of course, you volunteered." Nial's jaw ticks in a way that's starting to be familiar when I try him too hard, which is basically always. "And you were going to come here alone? To attempt a rescue from a mining planet overrun with one of the most violent, ruthless, and merciless races of beings to exist."

I shrug. "I was going to do my best."

"Your best." His eyes seem to daze as he looks at me. "You were going to do your best against the Fein, who are so adept at subjugation that they make the slpoi that controlled my mind seem like the games of youth?"

"Hm," I tilt my head. "We call that child's play."

"I'm serious, Fola. You are *mine*, which means you don't take risks you don't have to, and you don't take missions alone that will get you captured and tortured in ways that will make you wish you were dead. But you won't be. You'll have to live with it, wondering when it will end, hoping you'll be put out of your misery by some fate."

"Hey, hey." I step close and take his arms, pulling him back from whatever void of memory he's falling into. "I was being a smart ass. I wasn't going to come alone, and I was always going to ask you all to come with me."

I lean up and press my lips to his, moving against his mouth until his muscles relax beneath my palms. His arms come around, holding me tight as he strokes his tongue against mine, leaving me breathless. "I'm not taking any risks that would take me away from you if I don't have to. I finally have you all, and I don't want that to end so soon. But I think we can do this."

Hail snorts. "Of course, we can, and I'm going to talk with Fi'r about why this wasn't on our radar sooner. There's no reason why this Lyqa has been languishing here for so long. But we need to devise a plan."

I press one more kiss to Nial's lips, sinking into it because he feels so good, before turning with a self-satisfied smile. "Actually, I already have a plan."

"Does this plan include bum-rushing this place?" Syree is mocking, but his expression shifts to horror when my grin widens.

"Funny thing. It does."

Hail and Syree sigh in unison, their displeasure clear, but Nial merely stares at the surface of the planet, his expression troubled.

I approach and rub a hand up his back, letting my fingers slide between the firm, muscular grooves. "Hey, if you want to sit this one out, I'll understand. I get that this might be triggering for you, and I'm sorry I didn't think about it before."

He gives a short smile and faces me, pulling me close once again. "I'm not triggered. I'm just thinking about how I never thought I'd be on this side again. I was no better than the Fein not too long ago. Worse, perhaps."

"Not you." I hug around his middle, breathing in his scent. I love the way he smells. "That wasn't you. This is you. You're a person who helps people and does the right thing. You're a hero, baby."

He hugs me back but doesn't acknowledge what I've said. After a moment, he palms my butt, giving a quick squeeze and pat. "Let's get you ready."

***

"I vote to send Fola back to the ship."

I cut my eyes at Syree, who's staring at the smoldering entrance to one of the mines with a glower.

The same opaque, yellow smoke billows out in rolling plumes, providing the perfect cover for us to break into the side wall of the main compound. My throat is thick with the taste of metal as I inhale the bitter fumes.

I swallow past it and force my voice to come out clear. "I'm senior on this mission, *mate*. Voting to send me back to the ship isn't a thing."

"I second."

I pivot my indignation on Hail before looking at Nial.

He watches me with an unreadable expression, but I can tell by the stirrings along the link that he's also considering it.

Narrowing my eyes, I dare him. He rolls his eyes like he couldn't care less about my threats.

"This is Fola's mission. It's not our decision to make. But —" he continues when I grin in triumph, "if there's even a moment when I think your life is in danger, I'm putting you in stasis until we're out of there. You can hate me later."

I rub a hand down his arm. "I'd never hate you, but you can't say that a Thresher fights or dies by the blade and not let that apply to me. That means you don't really see me as one of you."

Nial merely hums. "You can hate me later, but I'm not letting anything happen to you, Thresher or not." He doesn't look the least bit remorseful, and I want to feel some way about it, but I don't.

I've waited my whole life to feel treasured like this. "Fine, but I'm still in charge. I'm just asking that you give me a chance before you come in and swoop me off my feet. Plus, I hate that damn stasis field."

***

"Baby, you're amazing."

Syree looks back and smirks at my awed whisper.

When we get to the side of the compound, which is made of some gleaming, reflective metal that, despite the warm temperature of the planet, is cool to the touch, I pause, unsure of how we're going to get inside.

I imagined finding a side door and sneaking in, but Syree pulls a small, quarter-sized disc from his weapons belt and sticks it to the metal. A bright beam of light shoots out, cutting through the side of the building like a hot knife through butter.

As the laser completes its circle, I'm even more amazed when, instead of the hunk of detached metal falling inward, it disintegrates into dust and floats soundlessly away.

I look at Syree again and shake my head in wonder. "Damn, baby."

"It's a particle dismantling mechanism that uses air to —"

"Stop it." Nial slaps his brother on the arm with a roll of his eyes. "It is not as impressive as it looks. This is a rudimentary device. He thinks you will fuck him later if you are impressed."

I make a face when Syree shrugs like he had to try.

I'm still gonna fuck him, though. It's hot, no matter how rudimentary it is. And he knows it, which is why he winks at me before climbing through the hole.

Nial gestures for me to go next, but when I go to step in, he lifts me and hands me to Syree, who carries me over into the dark hall, ignoring my eye roll at them passing me off like I'm not a grown woman capable of using my feet.

I take the hilt of my standard Thresher sword from my belt when I'm on solid ground and trigger the blade. It springs up with a soft swish, and as Hail and Nial climb in behind me, I hear their blades release as well.

It wasn't too long ago that I didn't even know how to hold a blade correctly, and now look at me.

"We won't stay undetected for long. The way the Fein keep control of their captives is to overwhelm them. They replicate until the hive is nearly impenetrable. When we're confronted, we take each other's backs and stay close." Nial fixes me with a pointed look. "Stay. Close."

I raise my arms. "Why are you looking at me?"

He shifts his gaze away and moves ahead to stand shoulder-to-shoulder with Syree.

Despite the impending danger, warm pleasure blossoms in my chest. I love seeing them like this.

Once they got over their crap, they fell into sync like it was nothing, and they've been like three peas in a pod.

Three hot Threshers in my bed every night.

Three hot Threshers taking turns—

Nial starts down the hall, snapping me out of my fantasy. His steps are measured and confident. A low hum emanates from ahead where the corridor turns, and a cast of light cuts through the dimness of the hall.

As we get to the bend, Nial turns just enough to glance over his shoulder. *"Don't hesitate. Take the first head you see— nothing below the neck. Don't stop until we've cleared the swarm. If you get tired—"*

"I'll be fine," I respond because I know he's talking to me.

Nial goes quiet at my declaration, but exchanges a look with Hail and Syree that doesn't need to be broadcast.

If I even look like I'm breathing heavily, it's stasis for me.

The entire time he speaks, Nial never stops walking, so that we turn the corner together to confront the eerily still forms of what looks like a hundred tall, lanky, pale beings.

Their slight bodies are covered in reflective scales, and the place where their faces should be is so nondescript they're almost a blur. There's nothing to distinguish gender, as far as I can tell. They're just *beings*.

In a uniformity that rivals the way the triplets seem to, at times, move and think as one, the Fein shift to face us, and a beat barely passes before they rush forward.

A surge of adrenaline floods my body, spreading from the middle of my stomach up and out through my limbs. It's like tiny bolts of electricity igniting my cells, and I tighten my hands on the hilt of my sword.

The last time I was in a situation like this, Hail and Syree were fighting an entire port of mercenaries, and I was left hovering fifty feet above them, watching from the nauseating protection of a stasis field.

At the time, it had been like my life before my hearing was corrected, my eyes tracking every silent slash of their blades, every bright beam of a blaster with wide, frightened eyes—a mesmerizing, soundless performance of death.

Now, it's similarly quiet. Nial and Syree take the heads of six Fein a piece without a word or heavy breath, and before one even manages to make it past them and get close enough for me to swing out and slice through its neck.

The thing slumps to the floor mid-step, its head rolling to hit my boots, the body twitching violently beside it.

It's the first time I've killed something. I pause for the briefest second just as another Fein charges from my left, its teeth bared in a jagged grimace.

"Fola!" My name cuts through the eerie quiet as Nial spins and decapitates the approaching Fein. "No hesitation, or —"

"Stasis, I know. Sorry." I mumble as I strike out at another Fein. It falls like the others, and then my body switches to autopilot, the kill mode activation triggered as I strike out left and right, stabbing through skulls when I need to, and using my foot to dislodge the limp bodies before moving on with the triplets.

It takes longer than I expect before Hail slices through the last of the horde, and we stand in a circle, our backs to each other. The floor is littered with bodies. The ground looks alive with their twitching corpses.

Hail takes me by the elbow and pulls me along as Nial and Syree start to move through to the next part of the compound.

"They won't stay down for long. We have to hurry and find the hive leader." We run through the halls, Syree throwing small disks at the intersecting corridors we pass, which eject wavy stasis fields that block the oncoming Fein.

The few who get through before the fields can be erected are quickly dispatched by Nial, who fights with almost beautiful efficiency. Unlike his brothers, he forgoes the flair of Syree's flourishing decapitations and the grotesque finality of Hail's cleave-in-two technique.

Nail is like a machine, his reflexes sharp and accurate as he seems to sense his targets before they appear, swinging without looking, his body relaxed and fluent as he evades our enemy's clawed talons and sharp teeth.

I don't realize I've stopped, that I'm staring, slack-jawed, at how his broad back shifts and flexes until I hear my name being called again. This time, Hail shoves me out of the way just as a Fein appears from the shadows at my right, swiping out with his claws and catching my Thresher on his side.

Hail hisses and twists away, but not fast enough to avoid the other hand coming for him. I quickly get it together and intercept, lobbing the thing's head off before it can touch my man.

"Fola!" The word is tight, and I slap my palms together in apology.

"I know. I know. But I've never seen him fight before. He's—amazing." If my eyes could go dreamy, I bet that's what they look like.

Hail groans in annoyance and pulls me along after his brothers.

After that, Syree runs out of field disks, and we have to take another wave. To their credit, the boys stay at my back, close enough to intervene if they feel it's needed, but giving me space to do my thing.

I remain near Hail, aggravated at myself that he got hurt because of me. Of course, I can't tell as he cuts through bodies with ease, never faltering and never giving any indication that his wound is bothering him.

We've come to the end of the hall, and I can see the entrance to an open space up ahead.

"Nearly there." Syree twists to meet my gaze. His eyes narrow, and I think the look is a warning, but then he suddenly pivots and comes back, grabbing me around the waist and smashing his lips to mine in a swift kiss.

"You were amazing, and I'm going to bury my dick so deep inside of you the moment we are out of here, but don't make me—"

"Use the stasis. I got it. Geez." Playfully, I shove him away, and we step into the large central hall, where we finally come upon the hive's center.

Every Fein we've fought so far is connected through a web, like my link with the triplets, except this web keeps brain function active even after mortal wounds.

We no longer have the element of surprise, so when I see an opening leading toward the center of the room, I don't wait to take it. I break away from the triplets before they can stop me or activate the stasis field and make a beeline through the gap.

"You three cover me!"

"Fola—hu'l!"

Nial's warning, or more likely threat, is cut off when I run my blade through the Fein standing guard at the base of the throne where the hive leader is seated, triggering the other Fein into action and drawing his attention back to the fight.

I didn't have time to do too much research when I took this mission, but from what the triplets told me, the Fein's entire structural stability is reliant on the being staring down at me with an expression that in no way acknowledges that I have a blade sticking out of the head of one of its colony.

I pull my sword out, pushing the Fein's body aside.

"Fola, get back here!" Hail's voice is strained as he fights off the Fein who flood the room behind us.

I don't risk a glance back, trusting they can handle what's happening, because all my focus is on the head Fein.

* * *

MEANWHILE IN THE ROOM WHERE THE FEIN HOLD THE CAPTIVES...

BA'IR

Something is different.

All around us, the Fein scramble toward the main hall in a flurry of screeches and scaled skin.

I, along with the other captives, stare in confused shock as we're left alone.

In my time being held by the Fein, we have never been left alone. The closest has been when they occasionally go dormant, falling into a sleep-like state, but even then, they are easily roused.

A painful scream sounds from the corridor leading to the main hall, and instinctively, I step forward, my heart thumping.

"Don't." One of the other captives, an Orshka, calls out when I would go toward the hall. After nearly ten rotations, I still don't know his name, but we have shared commiserating looks over our time together.

I turn back and meet his gaze, or rather, the single eye he has left.

One of our captors caught him winking at a female who was kept here for a time and thought it was a signal of rebellion. They tore the Orhska's eye out with their claws and ate it.

I stare into the jagged hole where the Orshka's eye should be and down at my mangled arms. With a shrug, I continue forward. "There's nothing more they can do to me, but if there's a chance of escape, I will take it."

The screams of my captors continue to draw me further down the hall, my steps emboldened by the fact that I have not been stopped. No one has come to rip out a chunk of my flesh for daring to attempt an escape.

When I finally enter the great hall from a partially hidden walkway, I am already salivating in anticipation of savoring the gore that meets me.

Dismembered Fein are scattered about the room, being dispatched with almost graceful efficiency by a trio of Threshers. I never met a Thresher before my captivity, but I recognized their deadly skill immediately.

With every *swish* of their blades, a satisfied tingle travels down my spine, lulling me into such a sated trance of retribution that by the time I see the dais where the Fein hive leader sits, I barely register the small being approaching them with a long blade gripped tightly in her hands.

"I'm looking for someone—Lyqa, probably gorgeous. Goes by Ba'ir."

I freeze.

She is human.

I focus on the face of the woman standing before the Fein leader, and an old memory takes over. It holds the same brown skin and beautiful eyes. The hair is different, but who knows what has changed in the past twenty turns? There are similarities to the voice—light but rich.

It's *her.*

She doesn't see me, but the Fein feels my presence, and their face registers satisfaction. It curls along the thread of control they have over me.

The Fein nods, triggering my legs to move closer. I try to resist, a sudden shame coming over me at what the woman will see when she notices me, but I have no control, and the shuffling drag of my feet draws her attention.

Her gaze moves from my shackled feet up my exposed chest to my face, which is mostly shadowed by my mass of curled hair. I keep my head low, but because I am so much taller, I can see the moment her expression settles in horror before shifting to a tight rage. She faces the Fein again, raising her blade, and rushes up the stairs, removing its head in a swift arc of the sword.

The moment the Fein is dead, I realize the woman is not who I thought.

She hurries over, her face a mask of concern, to break my chains—a precaution that was mainly symbolic—freeing me for the first time in twenty rotations.

"Hey. Ba'ir? Is that your name?"

I nod, still too stunned to believe that after all of this time, all it took was the blade of this small, human woman to free me. I look over her shoulder to where the Fein's head rests on the floor, their razor-filled mouth gaping wide.

So many times, I dreamed of this moment, but they were always dreams I would awaken from to the renewed horror of my captivity.

The Threshers and the woman take me to their ship, where I perch awkwardly in one of the seats while the woman, who appears to be the leader, prepares to depart.

The Threshers, who are triplets, move about, tending their wounds and alternating between teasing, scolding, and touching the woman in a way that makes it clear she belongs to them. They love her. Even with their small touches, they honor her.

My rescuer busies herself with preparing the ship, but I

feel her eyes sliding over to where I sit as she checks random outputs on the ship's control panel. She tries to stop, but her gaze strays back, hovering over my face, discomfort evident in the pained tilt of her brows.

"Sorry." She blinks and looks away. The skin of her ears tints lightly when she realizes she's been staring.

"Thank you for saving me." My voice is harsh from damage to my throat caused by the impure air of the mines and scarring, and I attempt to clear it.

One of the Threshers approaches with a water pouch and a medi-pen. It's a new design, much more sophisticated than what was available when I was younger. His gaze holds sympathy, an emotion I'd almost forgotten the look of. "There is no thanks needed. I'm sorry it wasn't sooner. If you let me, I can heal the more superficial of your wounds. The deeper scars can be corrected once we reach your home. This shot will also replenish any vital nutrients you are missing."

I look up then, revealing my face fully for the first time, and the woman gasps, the breath catching before emotion wells in her eyes.

She saved me. I will allow her pity, but that is all. "I will take the replenishment, but the reconstruction is unnecessary."

The Thresher frowns. "I am not sure what technology on Lyqa was like when you were taken, but all of what has happened to you can be remedied without pain. This is an easy fix." He glances at his brothers and mate in confusion before moving toward my neck to administer the shot.

Half a life of being on edge rises in me, and I react, jerking to the side and baring my teeth in a way that surely makes me appear like an animal before I manage to contain myself. Calming, I attempt again to make my wishes known. "The replenishment only, please. I've had no choice in my fate for a long time. Please give me this."

"Do as he says, Syree." The Thresher closest to the woman intercepts. He's moved in front of her. It's a subtle shift, but I see it. He seeks to protect her from me as a good mate should. When I meet his gaze, there is something in his eyes, and his voice holds a knowing that has his brother nodding.

"Of course." Syree taps his comm band.

I'm flooded with a tremendous rush when he presses the pen to my neck. My eyes, which were tight, gloss over with lubrication, and my vision clears. The lingering strain in my chest from inhaling the clay-clouded air for all of these rotations releases, and I feel almost Lyqa.

That the deep breath I take doesn't burn is its own relief, even as a twinge in my side accompanies it. I meet the Thresher's gaze. "Thank you."

He nods and steps away, going over to his station.

The one who supported my decision not to be renewed comes to stand over me. In his eyes, I can see the shadows of the suffering I've endured. "Do you wish to go home? If not, we will take you wherever you wish to go. You owe us nothing, and we require no explanation."

I stare back, thoughtful, but I know the answer.

It's what I thought about every day I was captive of the Fein. It's what kept me going when I would rather have died. "I'd like to go to Earth. I'd like to find the one who betrayed me and got me held in captivity for twenty rotations. I'd like to find my *lehti*."

3

BA'IR

"I see that your last work experience was some time ago. Can you tell me what caused the lapse in employment?"

The human male assessing me for the position at a lifestyle market on Earth looks up from the manufactured "resume" I created in my pod. The craft model the Threshers provided me with is modern, bordering on luxurious. It has been my home as I've acclimated to technological updates throughout the Greater Universe and plotted my course of action against the lehti who betrayed me.

Obtaining this job is the first step, and since my memory is often unpredictable as a result of my torture, I have kept most of the details of my previous experience vague but close to the truth.

Meeting the man's gaze, I force myself to look into his eyes after twenty rotations with my head bowed. "As you can see, I endured some physical hardships for a time. They kept me from participating in society. I am now stronger and looking to find my place again."

I swallow around the reference to my freedom. I'm still unused to it.

After so many years as part of a captive society run by a psychotic and ruthless hive of beings, freedom feels tenuous, like a dream or illusion. At times, a flicker of shadow in the corner of my eye convinces me it's the Fein.

Those tormentors may be gone, but the one who cast me into purgatory is not. She's *here*.

"Well, although you didn't disclose, as is your right, we thank you for your service, and we're happy to have you join us. I know something about the things we lose in war." My interviewer lifts his pant leg to show the bar of a metal appendage. It seems he lost his limb during combat and assumes my injuries are of the same source.

I should correct him, but I don't. I gather his assumption is based on the need for solidarity, and as someone alone for longer than I want to recognize, I understand.

"Thank you for the opportunity. I will do my best."

The man shrugs. "No problem. Let me know if you need anything else. I know a few places that have great resources for veterans."

"I need nothing else." While I won't correct the man's mistaken belief that I was wounded in combat, I also won't take resources away from those who were.

He nods. "Well, Karen will get you settled once your paperwork is completed. She'll get you your uniform shirt, too. We wear it with khakis or black pants, but if you need time to get those things, you just wear what you have."

He is being very generous, and when I stand and take his extended hand, stilling the urge to flinch away as our palms make contact, he smiles and shakes his head. "You sure are a big dude," he chuckles. "I think you'll fit in just fine."

***

"Jesus." The horrified whisper of the woman, Karen, who is gathering the uniform I am meant to wear, doesn't faze me.

At one point, many rotations ago, when I was still mostly a youngling, having someone look at me and call upon their deity would have bothered me, but I have long lost any sense of caring.

At least when it comes to how I look.

I know what I look like.

Not only am I keenly aware of every jagged etch and groove. I can remember, like it was only a turn ago, how they were made with claws and teeth, sometimes broken metal and stone.

The worst of the damage was done with blunt weapons, digging into my flesh until the skin finally broke. Those wounds took spans, and for the moments when I was conscious, they were agonizing.

"So, here is your T-shirt. The largest we have is a triple-X, but it should fit. It might be a bit short." She turns back, holding a dark blue tunic, and her gaze trails from my feet up my body, stopping short of my face.

In the few months I've been on Earth, most humans who see me, after an initial glimpse, avoid my face.

When aimlessly walking the streets as I often do, they avoid me altogether, moving to the other side of the road or huddling into the shelter of buildings until I pass. As if they think the violence that brought on my appearance was transferred to me with the scars, and I might lash out at any moment.

Their behavior serves me more than offends. If no one is

25

looking closely, I am less likely to be discovered or recognized. Not that I am recognized readily as Lyqa or human. In this way, my scars are a blessing.

Still, Karen's blatant lack of empathy or regard for the fact that I can hear her expressing her distaste makes me snatch the shirt from her hands.

She recoils with a curl of her nose. "Once you're changed, find Roger, and he'll show you where to go."

"That's fine," my mumbled reply meets her back as she exits the small changing room, her shoulders shuddering.

I turn toward the narrow cubicle where I have been instructed to leave my belongings and pull my top over my head, tossing it inside. In the same way the woman jerked her shoulders in disgust, mine twitch as a searing burn travels along my shoulder blades when the air touches my skin.

A grave sensitivity to the lightest touch is another gift from my time with the Fein. Many of the objects used to inflict my torment left particles beneath my skin that cause me constant, nearly unbearable pain. It's a discomfort that I've come to live with.

I shake out the new shirt and shove my arms in, wincing when the poorly sealed skin across my sides and arms stretches.

I'm just tucking my head inside when a startled gasp halts all movement, and I still.

The slight sound is sucked back before it even finds its wind, but I would know the issuer anywhere. It's the same sound she made when I entered her during our first fumbled joining.

We were both inexperienced, and I'd moved too quickly. The stretch of her taking me made her draw a sharp breath, followed by a cry that still echoes through my mind, as do the moans that eventually followed.

"Oh, I'm sorry. I didn't know anyone was in here. I—" She pauses, and I can feel her gaze traveling over my back, which is exposed and objectively worse than my face if that is possible. "Do you need help?"

A bolt of electricity slices through my brain, and I'm transported back to when the Fein dragged me onto the jagged clay rocks. I'd watched the pod lift higher and higher, convinced until the moment it blinked out of sight that it would lower and save me.

The pain in those first turns was unbearable. It rended my mind as much as my flesh while I held to the belief that Ivy would return. She'd gone to get help. She was a human, unable to rescue me herself.

But after rotations and rotations of captivity, I had to accept that she wasn't coming back. My need to believe she would return was just a vain attempt to keep faith in the leht —which was also a lie. If the leht had been real, if it were more than an inconvenient biological trigger, it would have saved me.

I've waited so long to see the woman of my useless First heart again, to look into her eyes and ask the questions seared into my brain—Why did you close the door? Why did you leave me to a fate that made death seem a mercy?

I should turn and make her see what she did to me. I should confront her the way I imagined doing so many times when I was being tortured. Then, the only escape was the corner of my mind where I made Ivy pay for betraying me.

In that place, she was being ripped apart, not *me*.

"I'm fine." I keep my back turned, expecting her to leave, but I can hear her heart beating.

I can *feel* it.

My own First heart thumps in tandem, and I wonder if she'll notice even though it didn't skip the way it should have when she appeared.

That part of me is long dead.

Now, my connection to the muscle in Ivy's chest is just an automatic function, an unintentional curse. The strength I gained from my First heart is what kept me from dying when others would have perished—when all I wanted was to perish. There is no joy associated with its beat.

"What did you say?" The voice is different—huskier and more mature. There's a tremor in it, and I wonder if she recognizes me. Did I just trigger some long-buried memory, or is it fear I hear at the thought that her transgressions may be coming back to find her?

It's unlikely she recognizes my voice since my vocal cords were damaged along with the rest of me. When I speak, it's little more than a growl.

I snort softly and pull the shirt down to cover my back.

She probably wouldn't remember what I sound like anyway. From what I can tell, she's gone on with her life, never thinking about me, never trying to have me rescued. If the tracker in my comm bracelet hadn't let my fathers know where I was, there probably never would have been attempts to extricate me from my captivity.

That's something else I cannot forgive—that she ran like a coward and didn't even have the decency to charge someone else with my rescue.

I want her to see my reality. I need her to know what she did. I need her to see my hatred of her in the grooves marked across my skin.

Slowly, I pivot to face the door, my gaze lowered until

the final moment before I focus on the woman standing with wide eyes just inside the threshold.

My own eyes widen as everything in me *lurches*. The room sways, like reality itself is bending, then rights itself until she's all I can see.

I step back, suppressing a groan when my back meets the locker, but using the pain to subdue the sensations threatening to overthrow my disdain and make me run to her. I shouldn't be responding this way, but the sight of Ivy after twenty rotations stirs something in me that I thought long deceased.

I need it dead.

I need it beneath the ground, rotting and putrid, and yet…I take her in like my first breath of fresh air after leaving the Fein.

She's changed so much.

I wish I could say that the twenty rotations between the last time we saw each other have left her as physically altered as I am, but the beauty that mesmerized me before my first heart even thumped a beat has only blossomed.

We weren't long in our maturity when we first were leht.

It doesn't happen often that my kind is bound to someone when they are just in adulthood. But while I visited Earth with my parents for a renowned food celebration in Ivy's hometown, I'd seen her through the crowd and knew she was meant to be mine.

She'd been laughing, her teeth encased in a metal wiring meant to correct a misalignment that she thought made her less attractive.

I would have taken her just as she was, with no enhancements or modifications, no corrections of perceived flaws.

She was perfect.

And though another sharp pain lances through my head as my mind tries to reject the truth of it, she still is. She's so perfect that for a moment, I nearly forget my pledge for vengeance.

My gaze is hungry as it takes in the changes. Her skin is still a creamy, warm brown, leaner in a face that shows maturity while still appearing youthful. Her hair still hangs around her shoulders, but is styled in loose waves, half of it clipped out of her face at the crown of her head. Everything else is the same—angled eyes, fringed with heavy lashes, a round nose, and full lips that rest in a naturally sensual pucker. She did things to enhance her features when we knew each other before, coloring her lips and eyelids. The skin of the woman facing me is bare.

She's also shorter than I remember, but other parts of her are curved with maturity. Her chest, which she bemoaned as being too slight when we first joined, is fuller. The mounds are enticing enough that my gaze lingers, wondering how they would feel in my hands.

Beneath her uniform, her belly is soft. Her hips flare wide, but she still possesses the athleticism that earned her a merit award to attend a higher learning institution. She had been so excited about her "track scholarship."

She'd also worried that I wouldn't want to stay on Earth while she completed her studies. She'd been set on becoming a dentist.

I told her then I would stay wherever she was, and I meant it. She'd said many things as well. None of which turned out to be true.

She stares at me now, her expression devoid of the

disgust that usually appears on others' faces.

Those looks I can bear. Hers makes anger, molten and dripping, roll through my gut, colliding with the lust that has me staggered.

She looks sad for me, pitying even. Her mouth opens like she wants to speak, but closes just as quickly. Will she tell me how sorry she is that I look this way? Will she ask what happened and try to comfort me?

I save her the trouble.

"Take a picture. It will last you longer." These were words said to me long ago, the first time I saw her and couldn't look away.

She blinks, backing away. "I didn't mean to stare. I'm sorry."

Sorry.

A useless word coming from her. I turn my back, ignoring the thing inside of me that wants to look at her one more time. We aren't bound in that way, I remind myself. Any love I had for this woman died in the dust-filled mines of that planet, choking on a throat full of blood and red earth.

"Roger asked me to show you around and get you set up with your post."

"Then let us get set up." When I turn this time, I avoid her gaze and follow as she leads me from the room.

My stomach tingles as I watch Ivy's hips sway, and I lie to myself that it's deserved excitement that my plan for revenge is in sight. She doesn't recognize me, and she'll never see my retribution coming.

She takes me into a room filled with pallets topped with boxes. "This is where you'll start. Your job is pretty easy. You just move the stock to the shelves where it goes. There's a guide to show you. Everything is labeled. Here, I'll get you started." She walks over to a pallet piled high with boxes and grabs the lever to pull it along. I can tell the weight is significant from the way her knees brace slightly to gain momentum. My body reacts without conscious effort, and I rush forward to take it from her as she strains under the burden.

"You should not be pulling things so heavy." I grab the handle, anger making me jerk it from her hands so that she stumbles forward, and when she reaches to steady herself, I move out of the way. "Don't touch me."

It's a growl. She avoids using me as a brace and manages to right herself.

"I'm sorry." Her eyes are cautious but kind as she watches me. "Does it hurt to be touched?"

"I don't want *your* hands on me."

She sucks in a breath, and I worry that the emphasis might have given me away, but then she nods and steps to the side.

"I can show you where to put that." She turns and leaves the storage room, and I follow her to one of the aisles where another employee is unpacking a pallet and putting the items on the shelves. "This is Elliott. He stocks, too, so you two will probably work together a lot. Elliott, this is—" She looks to me in question.

"DaQuan." I cannot stop the challenging rise of my brows, but her expression remains blank.

She shifts back to Elliott. "Do you mind showing DaQuan the ropes? I told Aliyah I'd cover her shift in media."

Elliott snorts and straightens. "Damn, girl. You're always up in someone's department doing something. You might as well have taken the management position they've been offering you for the past fifteen years."

Ivy smiles, but I detect the hint of embarrassment that colors her ears. "I couldn't be on call like that. If I need a day off, I have to be able to take it."

Elliott snorts again. "Says the woman who never takes a day off and only works in doubles. Okay." He waves a hand to usher her away. "Go'on ahead. I got this."

Ivy's gaze lingers for a long moment before she walks to the end of the aisle and disappears.

"Man, that girl is going to drop dead from exhaustion one day." Elliott's comment draws my attention, and I feel my lip curl against the scars tracing my mouth.

"It could be hoped." The poison-laced words turn to nausea in my belly. My chest pinches, and I shake my arm to ward off the numbness spreading upward from my fingers.

Elliott frowns, his expression confused, like he wonders if he misheard me. "Uh, let me show you what we're supposed to do." He waves me toward the open box he's working from, his expression still wary. "So you just take the product out and put it on the shelf that matches the product code for what's in the box. It's not rocket science."

"I would understand it if it were." I was in my second year of such study when the Fein took me. In all likelihood, I would be a leader in my field if my life had gone as it should.

Another thing Ivy took from me.

Elliott cackles, slapping my back with a weighty hand. I grunt around the pain. "You're funny. I'm glad cause the last guy I worked with was boring as hell." He leans in to speak in confidence, and the easy familiarity with which he's taken to me is confounding. He has not looked twice at my scars. "I'm in college right now to be an electrician. Shit's hard, but it's kinda fun, too, you know? Not rocket science, but..."

"The knowledge around electrical systems is very

sophisticated. It is an impressive path."

His expression shifts to pride as he smiles widely. "Damn. Thanks! I'm excited about it."

I nod and begin awkwardly removing items from the boxes and placing them as he's instructed. I haven't had a casual conversation with another being in a long while, but I find myself relaxing as Elliott shows me the procedure for stocking the store.

He also talks—a lot. Mostly about his path of study, an occurrence he didn't believe would be possible for him based on the prospects of his background. Apparently, he and a young woman he fell in love with conceived a child while they were both in their foundational years, an occurrence that created great financial difficulty for them both.

"Sixteen, and it was crazy. We didn't know what the hell we were doing, and kids are expensive, man. Everything costs something, and to make money, you gotta pay someone to watch them. It's hard, but we figured it out. It took a while. If we hadn't slipped up, I'd be done by now. She really wanted to be a dentist, though. That's her dream, so I hustled for a few years until she could finish dental hygienist school and get an undergrad degree. Now, she makes good money, so we can pay for daycare while I start working on my career. Really, all of this is for our little girl, you know?" He peeks at me from the side, and I detect the scent of emotion on him. His eyes shine with it, although he blinks it away. Clearing his throat, he picks up another box and places it on the shelf. "You got any kids?"

"I do not."

"Hm. Well, I don't want to overstep, but you got a good look even if your face is messed up. You're tall, built. Women like that shit. Some girl is going to fall for you if women are your thing."

"They are, but I have no interest in finding a partner." Even if I did not look the way I do, any trust I could have for a potential lover is shattered.

"Hm, well, I saw Ivy looking, and I've never seen her look at anyone."

I dismiss the secret thrill his words cause, knowing it is only the remnants of the leht that want to be pleased with the idea that she may still find me desirable, and continue our work, moving quickly. "I am sure she was merely gawking like everyone else."

He makes a face and shakes his head. "Nah, Ivy's not like that. That woman has more empathy than the world combined. She's a saint. My life would be in shambles if it weren't for her."

"How do you mean?" I don't really care about this man's misconception of Ivy's character, but I am also curious to know how she has managed to mislead him, since there is no doubt in my mind that she has.

"I met her when I started working here. That was a minute ago, back when I was in high school. We used to talk and stuff, and I told her about how my girl was pregnant, and we kind of felt like we'd messed up our lives. Man, she told us everything to do. What programs we could get on to get assistance while we got it together. When she found out my girl wanted to be a dentist, she basically walked her through the plan to get into a program since that's what she wanted to do at one point. For a while, she changed her schedule so she could watch our kid and we could work. She's been amazing, and she's like that with everyone."

I snort. "Impossible."

"Nah, really."

I refrain from trying to convince him that the woman he admires so much is an impostor. He'll learn soon enough. Hopefully, not before it's too late, like it was for me.

"Why did she not become a dentist as planned?" The question springs from deep inside a corner of my mind where I once cared. It annoys me, but I tell myself that any information that will help me get revenge on Ivy is useful.

Elliott shrugs. "Life. She doesn't really talk about it. Just said things changed."

"I am sure her life has been very difficult."

Again, Elliott stares in confusion at the vehemence in my tone but doesn't remark on it. After this, I ask no more questions about Ivy, and we complete our work in silence.

When it comes time to take a break, Elliott slaps a hand on my back. "Damn, dude. You're fast. We almost stocked everything for the day."

I make a sound of agreement as we walk toward the break room, my body flinching at the sharp clap. Before we even reach the room, where I can hear several animated voices sounding from the open door, I smell her.

The smell is the same—light and delicate. It carries other notes, which are sour and acrid. Probably the deceit seeping from her pores.

Ivy's laughing as she speaks to another worker, her hand suspended at her mouth. Between her fingers, she holds two long sticks, which she uses to grip some kind of food roll.

"But, sushi? That must have been like six bucks a roll! Did you win the lottery or something?" Another worker taunts her, and she rolls her eyes and throws a napkin at him.

Beneath her brown skin, she reddens, but only I can see it. She's embarrassed, but why? She has spent twenty rotations enjoying the pleasures of edible food. If I were to describe what I was forced to eat while with the Fein, it would turn the stomachs of everyone in the room.

"Shut up. It's only this one time. I'm kind of celebrating."

"Woooow! You're celebrating? Who are you, and what have you done with our frugal, fun-less friend?"

"Excuse me." Another employee comes in, forcing me to move into the room, which draws the attention of Ivy and the others.

As expected, most of the people react with shock.

The male who was speaking to Ivy drops the piece of food he was eating and pushes it away with a grimace. "Appetite lost, fuck."

"Chris!" Ivy admonishes, the mirth of a moment ago vanishing as she glares at the younger man. "Abso-fucking-lutely not."

The word is final and imparts the shame she intends. The male lowers his gaze before glancing up at me. "Sorry, man."

I say nothing. I need neither the pity nor the empathy of anyone in this place, least of all the woman looking at me with kind, apologetic eyes.

"Hey, do you want to sit? I've got some extra sushi if you want some."

"He looks like sushi," another woman with a surly expression and a scent tinged with bitterness—a look and smell I imagine follow me as well—mumbles as she walks out of the room, making it a point to throw her half-eaten meal in the garbage on her way out.

"Hey, fuck you, Patrice!" Ivy shouts after her.

The woman pauses only long enough to raise her hand, the middle finger extended.

Ivy sucks her teeth and stands, coming over to grab my

arm and pull me toward the table where she was taking her meal.

Caught off guard by the contact, I go with her, letting her push me down into the seat just to her left. It isn't until she releases me that I remember that I don't want her hands on me ever. Still, warmth hovers between the sleeve of my shirt and my skin where her hand rested.

"She's so ignorant. I knew she was going to be rude." Ivy stabs at the circular sushi and drops it onto a napkin in front of me. "Here. Try this. It's avocado."

I stare at the offering, everything in me rebelling at the thought of sharing a meal with her. And yet, I lift one of the pieces with my fingers, the rough scars on my hand coming into view.

She watches me expectantly, her eyes wide, as I bring the food to my mouth. At the moment I push the segmented roll between my lips, she sucks in a soft breath and holds it.

I chew slowly, testing the textures. After rotations of waste being masked as food, and only enough to keep me alive so that I could work and be tortured more, my mouth is almost confused by the salty, soft, savory maelstrom.

The bouncy beads surrounding the roll bring a particular delight, and I begin to chew too quickly, savoring the feel of them compressing between my teeth. I swallow, and the feeling is gone too soon.

This is delicious.

There is another in front of me. This one is slightly different, and I eye it warily, inspecting the bright bits wedged into the fold.

"It's carrots, spinach, and asparagus." My gaze jumps to Ivy, her brows raised in encouragement.

The temptation is a swirl of flutters in my stomach, and I

yank my hand into my lap, fisting it so tight that the scars stretch in stinging pain. "I do not want it."

"Oh." Ivy seems disappointed, but then her mouth sets in a way that I remember from our time together. She will be stubborn about this, but I am a different male now.

I don't care.

Ivy pushes the napkin closer. "Just try it. You might like it."

"Is there a part of 'I do not want it' that you do not understand?" The words are tight and stabbing. It's a petty retribution, but I savor it as an accoutrement to the treat she shared. Being this close to the woman who betrayed me leaves little room for simple enjoyment.

"Hey. She's just trying to be nice." Ivy's younger companion extends an arm before me as if he expects me to attack her.

I wish I could.

I should.

"It's okay. Have you ever had sushi before?" Ivy picks up her sticks and relieves me of the roll, popping it easily into her mouth, though I catch the tremor in her hand. "I don't get it to have it much, but it's good."

The inflection of her voice is high and unnatural, and my eyes narrow when I catch the sting of her hurt on my nose.

I still don't care.

Let her be hurt that I didn't like her food.

"Unfortunately, the place where I came from didn't have such luxuries as *sushi*—or food often."

Ivy's eyes shine even brighter as we watch each other.

"Damn, dude. Where'd you come from, a third-world country or something?"

Ivy clears her throat at her companion's interjection and

looks away. The sticks she was using to eat clatter to the table, and she pushes the tray, still laden with the intricate rolls, across to the man. "Here. You can have it. I'm full."

"For real? Thanks!" He stuffs piece after piece of the sushi into his mouth, never noticing how Ivy looks at the food with longing.

Luxuries.

Things I would have gladly given her if she had been loyal, but now I know she never deserved it. And yet, my First heart clenches briefly, a painful twinge at her sorrow.

"Where's the new guy?" A voice I have never heard booms from the corridor, and I turn, stiffening at the note of threat. A large human male with stringy hair hanging about his ears storms into the room, his gaze finding me almost immediately. "Who the hell told you to stock the aisles? Eggs were sitting in the back for the past four hours!"

He marches up to where I sit, and on instinct, I rise to tower over him.

To his credit, he doesn't shrink back.

"Well?" His voice rises, and I can smell from the apprehension and annoyance scenting the room that he uses this tactic to get those beneath him to do his bidding.

One thing about being held captive and tortured. A little yelling doesn't fluster me.

Instead, I look for some indignation to aim at him—he is being rude and unnecessarily antagonizing—but discover that the only rage I can find is toward the woman rising from her seat across from me. She is probably all too ready to absolve herself and blame me, to throw me to the merciless once again.

This surety fuels my reaction as I speak before she can. "This woman told me to work in the aisles. If there is fault, it is hers."

The man shifts his gaze to Ivy, and the scorn only increases.

She clears her throat, her tone placating when she speaks. "I was just going to say that I was the one who told him where to go. That was my mistake."

"Why are you telling anyone to do anything? You're not the manager, *Ivy*, remember? Stay in your lane! I'm writing you up." He storms away without another word, and the following silence feels like a metaphorical dagger in my back.

Better metaphorical than literal. Literal daggers bleed and leave scars.

"Damn, dude. You didn't have to throw Ivy under the bus like that." The young male sitting with us stares at me with disdain, and despite myself, the heat of shame washes over me.

I staunch it, leveling a hard stare at her, not him.

Her expression is gentle, understanding even, and it makes me more upset. Of course, she doesn't care about repercussions.

"Whatever this write-up is, I'm sure it won't be the burning sear of molten metal being poured onto her skin until it reaches the bone. She'll survive."

I leave, but not before I note Ivy's flinch at my words.

But, again, why should I care?

4

IVY

Fuck, I'm tired.

I had to spend the rest of my break kissing Michael's ass so that he wouldn't write me up. Not that I have to give a shit anymore, but habits are hard to break. In the end, only a promise to cover a week of his shifts so he could go on a trip to Cabo—something only another manager is supposed to do —and the assurance that I would get us caught up appeased him.

I spent an extra two hours checking the eggs myself to confirm they were still salvageable, and I stayed late to ensure they were stocked. Michael was begrudgingly satisfied, and I had a couple of hours of overtime, so it wasn't a complete loss.

The street is dark as I get off the bus. I walk quickly toward my house, thankful it's only a block away.

"Hey, lil' mama." One of a group of teenage boys croons

as I pass, and I roll my eyes.

"Old enough to be your mama." I don't bother turning, but I see one of them slap the cat-caller's arm and lean over to whisper something.

"Oh, shit. Sorry, ma'am! I mean, shoot."

His friends laugh, and I raise a hand to dismiss the offense before continuing on to my house.

"You still look good, though!" He hollers when I'm a little further away.

"Jesus," I snort, shaking my head and carrying on.

As it has been for the last three months, my house is dark when I arrive. I let myself into the complete silence of an empty home and drop my bag to the floor.

Beneath my feet, new mail litters the hardwood. I pick up one of the envelopes, immediately recognizing the tell-tale branding of junk mail.

I sigh and shovel the rest together with my feet, gathering them in my hands and putting them with the stack already set to the side. I'll get through them tomorrow now that I have the space.

My feet shuffle along the floor as I trudge to the bathroom, mentally going over my schedule for the week.

Thankfully, I don't have to worry about rent, so if I wanted to take some time off, I could. I lucked out being able to afford so much space when I ran into an old teacher one day years ago. She was my favorite teacher in high school, and after a brief chat, she offered me this rental property at a great price. She hasn't raised the rent on me in almost two decades, and I know it's because she thinks I'd probably end up on the street if she did.

She's not entirely wrong.

Things have always been a bit tight financially, and

unfortunately, there are only so many hours in a day that one person can work without falling over. I know from almost falling asleep at the wheel, offering ride shares in my old dinky car.

My reviews were unsurprisingly crap.

Not because of my driving, but when people call for a car, they expect something that was at least made in their generation.

Didn't matter, though. The money wasn't that great, anyway. The ride-share company took most of the fare, and I rarely got tips.

I hardly drive now, so I don't have to pay for gas.

Leaving my scarf, jacket, and hat on the floor in the hall, I go to my bathroom and toss my clothes toward the hamper in the corner. Turning on the shower, I make sure the water's scalding.

"Ahh," my sigh cuts through the steam as heat relaxes the tension in my shoulders and lower back, which hasn't been right for decades. The hours I spend each day bending over to pick stuff up haven't helped, either.

Nothing helps, but after today, it feels like there's finally something to look forward to.

It's silly to smile over sushi, but that's what I do as I wash off the day's grime.

My lunch has consisted of cheap turkey bologna sandwiches for years. Dinner is usually a bowl of rice and whatever frozen veggies were on sale at the market, but today, I ate sushi, and that's the third best thing that's happened to me in forever. Not so much because I deserve it but because of what it signifies—an ending, and hopefully, a beginning, too.

I finish my bath and am drying off when the doorbell

rings. I pause, listening to be sure that's what I heard. Sure enough, the bell sounds again.

Wrapping the towel tightly around my chest, I go to the front door and peek through the side window, my heart ratcheting at the sight of the tall form standing on my porch.

He's cast in shadow, but there's no mistaking the imposing height, his broad torso blocking out the light from the street lamps. The dense mop of dark coils fluffing out from his head is glorious and shiny. It shields his face, which he keeps perpetually lowered, though I don't think he realizes it.

There isn't much to go by on what DaQuan may have looked like before his trauma. His skin is a patchwork of scars and gouges surrounding his beautifully haunted brown eyes. His lips show the clearest indication of their original appearance, full and soft, though dissected by deep scars.

He's shocking. There's no way he can't be, and no one would be faulted for thinking it, except for Patrice; that bitch is on my list for the shit she said. But from the moment I saw DaQuan, beyond the shock, his eyes showed what his scars obscure.

He's hurt, hurting even. There's a tension in his face that makes me wonder if the snide remarks and biting retorts are less about people's reactions to his appearance and more from some lingering pain he still experiences.

Nervous tension tightens my belly as I turn the lock on the door and pull it open a crack. "DaQuan?" His face is cast in darkness, and with just the shine of his brown eyes, he looks unblemished. "What are you doing here?"

"You live alone?"

The question gives me pause, and I fumble for a response,

still too caught off guard by his being at my home. "I, uh. Yeah. Are you okay?"

His lips twist to the side, and he looks away briefly before focusing on me again. The hardness is still there, but there's something contrite in his tone when he speaks. "I came to apologize for putting you under the bus. I am not a coward. I own my mistakes, and I should have owned that one."

He doesn't want to be saying this to me, but I smile anyway, offering a slight shoulder shrug. It's cold, and I'm still in my towel. His big body blocks most of the wind, but the chill hovers over my exposed skin.

"Don't worry about it. I told you where to go, so you weren't wrong. Anyway, Michael can't do anything to me. He got drunk like two Christmas parties ago and put his hand up my skirt. He's all bark."

DaQuan's eyes darken, and he steps forward, inadvertently crowding me into the house. "He touched you?"

"Not really. I mean, he definitely grabbed my butt, but that was ages ago." I try to wave it off, but something I've said seems to trigger him because he tenses, the shadow falling over his expression once again.

"Just because something happened long ago does not mean it no longer has an effect. Even old things can hurt. They can cut as freshly as a new wound."

There is nothing to say to that, so we stand in silence until another gust of wind reminds me that I'm damp. I wave him into the house. "Want to come in?"

"No." It's the abrupt response I've come to expect.

"You sure? We can talk more. It's cold out, and..." I gesture to my towel-clad body.

His eyes dart quickly to my bare legs, and he looks like he'd rather be doing anything else in the world than stepping through my door as he crosses the threshold.

I close it behind him and turn the lock. "Can I get you something to drink? Tea? Water?"

"Why do you live alone?"

I turn to find him frowning at the inside of my house and chuckle. "I just do. Does it matter that I live alone?"

"I don't care how you live." This time, the iciness of his tone is like a lash.

"Okay, let me get you some water." I press my mouth tight as I make my way to the kitchen, unexpected emotion stinging my nose and making tears cloud my vision. "Do you like ice, or —"

He's behind me, a wall of heat radiating against my body. His towering shadow curves across the porcelain bowl of the kitchen sink. "But you are still beautiful. Has no man attempted to partner with you?"

I face him, leaning into the sink away from his penetrating gaze. "I don't—I haven't had the time to think about that. That wasn't a priority for me."

"And what has been your priority, Ivy?" The way he says my name is a caress and a curse, and I feel both to my soul.

Swallowing, I search for a sufficient answer. I've been on autopilot for so long that I doubt any reason would be good enough, even if I tried to explain. "I've just been living or trying to."

Again, it's the wrong thing to say because the sneer is back, and he steps away like I'm diseased.

"Living," he snorts. "You say this as if that is not more than many are allowed to do. I should have known—" He gives me his back, and I reach out instinctively, grabbing his arm.

He makes a sound of unmistakable pain, and I release him, looking down at the place where we touched to see that the skin is twisted and missing chunks. The wiry cord of muscle that's exposed is darkened and scarred.

"Oh, my god." I reach for him again, gentler this time, lifting his hand to examine the damage. "Does it hurt?"

"What do you think?" I don't have to look at him to know the look he's giving me, so I don't. I keep staring at his skin, catching patches of smooth brown among the ruin.

"Why did you say I was beautiful?" I look up as his expression goes blank, and it dawns on me that he didn't realize he'd paid me the compliment.

"I say many things. Outward appearances mean nothing." I'm sure it's supposed to be shade, but his words make me smile as they give me the opening I was looking for.

"That's true." I smooth over his wrist, keeping my touch feather-light and watching for signs of discomfort. "You should know that none of this matters." I expect him to resist, so I lower my hand to a patch of skin less affected and tighten my grip, stopping him from moving away. "You're beautiful, too."

His chest heaves as he looks at me, but when he doesn't try to escape again, I step closer, raising his hand to my mouth. Some of his fingers are shorter than they should be, and from the uneven tips, it's clear that they were not removed cleanly.

I press my lips to the puckered ends, kissing each one.

He sucks in a breath. "I don't need your pity."

"Not pity," I murmur as I continue to brush my lips across his skin.

He's warm and has an earthy scent. The smell evokes a long-ago memory, one that began sweet and then transformed into something worse than a nightmare.

I keep my mind in the sweet spot and revel in the feelings it recalls. It was such a different time in my life, full of wonder and things I couldn't imagine.

I lift his arm higher and kiss my way down, feeling him watching me. When I glance up, he's sneering, but his chest rises and falls rapidly, matching the huffs of breath pushing from between his lips.

"What are you doing? You have no right."

"Do you want me to stop?" I tsk when I get to the raised line of a healed gash. My tongue darts out on its own to trace the scar, and this time, the sound he makes is a moan. "You said before that you didn't want my hands on you, so tell me to stop."

I don't know if I want him to say it. I don't even know why I'm doing this. He's right that I shouldn't be, but I can't seem to help myself, so when his nearly pained response comes, the relief that crashes through me feels like a lifetime of waiting.

"Don't—don't stop."

5

BA'IR

Those are not the words I mean to say.

I mean to wrestle my arm away, to push her off and make it clear that I would rather die a thousand deaths, more deaths than I've already died, than have her caress me.

But with every brush of her lips across my skin, the words disappear.

I don't want her to stop.

I should, and I don't.

When I tell her to continue, she raises her gaze to mine, and in her eyes, I see the same relief I feel, as if this is also something she needs.

I shouldn't care about her needs, so when I pull her against me and clash my mouth to hers, I tell myself that this is for me.

Lyqa are not violent, and not even my captivity has stripped me of the nature that keeps me from harming Ivy in the ways that I have been harmed. Even my original plan, to insert myself into her life and make her suffer in other ways, seems futile after one day of viewing how she lives.

As far as I can tell, she has nothing. She has this home, which a basic bit of research revealed belongs to someone else. Her employment pays her minimally, and she has even less of a digital footprint, which can only be achieved if one is insignificant.

It would seem that the Universe has done my revenge for me.

She is not the tooth doctor she wished to be. She is demeaned in front of her peers for the slightest mistakes, and the weariness around her eyes suggests she gets little rest.

But she is still beautiful, and perhaps the better revenge would be to allow her to give herself to me.

I'm sure she would be less pitying, less eager to search out my tongue—cut short long ago, and therefore less identifiable as Lyqa—with her own if she knew I was the lehti she betrayed.

I wonder if she offers herself to me to convince herself that she is not the terrible being I know she is. Or perhaps she gets some gratification from being with someone who looks like me.

That sounds more correct.

I kiss her harder, punishing her for the thought, bending her over my arm until she grabs my shoulders for stability. The pain of her gripping the exposed nerves of my torn flesh makes me hiss and pull away.

Spinning her around, I push her belly into the stone sink and rip the drying sheet away from her body.

She is so smooth and brown. The rounds of her bottom bounce as I fumble between us for my waistband and pull out the straining length of my dick.

I haven't held myself in a long time.

This is the singular part of my body that the Fein didn't touch, and I only believe it is because they knew the fear that they would maim me here was more torture.

I stare at the unblemished flesh, pulled taut by my desire for the woman before me. From the angle of her hips, I can see the slick flesh of her cunt. My gaze fixes there, a place that once held the greatest rapture of my life.

"I can't be gentle, and I don't care if it's good for you." The need to insert the animosity that's brought me to this point makes me give this assurance.

I expect her to recoil in indignation or even disgust, but she angles her face over her shoulder and meets my gaze. "That's okay."

Anger glides along my desire.

Like almost all of my emotions since I've seen Ivy again, her acceptance of whatever I send her way, be it mean or vile, fills me with annoyance and makes me line the dripping tip of my dick to her opening and fuck up hard, filling her with a single, brutal thrust.

She smothers her cry, but her head drops down, and her shoulders tense as I stretch her.

My eyes close on their own as her slick heat cushions my length. The groan that rumbles in my chest feels good—like a cleansing—and when I ease myself free to the tip and plunge back inside, pitching her into the basin, the rhythm of our bodies colliding feels like the violence I needed to happen.

It feels like war.

I get lost in the tugging slide, the slick sink, the scent of her, and the flesh bruising beneath my brutal grip. I experience all these things while urging myself to ignore the woman they are attached to.

She means nothing, and, anyway, she is quiet as I slam into her, but the knuckles of the hands that grip the sink are tight.

My First heart twinges, sending another sharp warning through my chest. The connection that should be with our joining is missing, and it's noticed.

I release one of her hips, noting the mottled discoloration already forming around the curve, and grab her shoulder, pulling her upright. "Take what you need."

She doesn't respond and remains passive.

"Take it! Would you continue to deny me everything? Take it, Ivy," I punch my hips forward, and her mouth opens with a moan.

She reaches back to cover the hand still on her hip with her own and starts to rock her pelvis to meet my thrusts. "Yes."

The satisfied hum accompanies the relaxation of her body, and then we're moving together, each of us seeking our end. A thread of connection forms through our touching hands, and when she shifts her fingers so they lace through mine, I squeeze back tight.

It doesn't take long for the tingling anticipation of release to form, and I lose all sense of myself, thrusting wildly into her, rattling the dishes on the sink.

She chokes out a sob, her knees buckling as she starts to gush and contract around me.

Her release sends me over the edge, and I seat myself to the hilt and let go, filling her in a torrent that seems to go on for spans.

"Come on."

Our hands are still joined. I stare at them as Ivy tugs me toward a room down the hall.

The space is sparse.

There's a bed and an entertainment console across from it. In a daze, I follow her over to the former, and when she eases down and urges me with her, I go, fitting myself around her body. We lie in silence for many moments, and in this silence, the reality of what just occurred settles like a stone in my gut.

It does not matter what I told myself as I took her.

It does not matter how roughly I drove into her.

What I did wasn't punishment. It wasn't revenge. It was what I'd longed for over nearly twenty rotations, and the sense of contentment that fills me now as I mold my body to Ivy's is mocking.

I'm weaker than I thought.

I had one task: to avenge myself for Ivy's betrayal, and I could not even do that. It is no wonder I was easy prey for the Fein.

Disgust slowly replaces the satisfaction I feel, but it still takes effort to ease myself away from her sweet scent and sit on the side of the bed. I need away from her. I never should have come here.

Standing, I leave her room and go into the main part of the house. She pushes off the bed to follow, and I rush to locate my clothes and pull them back on.

"Hey, you okay?"

"It would be best if you did not speak to me right now." I feel many things, none resembling the hatred that should be aimed at her.

This is a problem.

"I just—I wanted to say that this was nice. I mean, I'm

glad we did this."

I whirl on her, crowding her back as rage heats me from the inside. "Why? Do you feel good about yourself now? Does fucking me make you feel like you've done some good deed?"

"What? No." She shakes her head. The bedding she's wrapped around herself is clutched tightly in her hands. "I just don't want you to feel weird—"

I snort, giving her my back, and stride to the door. Yanking it open, I step out and slam it behind me.

The sound of splintering has me turning to find the glass in the door, and the windows alongside it, webbed with deep cracks.

Ivy looks through the damage in shock, and I nearly turn back before storming through her gate and down the street.

The cool wind serves as a balm until I realize it's kicking up the scent of her on my skin.

I hold my breath, inhaling shallowly until I reach the vacant lot where I've hidden my pod not too far from where Ivy lives.

Inside, the door is barely closed before I fight with the fastening to my pants and roughly jerk my dick out.

It hasn't been half a span since I had her, but her *scent* is like a shroud around me, making me ache in ways that have nothing to do with my wounds. I groan as I fist my length, stroking over the stiff flesh with rapid movements that have the muscles in my forearm twinging.

My mind replays the smooth sheen of Ivy's brown skin, the moment I sank inside of her, the slippery lips of her cunt parting to take me deep, the full globes of her bottom bouncing back as I fucked her, the enticing view of my shaft, glistening and swollen—unblemished, the only whole part of me—as it disappeared inside of her over and over, her soft moans and then louder cries when I made her open her mouth so I could hear just how good it felt. All of it wars with my other memories, the ones that drive my hate, and on the next rough stroke of my dick, I unleash a surge of semen onto the floor of my pod.

My knees give, and I collapse to the floor, scooting away from the spreading puddle of shame until my back meets the wall.

Looking at it reminds me of what I left inside of her, and it makes me angrier.

She did this.

Lying with me probably wasn't pity at all. That would imply that Ivy, at least, is capable of empathy, but knowing her, the only reason she would lie with me is selfish.

Her motive becomes clear.

She thinks this will make me kind to her. She thinks gracing someone like me with her body is enough to pacify me, to have me spouting her praises as everyone else does, but she's wrong.

She may think this is enough to appease me, but I've had what's between her legs, and I know it comes with nothing but empty promises and betrayal.

I sit on the floor for a long while, my dick flaccid against my thigh, my mind in turmoil. When I finally rise and right myself, it's only to gather something from one of the ship's compartments and exit the pod.

It's dark when I emerge. Most of the people in the area have retreated to their homes, so no one sees me make my way back to Ivy's house. I climb the steps in silence, pausing when I get to the door. The device in my hand fits into the lock, opening the door with ease. Looking back to be sure I'm not seen, I slip inside the darkened hall, closing the door behind me.

6

IVY

"Xuh!"

I gasp and wake with a start, my eyes peering into the darkened hallway, searching the shadows, which for a moment seem to move. The phantoms of my past have finally come to drag me away.

My mind flashes with honey brown eyes, an outstretched arm trying to reach me.

The pulse in my neck pumps blood to my head in a deluge that echoes through my ears, the sound loud in the quiet of my bedroom, even as my head reverberates with the screams of terror that have pulled me from the prison of nightly slumber for the past twenty years.

The bright lights of a car passing outside cut through the hall's shadows, dispersing the illusion and leaving me with the relic of my regret.

A glance at the clock tells me it's two in the morning, and

I chuckle. I've managed slightly more sleep in one go than I usually do before those screams wake me up.

Another shift in my periphery, and my gaze strays back to the hall.

Someone's there.

Beneath the nocturnal noise of the house—the old mantel clock ticking in the living room, the dull thump of bass from an after-hours party at one of the neighbors', the screeching battle cry of two raccoons fighting over whatever takeout scraps they've discovered in the alley—the pulsing beat of a heart reaches me.

I press a hand to my chest, feeling the thud of the muscle there, but the thump beneath my breastbone isn't in sync with the beat I hear. It's a fraction of a second before, and there's a reluctance to the beat that follows, as if it's there outside of its will, an unwilling accompanist.

"Hello?" The moment I say it, I shake my head.

There's no one out there. It's just the dream chasing me into reality, the same way it's nipped at my heels since I was a naive eighteen-year-old who thought she'd lucked out on the adventure of a lifetime. I'm hoping now that the dream can finally rest, too. That, despite everything, I'm on a path to peace.

Falling back on the pillows, I exhale the years of waiting, glad I can finally breathe just a little.

So much has changed in the past few months. After years and years of thinking nothing would ever change, *everything* is different.

I've been slowly trying to come to terms with it, to accept the strange relief I don't even know if I'm allowed to feel, but which is manifesting itself as a certain recklessness. In the span of one day, I've twice done something I never would have allowed myself to do before now —I've indulged.

First, the sushi, which felt almost blasphemous as I ate it, and once DaQuan reminded me of the injustices in the Universe, became no better than an affront against a Lord I didn't believe in.

DaQuan.

This man, who's appeared like a walking symbol of a torment I've only been able to have nightmares about. This man, whose pain is so palpable that even if it weren't literally carved into his skin and sewn like poisonous thread into every word he speaks, I'd know it was there because it's a pain I've fostered for decades. It's a pain I've sought in overworking a free and able body that felt dead inside. That is, until I met the honey brown eyes of a wounded man in the staff locker room, felt the loathing in his touch, and couldn't make myself believe it should be more merciful.

I've lived in the shadows for so long—a cave full of glowing eyes and sharp teeth, dying inside little by little with every passing year—that it wasn't until DaQuan stormed out, letting his resentment at the world drive him away from what we'd unexpectedly shared, that I recognized the tingling remnants of my orgasm as proof of life.

Stretching, I groan into the sharp aches that pinch my inner thighs. A hand between them finds my folds puffy and tender. I tilt a hip into the light from the open blinds, revealing palm-sized marks on the curve. I can feel the twin mark on the other hip, too. It flares with vibrant heat beneath my skin.

"I can't be gentle, and I don't care if it's good for you."

I hadn't needed gentle, and my hopes weren't high enough for good. I just knew in that moment I needed *something*, to give something, to offer something, and I suspected—despite the sting of his tongue—DaQuan needed it, too.

In the end, he'd made me take what I needed anyway, forcing it on me even as he cursed his benevolence. The tremors of that offering still rack my body, vibrating through my fingertips and making me tremble between the cool sheets.

I bask in the sensation, once again indulging because I know I'll be back to questioning if I deserve it tomorrow.

My hand sneaks back between my legs to worry the sensitive flesh. The memory arises of how completely he filled me, stretching me with every deep thrust, the cruelty of his movements defied by how perfectly he felt inside of me.

My fingers move on their own, slipping along my labia and spreading the wetness my thoughts have triggered across my pussy.

I gasp, parting my trembling legs more as I press circles over my clit, uncaring that every movement abrades my already battered flesh. Like when DaQuan took me against the sink, the tenderness is secondary to the deep void it fills as I push myself over the edge, crying out as I orgasm. My core contracts, and my fingers are overcome with a flood of liquid pulsing from inside me, and the realization that it's DaQuan's cum sends me into another flurry of release that leaves me limp and breathless on the bed.

Thump.

I start, instinctively yanking the covers up, my heart racing for the second time tonight.

This time, I know the sound came from the hall. A harsh grunt preceded the bump against the wall. I didn't imagine that.

"Is someone there?"

Slowly, I rise from the bed, grabbing my robe from the end and pulling it on. Tentative steps take me toward the hallway, and I wait until I'm close to the door to flick the light switch on the wall by the threshold.

Soft yellow light floods my room, spilling into the empty hall.

There's nothing there but the blank walls, which speak to my life priorities of valuing the moment over documentation.

Cautiously, I peer down the hall, making my way to the front door.

It's only when I've stepped back from looking out and scanning what I can see of the street, satisfied that the noises must be in my head after all, that I realize the window is whole again, the webbed splinter gone from the glass like it never was.

7

BA'IR

She's laughing with Elliott when I arrive at my scheduled station the next morning.

Laughing as if nothing happened.

She doesn't see me approach, so I relish the look of nervousness that appears on her face when Elliott notices me and stands, holding out a hand for me to clap.

"Hey, DaQuan! You here with me again?"

"It appears so."

Roger has assigned me to the aisles with Elliott, noting how efficiently we worked together the day before.

I shift my gaze from Elliott to Ivy, anticipating the familiar heat of vengeance scorching through me, hotter than before, after what she pushed me to.

And I do feel heat, but it's not the heat of revulsion. It's the heat of want and need. It's the residuum of the combustion that had me bending Ivy over her sink when I should have been telling her exactly how much I loathe her.

It's the heat that made me walk back to her home to repair her door for fear that someone might see the crack and think her home vulnerable. It's the inferno that scorched my insides as I watched her finger herself to release as she whispered the name I've given myself.

It's the leht, and as much as it's resurrecting in me, I still despise it.

My nostrils flare with her scent, and it's there—me—or what I left inside her. A groan rumbles through my chest, and her eyes flare with awareness. She knows what's in my mind. Does it disgust her, or has she been reliving each moment of our frantic joining as I have?

"You hungry? I got some jerky. Here." Elliott reaches into his back pocket and produces a bag of meat product.

Holding Ivy's gaze, I reach inside and pull a strip out, folding it into my mouth.

I don't eat flesh, but flesh is all I think of as I chew.

I should have tasted her first.

The image of me kneeling behind her and pushing apart the plump rounds of her bottom to expose the slippery slit of her cunt—

"You don't have to chew it that long." Elliott snaps me out of the fantasy of licking through Ivy's slit.

I swallow, forcing the dry meat down.

Ivy clears her throat, looking away, but she colors beneath her skin. "Uh, when you all are done, Roger wants us to do takebacks."

"Got it, boss lady." Elliott opens a box with a blade he produces from his pocket and starts unloading the items.

"Not your boss." She colors more as she waves him off.

"You should be. Seriously, I was just talking to this dude

yesterday about how you basically keep this place and everyone in it running. Why won't you let them make you a manager already?"

She peeks at me before turning a wide gaze on Elliott in some silent communication.

He rolls his eyes, pushing another box onto the shelf. "Right, you gotta be able to put money on ya man's books and go visit him in jail when you want."

"Elliott!" She turns to me, shaking her head. "That's not what it is. I don't have—"

"Don't be ashamed. Look, I get it. If my girl got sent up for the rest of her life, I'd be trying to see her every chance I got. You're ride or die." Elliott continues stacking the boxes onto the shelf, completely unaware of how his revelation is affecting Ivy.

Her look is pleading as she stares at me. I stare back as the rage she nearly extinguished when she came apart around me bubbles back to the surface.

None of my examination of Ivy's life from public and private records showed a connection to a male. It certainly didn't connect her to any male who is incarcerated.

Which means...

"What is 'ride or die'?" I can infer the meaning of this human expression, but I want to hear it.

Elliott makes a face. "You know, dude. Ride or die. Like ya girl is going where you go, and if some shit pops off, she's got your back, or she's going down trying."

Is that so?

Ivy may not know who I am, but I'm sure that she can read my disgust, even through the scars.

While I was wasting away, being tortured over and over within a span of my life, she was claiming to be supporting a male she was too loyal to leave behind.

Suddenly, my body flares with a sensation I'd nearly forgotten.

It's what filled me in the first few rotations I was with the Fein. It's what I focused on when I was being torn into, when infections raged through my body until I was delirious and imagined a great winged warrior coming to save me.

It's hope.

Even when her betrayal has revealed another layer, I can imagine a reality in which she was loyal to me. I can imagine a life where she loved me enough to honor the promise of the leht—to follow me wherever I went.

I turn without a word, my feet carrying me to the back of the store and through the doors that lead to an area where only employees are authorized.

I can't breathe.

I lean against the wall, struggling to quell the panic that's paralyzed me.

The room shifts and fades away, reappearing as the dark tunnels of that horror planet, and I'm back with the Fein.

One of the many games they enjoyed was to release me—or rather, to make me believe I had found a means of escape—only to hunt me down and drag me back into the darkness.

It took me a while to catch on that I was being toyed with, but as I ran through the tunnels, every corner I turned, I expected to see Ivy leading a rescue team to me.

But she was never there.

No one was there.

"Hey." She sounds hesitant behind me, and I tense, my hands clenching against the wall where I've braced myself.

"Leave." I cringe at the frailty in my voice. I've survived horrors most beings could never imagine. I should not be this weak, and I certainly don't want her to see me this way.

"Are you okay?" She's closer, still smelling of me, and I close my eyes against the confusion this causes in my body, which wants to push her away, but also—

"You need to breathe."

"I *need* you to leave."

She doesn't. She moves closer. "I don't want you to misunderstand what Elliott said. He made it sound like I'm with someone, but I'm not."

I spin around, my nostrils flaring as I glare her down. "Oh, I *know* you are not this woman he's claimed. You are no *ride or die*. I doubt it would take much for you to decide someone wasn't worth the risk."

I know I'm speaking too brazenly to someone whom I've only known, in her eyes, for two days. But perhaps I've *wanted* her to recognize me, and I'm even more enraged that she seems to have so completely forgotten me. That I was so insignificant to her.

"Is that what you think, that I believe you're not worth the risk?"

I snarl, stepping close, even though, like every time I've attempted to intimidate her, she doesn't back down. "You think I care?"

"I think," she smiles, "maybe what happened yesterday was unexpected for us both."

"Because you'd never give yourself to someone who looks like me?" It's meant to bite, but the doubt feels real.

She chuckles, and my entire body tenses. "No, DaQuan. I would have never in a thousand years thought you'd want me back."

My deflation is visible. I shrink under the sincerity of her words.

Not want her back?

I spent twenty rotations telling myself I had every right to hate her, and since the moment I saw her, fight it as I've tried, I've wanted her as much as I did when we crossed paths all that time ago.

My First heart pulses, its muted beat expanding as I take the two steps to crowd her. I'm so hard that I ache, but I urge my anger forward. It's the only thing that has a place here. There's no room for the tenderness that shines in her eyes as she looks at me.

"'Want you back?'" I choke out a laugh; it's a harsh and unnatural sound. "As if last night wasn't some morbid curiosity for you. Did you just want to see if my dick matched the rest of me?" I'm snarling into her face, but she remains calm.

"DaQuan." Her hands flatten against my chest, and I flinch, not from pain but because any touch from her numbs the lingering suffering that lives beneath my skin. She smooths her hands upward until she must lift onto her toes to reach my shoulders. "I want you."

The sound I make is part derision and part disbelief. "Yes, of course. Let the one who looks like a beast fuck you in the cover of the night, when no one would suspect. But what about now, in the light of day, when anyone could come upon us and mock you for allowing me to put my hands on you?" I grip her hips and yank her against me so she can feel the betrayal of my body.

I expect her to push away or fight me off in panic that someone may see, but she *moans*. It's only a slight exhale of breath that carries the sound, but it's a torch to the vengeful lust flickering inside of me.

I smash my mouth to hers, groaning when she opens for

me.

The sounds of commerce beyond the door reach us as I walk her into a metal shelf. The items wobble and clank when her back meets the frame.

She moans *again*. "I want you, DaQuan. Please."

With a grunt, I spin her to face away from me and yank her hips back.

The form-fitting pants she wears, which I noticed earlier molded over her soft curves, are yanked down to her knees, and I have my own pants unbuckled and shoved beneath my hips before I realize it.

I pause, smoothing a hand over her skin as I stroke my throbbing length. "Still so beautiful," I murmur.

"Hurry." Her urgent whisper is preceded by her pushing her hips back to split herself on the tip of my dick, which I fuck to the back of her pussy with a single deep thrust.

My hand is already over her mouth, the split-second decision made before I fill her, and my palm catches the high-pitched mewl she releases as she takes me.

I groan, pausing when I touch her womb. Once again, I'm lost to this unacceptable draw I have to the woman who is my lehti. It's a need so in conflict with my hate for her that my head begins to throb.

This flaw in my biology makes me ease from the tight grip of her warmth and fuck back in, seating myself deep as I set a quick, brutal rhythm of tunneling through her cunt.

Her moans are hot and breathy against my palm. Her hand grabs mine, holding her waist as our bodies collide.

"Do you think I want this?" I huff into her hair right before inhaling so deeply that my lungs burn. Her light, floral scent fills me, permeating every cell in my body and making me fuck even harder.

I want it to be my rage making me take her so hard, but even if it is, the absolute satisfaction that comes when I slam up, seating myself against her womb and flooding her with my release cannot be denied.

Voices beyond the door, nearby but still a ways from the storeroom, indicate we are not long from someone walking in to find Ivy bent over the storage rack with my dick shoved into her from behind. I tense, and her body stills.

"Is someone coming?"

"It doesn't matter. I'm not letting you go until you come for me." It's a threat as much as a plea.

She peers at me from over her shoulder, her eyes wide with what could be fear, but then her gaze goes liquid as she rocks back, impaling herself onto my length.

"*Hu*—the Lyqa curse stalls in my throat as I rise quickly, jerking to meet her thrusts. A new release is already cresting,

She's close. I can feel her clenching around me, her thready gasps getting quicker in time with how she bounces back.

The voices are loud now. I can make out Michael's voice and another male voice I have never heard. Twisting my hand into Ivy's soft strands, I pull her head back, at the same time reaching around to press against her clit, countering the pressure of me driving into her core.

She goes with a shudder and a ragged moan, her upper body collapsing against the shelf. Breathing heavily, I ease away, letting the weight of my length slide from inside of her. With sluggish movements, Ivy tugs her pants right just as the voices come within range for her to hear.

I watch her cover her slick-coated thighs, my chest heaving, and when she realizes I haven't moved, she reaches for my pants, gently but quickly folding me back between the flaps and securing them.

She folds her hands in front of her as the men walk in. Her expression is carefully blank, but a tremble runs through her form.

Michael is the first to see us, and his eyes narrow as they bounce between Ivy and me. "What are you two doing back here?"

"Uh, I wasn't feeling well. DaQuan was just making sure I'm okay." She's broken into a thin sheen of sweat, and the scent of my release, combined with her residual arousal, is thick. My nostrils flare, and some primal part of me that I can't suppress is satisfied by having claimed her so publicly, even if we are the only ones who know it. Though the way Michael's gaze lingers, I sense he suspects something is amiss.

His mouth curls as he steps further inside the room. The other male watches closely.

"See what I'm talking about, Sam? This happens all the time. She's supposed to be working, and instead, she's off doing something no one asked her to do. Yesterday, she changed this fella's assignment without asking anyone, and we nearly lost a whole shipment of eggs." He flings a hand in Ivy's direction, and when I glance at her, she stares calmly back, giving no reaction to his accusation.

Sam shifts his focus to Ivy after listening to Michael. "I know you've been with us for a while, but you've still got to be clear about your role here, Ivy."

"Understood." She nods, her lips folding in as if to stop what she truly wishes to say. "I just needed a minute. I'll head back out now. Come on." She waves me forward, but I ignore her and address Sam.

"You are higher in rank than this man?" I nod to Michael

without looking at him.

"I am," Sam responds, and Michaels casts a nervous glance in his superior's direction.

"I was simply offering assistance to Ivy, and yesterday, she was following the instructions of the supervisor who was managing before this *fella* came on." I nod again to Michael. Again, not sparing him a glance.

Sam frowns and looks at Michael. "Is that true? Roger assigned him?"

Michael blusters, looking from Sam back to Ivy and me. "We'd just gotten a shipment of eggs. Roger should have known not to assign him to the aisles."

"So, Roger, not Ivy. Did you do your rounds to make sure everyone was stationed where they should be?"

Michael starts to panic, and I tilt my head as he searches for some excuse for his incompetence now that Ivy can no longer be blamed. "Roger leaves this place a mess when he finishes his shift. It takes damn near the whole day just to get things running smoothly again —"

"So that's a no?" Sam shifts his eyes away from a red-faced Michael and looks at us. "You all can go. Thanks for looking out for your team member, Ivy. Next time, just let someone know you're off the floor."

Ivy smiles. "Thanks, Sam." She taps my arm, signaling we should leave, and I let her lead the way to the door.

As we're passing, Michael's glare is hot, and the same instinct that was crowing a moment ago at having felt Ivy clenching around me as she came rears back up with the protective nature of the leht.

I pause, turning back and finally giving Michael my attention.

"Sam is your name?" I flick my eyes to him, and he nods.

I shift my gaze right back to Michael. "If a person of authority here were to touch a woman who works beneath him in an—intimate—manner that she did not wish at, let us say, a Christmas gathering, what would be the repercussions?"

Sam's face goes hard, and he shifts to partially face Michael. "If anyone on my staff were stupid enough to assault another staff member of any gender, they would be investigated, fired, and charges would be filed if the allegations were substantiated."

Michael swallows, and a visible shake moves through his body. "I don't think that's been the case—"

"So you're saying you didn't put your hand up Ivy's skirt at the Christmas gathering?" My feet move on their own, bringing me closer until he cowers back. "You didn't touch what's mi—" I blink, swallowing the words and shifting to Sam. "I have barely been employed here a week, and it is clear that this man is harassing Ivy. He has berated her at every turn, and for someone like me, who has suffered so much trauma, it has been difficult to witness. For whatever reason, Ivy has been reluctant to reveal his actions, but I do not have that reservation. Deal with him." *Or I will* is unspoken in the glower I turn on Michael. "Furthermore, this has been stressful for both Ivy and myself. We are going to leave for the remainder of the day."

"Yeah, of course. I'll get someone to cover for you. I'll be reaching out to arrange a conversation with HR." Sam nods us off and turns on Michael with a deep sigh. "What the hell, Michael..."

I don't wait to hear what is being said. I take Ivy's arm and lead her out onto the floor and directly to the room where we keep our personal belongings. "Get your things."

She hasn't said anything since we left Sam and Michael, but she faces me now. "You didn't have to do that, and I'm not taking the day off."

I step forward. "I don't like predators. Doing that wasn't about you. It's for the next female he tries that with. She might not deserve it." The insult is a poor attempt to wash away my possession of earlier, and the heat of guilt follows it. I swallow and look away. I'd be concerned that the physiological display of my face pulsing with color would give me away as Lyqa, but the thin skin camouflage I've applied hides it. "Of course, you didn't deserve this either. No one does. I didn't mean to imply otherwise."

She shrugs. "It's fine, but I'm going to go talk to Sam and tell him I'll stay."

"Don't. I've already gotten us free from the rest of the day. We should make use of it."

"Yeah?" Her brows raise. "And what should *we* do?"

"I didn't mean you and I—"

"You've already said it, so." She smiles shyly. "Besides, if I don't do work here, I'll just find work to do somewhere else." Our hands are already joined—I joined them. And when she tugs me along, I follow.

We're silent as she leads me from the building, hand in hand, onto the street and to a public transportation stop not far from the store. I willingly get on the bus that arrives, swiping my band across the payment pad for us both before she can, then sitting stonily beside her while the vehicle jostles down the street.

We pass people walking along the busy thoroughfare on the other side of the road, and Ivy's scent colors with the unmistakable sweetness of excitement. Her leg bounces as she stretches to look out the opposite window. "Oh, my god. I totally forgot this was now." She reaches above to yank on the cord that signals our desire to get off the bus before facing me with delight dancing in her beautiful eyes.

And they are beautiful—brown and gentle. They angle slightly at the ends, giving an allure to her otherwise soft face.

My memory flashes with scenes nearly forgotten—Ivy beneath me for the first time. Her full, bow lips parted as I eased into her snug heat. It merges with the memory of Ivy last night, just as snug, taking the force of my thrusts with a quiet passion that shouldn't make me want her all over again.

I blink away the thought just as I realize I've been staring at her, barely registering what she's said. She doesn't seem to notice; she's too energized with whatever has suddenly caught her attention.

"Let's get off here." She grabs my hand again to pull me off the bus and onto the street, and once there, she nearly drags me through the throngs of people who appear to be moving in the same direction to some sort of attraction happening in the sprawling open park that she was trying to see from the bus.

She's so eager, her torso angled forward. Her body forms a spear that cuts through the crowd, and by the time she pauses, dropping my hand to sigh at the sight before us with a wide grin, I'm intrigued.

"I almost forgot what this was like. I haven't been in so long." She looks back, transforming before my eyes into the girl I once knew.

When I finally tear my gaze away to see what has her so delighted, I'm not prepared, and my body seizes as I'm transported twenty rotations into the past…

Earth Twenty Rotations Ago

BA'IR

"Girl, he is looking at you again!"

"Shut up, Fallon. He is not."

I am. In fact, I have been unable to tear my eyes away from the young female standing several spans away from me at this festival on Earth. The only thing staying me from going to her right this instant and declaring my love is my Ap'hati's hand on my shoulder.

"Just breathe through it, dahni. It will feel overwhelming at first, but that will settle shortly. Vitem," he glances in worry at my other father, who comes to my other side.

"Ba'ir, you need to breathe. Your agitation is beginning to show, and we must maintain our cover while we're here. We will not leave until we have determined how to resolve this, but you *must calm.*"

I hear my fathers, but my attention stays fixed on the female who has triggered the rapid thump of my First heart, a biological urge that's so profound it paralyzed me the moment it was triggered.

The girl and her friend stand with their heads bent together as they whisper about me.

"Listen, I'm looking at him, and I'm telling you. He's looking at you."

"We're standing next to each other. How do you know he's not looking at you?"

"Because I'm looking at him, and he's looking at you! Look and see." She nudges my lehti with her elbow, and I flinch even though the motion isn't done aggressively. I just don't want anyone touching her. *I* want to touch her.

My lehti's nose scrunches. *"What? No! I'm not about to stare at him if he's looking at me. That's weird."*

"Girl, it's already weird. He hasn't blinked in like a whole minute. He's cute, though. Real cute, actually." The friend tilts her head as she stares openly back at me. *"His face is a little funny looking, but it works out."*

At her friend's words, my lehti's head finally snaps in my direction, and our eyes lock. Her lips part, and I hear the soft intake of breath, as my body finally relaxes. This small recognition is enough to sate the pining of the leht for the moment.

"I knew it! I knew you would look once I said that. You love weird-looking dudes. What do you think his name is? He looks like a DaQuan."

My lehti ignores her friend and continues to hold my gaze before her mouth tilts into a shy smile. She raises a hand and moves her flattened palm back and forth.

It's like dawn breaking.

I've lived a wonderful life so far, full of joy and the love of my fathers, but this simple smile and hand motion from my lehti is like being reborn into another kind of beauty.

I smile back, my feet moving on their own to finally take me to her, but my Ap'ha stops me again before I can take a step.

"Easy, dahni. You will get to speak to her, but we must do this with care. She is young. You both are. The leht is not usually triggered before full maturity. We must be careful not to scare her, and *you* must be realistic about what can come from this."

"But she's mine."

Ap'ha sighs. "I know it feels this way, but she must choose you also, and that means you cannot press her because you are sure of the leht. This is not her way. Let us attempt to create an opportunity for you to meet her."

Reluctantly, I nod but keep my eyes locked with my lehti.

Suddenly, her friend steps in front of her, blocking my view, and sending a surge of panic through me when my lehti is no longer visible. She cups her mouth with both hands, angling her head back as she shouts, "Take a picture. It will last longer."

Her announcement has most heads in the vicinity turning to look at us, and my fathers crowd me with their large frames and usher me away.

I drag my feet as they guide me from my lehti, but I've already determined that I'm not leaving without her.

***

"You should try this. It's called a Chicago hot dog." Ap'ha takes a large bite of the oblong food as my Ap'hati makes a face.

"That's flesh."

Ap'ha's brows lift in surprise before he shrugs and takes another bite. "I am a chef. I should not limit myself to tastes within my cultural range. Neither should our son."

Ap'hati snorts and goes back to tasting his dish of "sweet plantains." "Do you want to try mine?" He gestures with his utensil, but I only see it out of the corner of my eye. I'm still looking across the large festival space to where my lehti and her friend stand in line for another food vendor.

I have tracked their movements since my fathers forced me away.

"Dahni, your father and I brought you to this festival to try some new foods. You can look away for a moment to eat. It will help settle you."

"Okay, Ap'hati." I lift a long cut of root called a fry absently from my plate and fold it into my mouth.

It's quite good, but that won't matter until I speak to my lehti.

"Ew, you're both his dads?" The acrid scent of animosity, mixed with the tang of curiosity, has me looking up at the bearded male who's standing over where my fathers and I are seated on the edge of a fountain.

Ap'hati peers at him, his expression brightening. "We are! Rather than judge us, would you like to sit and speak about our very personal decision to partner with each other?"

Ap'ha smirks at my father's flippant response and takes another bite of his hot dog, but his brows raise as they wait for a response from the stranger.

"I don't care about who you choose to screw," the man spits, but this only earns him a nod of approval from Ap'hati.

"Ah, so your small, human mind does understand that our relationship is none of your concern? And, yet, you have come all the way over here to question it."

The man shifts, his posture becoming aggressive.

My ap'ha tosses the final piece of his hot dog between his lips, chewing leisurely as he rises to tower over the man, who flinches back, his eyes widening as he takes in my father's intimidating form. Ap'ha takes his time swallowing. He may look calm, but beneath his skin, his muscles vibrate with the power of the leht.

Using the distraction, I ease off the bench and start across the field, registering my ap'ha's response as I walk away.

"If you have questions, ask them. We are feeling generous and will respond. However, if you touch my lehti or otherwise behave aggressively toward him, I will kill you."

He means this.

The shift in the man's scent from bravado to fear carries on the wind as my steps quicken away from the confrontation. My fathers can take care of themselves. If I weren't so distracted, I'd be worried for the man, but my only concern is that it appears my lehti is leaving, and I may not see her again.

She and her friend are near the street, having enjoyed several small meals from the variety of restaurant stands scattered throughout the festival.

"*Oh, there's our bus.*" My lehti's friend points to an oncoming vehicle, and my heart thumps as it approaches, slowing to a stop.

I'm moving fast now, running almost at a pace that could appear unnatural.

"*Hu'l, Vetim!*" My Ap'hati's voice is alarmed, followed by the sharp thud of flesh hitting flesh.

Grunts and sharp words sound out behind me as my father makes good on his promise of harm, but I persist with a singular focus.

My lehti's so close. I couldn't stop if I wanted to.

The bus doors open, and my lehti's friend steps up first. My lehti steps up behind her, but I reach her at the moment her foot lands on the step and grab her arm, pulling her back before she can board.

She gasps, instinct making her twist to pull from my grip. Our eyes lock over her shoulder, and her defenses drop; whatever reproach was on her lips melts away.

"It's you." A hand flies to her chest, and I follow it, knowing what she's feeling because the rapid thud is being echoed in my chest.

Up close, her eyes are warm and brown. Her skin is an even shade of the same color, and there is nothing about her that isn't beautiful. Her hair hangs heavy and straight around her shoulders, the ends tucked under in a distinct curve. The thick but finely arched brows above her wide eyes are pinched.

I don't know what to say.

I've wanted nothing but to be close to her from the moment we were leht, and now that I'm here, I don't know what to say, so I say the only thing I can think of. "You make my heart beat."

She snorts, her lips parting to flash metal encasing her teeth. "I make your heart beat? And how do I do that—"

Three loud pops sound out, and my lehti instinctively ducks, triggering my own guard as I pull her behind me and take up space to cover her body.

"Somebody's shooting! Girl, get on!" Her friend waves a frantic hand, urging my lehti through the open door of the bus, but before my lehti can decide, the driver activates the door closing mechanism and drives off.

"Hey—" My lehti grunts as someone cuts between us and collides with her, shoving her back and to the ground.

All around us, people are fleeing in a panic, screaming and tripping over one another as they attempt to escape some unknown threat.

My lehti tries to get up, but is immediately knocked down again. She cries out, bringing her arms up to shield herself from the onslaught.

The leht rises fiercely as I watch her cower on the ground. I surge forward using my body to block those who would run into her. Her eyes are flared in fear, and I pull her to her feet and into my arms, holding still as I allow the people to pass.

She turns her face into my chest until the sounds of running subside.

The festival area has mostly cleared in a matter of moments. In the distance, two lone figures stand tall among the few who remain, and I set off toward them.

"Is she well?" Ap'hati's forehead is creased as they rush forward to meet me.

"She was knocked over. *Lehti*, are you okay?" I pull my chest back to see her face, and she blinks up at me.

Her bottom lip is split and glazed over with crimson. Without thinking, I lower my face to hers and lap at the red stain.

Her gasp is soft between our mouths as I lick at her lush lips.

My ap'hati clucks his teeth. "Goodness, he's just like you."

"Proactive?" Ap'ha returns with some amusement.

"Impulsive. Dahni, have you asked permission to touch her in such a way?"

I draw back, embarrassment making my face pulse with heat. My lehti looks stunned, and the flashing along my cheeks intensifies.

"*Lehti,* I didn't mean to—*M'ah qitah.*" I kiss the corner of her mouth, brushing my lips over the smooth skin of her cheek.

My lehti's eyes dance over my face. "Your cheeks are glowing," she remarks in wonder.

Ap'hati sighs. "Son, you are *still* touching her without her permiss—never mind. Let's go back to our pod. I can tend to your father's wounds there."

My gaze startles up, and I realize my father's holding a hand to his side. There's blood leaking from between his fingers. "Ap'ha, what happened?"

"Apparently," he grunts, pressing his hand harder into the wound, "the man believed it was very much his concern that your father and I love each other. Come, I called the pod. It's over here." He waves a hand at me. "You may as well bring her since you're determined to rush this revelation. Miss—" My father's brows lift in question, and my lehti shifts her attention to him.

"Ivy. My name's Ivy."

Ap'ha smiles, but I'm frowning because he's robbed me of the honor of asking her name first.

"Ivy," he continues, ignoring my scowl. "You are safe with my son. Can you trust us?"

She looks back at me, searching my face for something, before nodding. "I'll go with you."

My ap'ha's eyes shift behind his lids. He murmurs about "younglings" and turns away, moving toward a secluded area of the park where our pod is indicated on my comm.

I hold Ivy close as we follow my parents, and when I feel

her eyes on me, I look down.

"What's your name?"

Pleasure swells through my First heart, and I resist the urge to kiss her again. "Ba'ir."

Her lips part, flashing those metal encasings again. "Anywhere." My brow tilts in confusion, and she cups my jaw with her hand. "That's where I'd go with you. Anywhere, Ba'ir."

9

IVY

For a moment, I'm worried I may have made a mistake.

There are a lot of people here, and more than a few stop to stare at DaQuan, their gazes crawling over his scars and disfigurements. Most look awkwardly away, but others are not quick enough to hide their shock or openly pitch their mouths into sympathetic frowns.

I face him, my grip tight around his hand. "I'm sorry. This is a thing, a food festival. If it's too much, we don't have to stay."

I start to lead him back to the bus stop, but he resists, nodding to a nearby food truck. "Let's start there. I have been here once, but I didn't get a chance to enjoy any of the food."

"No? Why?"

He looks at me, his gaze lingering on my face but seemingly lost in some memory. "I was distracted."

"By what?"

He blinks, and his scowl returns as he releases me and waves an impatient hand at the food truck. "Do you wish to eat or not?"

"Sure." I walk ahead, trusting that he'll follow, and when I get to the truck, I feel him come up behind me. "What should we try?"

There's a tremor in my voice, partly because DaQuan's default mode as a hostile participant always has me a little on edge that I might say the wrong thing and scare him off, but also, he's stopped so close that the muscles of his torso press slightly into my back. The heat from his body sears through my shirt, making a flutter rush through my middle.

He places his hands over my hips and squeezes.

Like always, his hold is just a little too tight, like he can't decide if he wants to be gentle, but his grip gradually eases until anyone looking might think we're really lovers and this is a tender moment between us.

I don't let myself dwell too long on the thought. It's been taking all of me just to stave off the guilt that's trying to worm its way through my mind over how easily I've twice let myself fall into him.

"How about we try an empanada?"

The person in front of us steps aside after placing their order, and the hair-netted chef with a sweaty brow turns his attention on me.

"Uh, yeah. We'll have two orders of the—"

"Hot dogs. I'd like the Chicago hot dogs, please." DaQuan speaks up from behind me, his voice catching a bit.

The chef's gaze lifts behind me, and I wait for the shock that always follows someone noticing DaQuan's appearance for the first time, but the chef just nods. "Two hot dogs coming up."

I relax, realizing that I was tense waiting to defend DaQuan if the man said something rude.

"He understands." DaQuan's voice is soft, and I look back and up, noting not for the first time while staring at the underside of his jaw that, despite the severity of his disfigurement, his face is beautifully structured. He nudges his chin toward the food truck, and I turn back to see the cook working over the stove.

From the collar of his t-shirt, the ripple of burn scars marks his neck and down the back of his arm in a way that indicates his entire back is covered with them as well.

"When I first arrived, Roger believed me to be a war veteran. I am not, but there are many ways we become scarred, and the outcome is the same. Some of us just have the misfortune of not being able to hide them."

I swallow, warring with the question I've wanted to ask but haven't out of fear that DaQuan would think it mattered to me.

"Don't." His eyes are on me, and for once, they burn hotly with something other than anger. In fact, they're almost pleading. "Don't ask me how. Don't ever ask me how."

I press my lips tight and nod, shifting so I'm facing front again. The chef is just turning around with our order.

"Two hot dogs. Enjoy." He and DaQuan exchange another head bop, and we carry the paper plates to one of the benches set to the side.

"Oh. My. God!" I lap at some mustard that's caught the corner of my mouth as my jaw works hard to compress the multitude of ingredients on the hot dog. "Chicago hot dogs are so extra but so good."

A moan brings my attention to DaQuan sitting across

from me. His dog is already half gone, and he makes the rest disappear in a single bite. His eyes are closed, so he doesn't see me admiring his rapture. It's the first time I've seen anything close to bliss on his face. "Good?"

"Excellent." His eyes are already darting back to the truck that served us.

Chuckling, I grab his hand and urge him up. "Come on. Let's get more."

DaQuan gets three, and then he tries loaded fries, which he decides are the best thing he's ever eaten. But the Mexican street corn nearly takes him out.

"*Hu'l*." Like everything he's tried since the first hot dog, DaQuan savors every bite, chewing slowly like he's determined to experience every taste.

"What does that mean? I feel like I've heard it before." I stab some chili cheese fries and fold them into my mouth.

His gaze jumps to mine, and he pinches his mouth tight. "What does what mean?"

"That word. '*Hu'l*.'"

He stares for a beat, then blinks back down to his corn. "Nothing."

"It's not English, though?"

"Is there something about the word 'nothing' you didn't understand?"

I smile, forking more fries. "Sure." Looking out across the park, I see a stage in the distance where people are starting to take their seats. "Oh, I wonder what that is."

DaQuan grumbles, finishing his food quickly and crushing the cardboard tray in his hands. "I am leaving."

He stands, and so I do, holding out my hand for his trash. He hesitates for only a moment before dropping it into my palm.

"The food here was good." That's his goodbye. He's already several feet away when I call out to him.

"Let's check it out."

He pauses so abruptly that several people stumble to move around him. Turning, he fixes me with a cautious stare. "What?"

"The stage. Let's see what's going on. It might be cool. Come on." I start in the opposite direction, my heart thumping until I feel him catch up beside me.

By the time we get there, the seating is nearly packed, but we snag a couple of seats in the center of one of the middle aisles. DaQuan is annoyed as usual when we have to scoot past folks to get to our seats. I hear him knocking into people and grumbling apologies, and I try my best not to laugh.

"What do you think this is?" I smile excitedly as we sit, training my attention on the stage.

"Why would we take these seats where we are trapped if we did not know the topic of this event? Now, we are forced to stay if we don't like it."

I shrug. "Even if we don't like it, we might learn something new."

He offers more grumbling just as a woman comes to the stage.

My body tenses as I spot the most noticeable thing about her: two shiny prosthetics in the place where her legs would be.

She moves with practiced grace, her bearing confident in her pressed uniform. "Thank you so much for joining our Veterans celebration. Today, we're going to hear some stories from survivors like yourselves, and I hope it helps give you the assurance that no matter how hard things may seem at times or how deep the scars, you can push through with the same fellowship that brought you to the service in the first place. We're all here for each other."

Applause and hoots ring through the crowd, and beside me, DaQuan flinches at the sudden sound, but when I glance to the side, his gaze is riveted on the stage.

10

BA'IR

I am nothing like the humans who come one after another and speak of the sacrifices, often disillusioned, made for their homeland.

I did not volunteer for the risk of maiming my body and mind, and yet, as being after being stands to tell their story of life beyond the scars they now carry, I feel more connected to their experiences than I would have believed possible.

I am not these people—but for the first time, I wonder if I could be.

My hate for the woman beside me is real, but so is the fact that I have been unable to realize it in the ways I imagined while with the Fein. I want to blame it on her kindness. Even when I am horrible to her, she smiles at me. The two times we have joined, she's welcomed me into her body despite the coldness of my engagement.

At this moment, as she looks at me while I ignore her,

there is hope in her scent as if she wonders if the life free of revenge and rage that these people speak of is possible for me.

I know this hope is not for the Lyqa who was trapped on Fein, but I also know I am no longer him.

He was gouged out, picked away, shredded apart.

Here, on Earth, with the woman who betrayed me, I have become someone else. Maybe this new being can have a life of decadent food and free walks during warm seasons.

Maybe I can allow Ivy to smile at me. Maybe I can forgive her.

The thought is a sharp pain in my skull, and I stiffen when she slides her hand in my lap, but then my fingers curl around hers, squeezing tight, trying to hold onto a reality I suddenly wish to be real.

We listen to the rest of the speeches in silence, each one revealing a more splendid image of the life I could have. People speak of families and peace, of joy and self-fulfillment. It isn't until Ivy squeezes my hand again that I blink to find the stage empty.

"I think they're breaking down now." Her voice is gentle as she indicates several men collapsing and stacking the chairs onto a transport vehicle. "We should go."

She loosens her grip as she stands, and I clench tighter, keeping the contact. We walk through the nearly deserted park, and I inhale the sweet scent of Earth's polluted air.

It smells like a new beginning.

"What those people said up there was nice." She tries to keep her tone even, but I smell her anticipation.

My head twinges with a shock of pain that makes me want to lash out at her, but I quell it, inhaling deeply again and telling myself that Ba'ir is dead, so there's no vengeance on his part that needs to be satisfied. "It was."

Her breath quickens, her lips parting to say more, but she hesitates.

We continue to the underground public transport that will take us to our respective homes and stand at the entrance, neither of us making a move to enter the station.

"Do you want to come to my house?" Ivy shrugs. "It's okay if you're tired of me."

I want to say yes, but after so long of resenting her, I need time to come to terms with this new future and what it could mean. "I should go to my own home."

Her face falls, but so slightly that no one else would catch it. "Of course. I'll see you at work."

I nod but make no promises. It seems that I am unable to do what I came here for, and maybe that means I should go home—to my real home, Lyqa.

Ivy walks into the station, and I watch her swipe her payment card and cross the turnstile. She starts for the steps, and when she would disappear below, my feet carry me toward the platform. I swipe my band to activate the payment confirmation and push through, quickening my pace to catch up with her.

When I reach the bottom of the steps, she's just boarding the waiting train, and I rush forward, sliding between the doors as they close.

She's sitting in the corner, staring out the window as I approach and drop onto the seat beside her.

I don't know why I followed, why I did not go home.

She says nothing. She doesn't even face me, but her hand finds mine, linking our fingers, and we stay this way as the train pulls away from the station.

* * *

"God damn." The murmur cuts through the silent companionship Ivy and I have been sharing, and I glance up to see a man staring at me from his post near the doors.

His body sways with the roll of the train, and I hold his stare as he openly grimaces. "Your face is fucked up, huh?"

I blink, unbothered, but beside me, Ivy turns her attention to the man, her posture going stiff with hostility. "Why don't you shut up?"

The man snickers, looking around to see if he has an audience. "Don't be mad at me because you're fucking the Phantom of the Opera." He chuckles loudly, attempting to meet the gazes of the other passengers, but they ignore him, though the air fills with a general scent of unease.

"You're so ignorant, and you look stupid, so go sit down and shut up. Nobody's laughing with your goofy ass." Ivy cuts her eyes at the man, and a few people hum out their agreement.

The man's scent colors with embarrassment, and he steps around the partition beside the door and approaches us, his hand raised to point a finger at her.

Standing, I tower over him, halting him in his tracks. "Do you imagine it hurt, what made me look like this?"

He swallows, his posture deflating beneath my glare as I continue.

"It did, very badly. In fact, it was the worst pain any being could experience—being ripped apart and picked apart, being *torn*."

His eyes get wider the longer I speak, and I step closer until I can smell the bitterness of whatever inebriate he is under the influence of.

"If you do not want to learn what this feels like, take a seat and stop speaking."

The man trips backward and collapses into an empty seat, nearly toppling onto another patron.

I take my place beside Aida, who retakes my hand. "You didn't have to do that."

"I did."

Silence descends again as we make the long ride to her stop, where we transfer to a bus that takes us to the block where her house is located.

As we walk the short distance to her home, I ask myself again if I can do this. Can I forget the past? Can I forget her betrayal and live in this moment?

By the time we enter her home, I've managed to suffocate the vengeance that's fueled me until now, so that when she turns to me, her eyes wide with hope, I say nothing. I lift her into my arms, groaning when her legs secure around my waist, and carry her to her room.

This time, when I peel her clothes away and settle between her thighs, it's not to punish her. She isn't facing away from me so that I can distance myself from the desire beneath my loathing.

When I sink into the wet grip of her cunt, it's not with bitterness. And when I flip us over, settling her astride and urging her to ride me, I close my eyes and imagine it is twenty rotations ago, and my life has not been what it is.

11

IVY

Something's different.

I hesitate when DaQuan rolls us over, his hands taking my hips as I straddle him. "What—?"

"You take your pleasure this time." His fingers flex against me, and he shifts his hips, driving himself deeper and making me gasp.

I move hesitantly, my grind at war with the sudden power I feel being the one in control.

DaQuan watches me, his gaze heavy, his hands gentle for once, and I don't know if I miss the grounding of his aggression, and the way it let me know just where we stand, where we should stand, but this new freedom feels unpredictable in a way his anger never did.

Still, I can't stop myself from rocking against him, loving the drag of his thick length gliding through my core.

He's patient, letting me find my rhythm, his only

movement a gentle thrust when I seat myself, heightening the stretch that ignites a tingle behind my clit.

"Oh, god." My head falls back as I move faster, bouncing to catch the feeling.

I need more, but when I lower my chin and open my eyes, DaQuan's watching me with the same even expression. It's almost like he's giving me this, so he doesn't have to take anything for himself.

Or maybe this is the only way he can take this, if he shuts everything else away.

Suddenly, I want the aggression because at least it could have been mistaken for passion.

I cover the hands on my hips and hold his gaze. "Come with me."

He doesn't respond, but when I grind down, rotating my hips to take every inch of him in, his eyelids flicker, and his nostrils flare.

Bracing myself on my toes, I slap my hands onto his chest, savoring the sting of my palms meeting the hard muscle as I work myself on and off his dick.

"*Ivy.*" My name is ground between his teeth. Light flares in the deep brown of his eyes, and his hips buck, pitching me forward so my breasts press against his chest.

He growls, the sound vibrating through our touching chests, and then his arms band around me as he fucks hard and fast into my pussy. The sharp slap of our pelvises tosses me over that precarious edge into a blissful pleasure that nearly renders me unconscious.

Through the white noise filling my ears, I hear him grunt, then feel him swell inside of me right before a flood of warmth rushes through my core.

* * *

In the long moments after we both come down, I tell myself that DaQuan's arms are still around me because we're cuddling. It isn't until he stiffens, letting his arms drop to the bed, that I allow the disillusion to fall away.

"I should go." He rolls to the side, avoiding my gaze. Reaching for his pants, he starts to pull them on, but I sit up, too, and place a light hand on his jagged back.

"Don't go yet."

DaQuan stops, his broad back expanding as he takes in a breath, and I struggle to find something to say to keep him from running away or from thinking that I regret what happened.

I don't.

I've regretted a lot of things in my life, but sharing what we just did isn't one of them.

He shifts, angling his gaze over his shoulder, but at the bed. "I tried to pretend, but I'm not sure this should have happened again or that I should have let it happen."

I don't know if there is anything I can say to convince him that this was right, so I say the first thing that comes to mind. "Stay. Watch a movie with me."

His eyes finally meet mine, and a frown creases his brow. "What?"

"A movie. Stay. Watch one." It's not what he's expecting, I know, and it catches him off guard enough that he scoots back on the bed.

I've leaned against the headboard, and he settles beside me, glancing at my nakedness with a nervous gaze.

"Hold on." I get up, put on panties and a pair of pajamas, then find the remote and settle back on the bed.

He sits rigidly on the edge, but I get comfortable against the pillows.

"Let me turn off the lights."

I scramble up again and hit the switch. The room is shrouded in darkness as I press play on the movie already pulled up on my streaming service.

The opening scenes to *Titanic* begin, and I peek over to DaQuan as he frowns but watches without comment. Settling in, I let the wistfulness that always comes with Rose and Jack's love flourish over me.

The first time I saw this movie as a kid, it took me two days to cry. It was two days of me thinking about what happened in the film, and it wasn't until I started considering what could have been if Jack had somehow miraculously survived that I got sad.

So much loss.

We're quiet for the full three hours. During the parts where the couple is being mischievous, I tap DaQuan's arm, and he scoots closer so I can rest against his shoulder.

As the movie progresses, his arm comes around my waist, and I hold him back, careful not to squeeze too hard. When Rose is on the door, and Jack stays in the water, a pained sigh rumbles through him.

It isn't until the final scene, when Jack turns from the ship's clock and holds his hand out to a young-again Rose, that I speak. "I love this movie, but I never liked this part."

DaQuan doesn't reply, but his chest lifts and falls heavily. Maybe he gets it. Maybe he knows I get it. Maybe I did this right, and this is the moment I've been waiting for.

"I always wished they would have shown her at the end like she was when she died, old and so physically different than when Jack knew her. It would have been a better representation of their love. That he loved her no matter what she looked like or how much she'd changed." I swallow.

"I feel the same about you, Ba'ir."

He goes so still. "You knew?"

"Did you think I didn't?" I can't believe that he thought all this time I didn't know who he was, that I didn't realize it the first time I saw him in the employee locker room.

He doesn't look at me, and I resist the urge to make him show me the beautiful brown eyes that belong to the Lyqa I fell in love with as a nineteen-year-old. "I'd know you anywhere, Ba'ir." He says nothing, just stares ahead. Hoping this means he's ready to hear me, I press on. "No matter what you looked like, or what name you went by, I'd know you. You're all I've thought about for almost twenty years."

He has to know I don't give a shit about his scars, and if he doesn't, I'm going to make it clear.

But then he snorts, and I think I must be mistaken because it's laced with derision. "And what did you think about during that time, *lehti*? Did you wonder what was happening to me? Did you wonder if I was still alive? Did you try to imagine what I might be going through?" He shifts until his eyes blaze down on me. His mouth is curled into a sneer, made more menacing by the scars pulling it tight. "Well? Do I live up to your imaginings? Or are you disappointed?"

"W-what?" Instinctively, I pull back, pushing up until I'm sitting on the edge of the bed. "Ba'ir, that's not what I meant—"

"Or," he seems to be in a trance. His eyes glaze over with a rage I didn't think Lyqa were capable of. "Is this *exactly* what you knew would happen when you closed that door and left me to the evil of the Fein?"

"Ba'ir—"

"DON'T YOU SAY MY NAME!" His roar makes me spring

from the bed. I fall back, my shoulder blades slamming painfully into the hardwood. I scramble to my feet with my heart pounding as I retreat into the wall. "You promised to love me, to stay with me, and you LEFT! We could have both made it, AND YOU LEFT!"

I clamp my hands over my ears at the deafening pitch of his voice, and a frightened scream escapes me. I'm back on that planet, that terrible place where my entire life changed, and my brain searches for the memory that's never too far away. It's haunted me for two decades.

I wander through the jumbled scenes, hunting for the reality he's insisting on. "Ba'ir."

He stands abruptly, moving around the bed and forcing me into the corner. His big body cloaks me in shadow, and I shrink back, unsure of how to reach him.

What he's been through is terrible, but it's not like he says. I've replayed that nightmare every day, awake and asleep, and I don't know how I came to be on that ship without him, but it's not because I *wanted* him to be left behind.

Finding my voice, I lower my hands, shifting to straighten as much as possible with him crowding me in.

He's not going to hurt me. He can't. I won't believe it.

"Ba'ir—baby, that's not what happened. I never wanted to leave you." My voice rises in a plea, and his expression shifts until I'm no longer sure that the Lyqa I knew even exists anymore. I'm no longer sure I'm safe.

All this time, I thought Ba'ir was afraid to reveal himself to me because of how he looks. I thought he was angry that I didn't recognize him or just angry about what he'd been through, which would be fair. But it wasn't that.

He hates me.

I can see it in the eyes that once held so much love for me, I thought I was the luckiest girl in the Universe.

"You are a LIAR!" Ba'ir's chest expands, his hands curling into claws at his sides. The muscles beneath his skin tremble, and my eyes widen in genuine terror.

I cover my face, both because I can't deal with this version of him and because I don't want to see what's about to happen.

"Get away from her!" A voice cuts through the ringing in my ears, and then Ba'ir is gone, his body flying across the room to slam into the television we were watching not ten minutes ago.

Now, the only thing I can see is the undulating expanse of a broad, familiar back.

"I don't know who you are, but if you touch my mother again, I will *kill* you."

12

BA'IR

This youngling has my face.

Not the face that makes others cringe, but the face I had so many years ago that it feels like a memory, a memory that's standing between Ivy and me.

I push myself up from the floor, the jagged bits of debris from the broken television digging into my hands.

Across from me, blocking Ivy from view, though he can't block the stinging scent of her fear, is my son.

Our son.

"Get out."

"BJ—"

"I said, get out." The boy ignores his mother and shifts so she can't move around him, his brown eyes blazing with intent. "Now."

The lehti'an has been triggered, and if I were to make any move, even perceived as threatening, this boy would do precisely as he's said and take my life.

Good.

He's a good son, then.

The rage, an ever-present hand around my neck, urging me toward my revenge, recedes enough that I can see the image I must have presented when he walked in.

I must have appeared like a wild beast, and that is aside from my face.

I don't want to think that I could ever hurt Ivy; that was never my goal, at least not physically. I only wanted her to understand how she had hurt me, how she had betrayed me. Instead, I finally became what the Fein tried to make me—an animal.

"I will go."

"Yeah, you do that."

I walk quickly toward the door.

As I make my way down the hall, the soothing voice of my son follows me, all of the threat gone as he speaks to his mother. "Crap, Mom. Are you okay? What the hell is going on?"

I pause, my First heart thumping as I wait for her to expose me to the son I didn't even realize I had.

"Don't worry about it, sweetie. It was my fault. We just had a misunderstanding. I didn't expect you to be here. You shouldn't have had to see that. I'm sorry."

"Did he hurt you? Let me check you."

"No, baby. I'm fine. Just give me a minute to get myself together. Why aren't you at school?"

"Mom, forget about school. Are you sure you're okay? Who was that?"

There's a pause before Ivy answers. "No one. It wasn't anyone."

I breathe a sigh of relief and leave.

***

"Welcome back."

I pause at the greeting of the transport center assistant as I leave my craft in his care.

I *am* back.

I was rescued from my enslavement nearly four spans ago, and it is my first time on Lyqa soil. Until this moment, returning home seemed less of a priority. All I could think of was Ivy and finding her so she could see what she'd done to me. But now that I am home, I don't understand why I didn't run here. After so long being kept from everything I held dear, why wasn't this the first place I went?

I acknowledge the attendant with a lowering of my head before rushing out into the world I once called home. I stand in the walking path with my face to the familiar constellations above and inhale the scents of my youth.

Back then, Lyqa was an easy but bustling planet, vibrant in culture and social life, and from the looks of things, as I start down the road, not much has changed.

Despite the late hour, several people, mostly pairs, are out. Everyone seems happy, and when the random person catches my gaze, they nod and pass. I hesitate in nodding back, still unused to free socialization. It isn't until I pause before a large home, which resembles the other homes I passed along the way, that I realize my feet have carried me along the path to my fathers' house. It sits on an incline that seems both steeper and shorter than I remember, and as I stare at the door, the memory of my last day here assails me.

Ivy and I, rushing down the steps, her hand held tightly in mine, my heart light with the excitement of the leht. And even though I know it's useless to think this way, had I known then that day would be the last of my freedom for twenty rotations, I never would have left.

It's a long while before I am able to climb to call at the door. My heart thumps as I wait for it to open, and when it does, the past collides with the present once again, making me sway with sudden emotion. I want to cry out, but the sound stalls in my throat.

I was nearly as tall as my Ap'ha at twenty-three rotations but not yet as broad. He passed his dark, curled hair to me, and while mine is now dense and long after years of having no way to maintain it aside from an occasional rough chop with a sharpened bit of rock, the tapered cut he wears is the same as it has always been.

His dark, reddish skin is as rich and shiny as I recall. He has not aged much, but fine lines etch his eyes and mouth, lending a weariness that wasn't there before. As a child, Ap'ha was a confident presence, warm yet commanding, a perfect complement to my Ap'hati's more exuberant, if worrisome, nature. It was easy to see why they were leht.

"Dahni?" Ap'ha's eyes widen before he grabs me and pulls me into a hug.

It takes a moment for me to hug him back, but not as long as it would have a week ago, before Ivy chipped away at my reserve and reminded me what it felt like to be touched with something other than cruelty.

"Ap'ha." I grip him tightly, overwhelmed by the comfort of his smell and the familiarity of his embrace.

I once let myself believe that I would never see him again. I'm glad I was wrong.

Reluctantly, we release each other and step back, and it isn't until his eyes begin to track across my face that I remember what I look like. My hands come up to cover my scars, but my father grabs my wrists before I can shield myself from the disgust I can't bear to see on his face.

"What are you doing?" His voice is harsh, admonishing. "Do you think in your home, where your fathers love you, we care what you look like? You're our son. We thought we'd never see you again. I will look at your face as much as I want."

"I thought we taught him better that shame wasn't something we did in this household." Another familiar voice sounds out as Ap'hati appears in the hall, his mouth tightening. "Come here, my beautiful son."

He is also the same but different. The time shows a little more in the lightened edges of his cropped red hair. His eyes, which are the same brown as mine, shine bright.

It occurs to me that I look like him.

I never considered the features my fathers passed to me, but while I received my height and hair from my Ap'ha, my general appearance is that of my Ap'hati.

I was barely of age when I was captured, silly and young, and just exploring on my own. Now, I'm a man, full-grown for many rotations, but I rush into my father's arms like the youngling I was when I last saw him, gripping him hard and sobbing against his shoulder.

"You're home. You're home." Ap'hati rubs over my back, and I'm filled with the sure and unyielding love I grew up with.

It's warm and bright. It's the yeasty smell of the bread Ap'ha cooked with my favorite stew. It's the crisp, feathery touch of the first dwal, spiraling down from the sky to land on the tip of my nose. It's a hug from the ones who raised me and gave me my name.

It's home.

I sniffle and nod, pulling away to run a hand over my warm face. "I'm sorry, Ap'hati. I'm sorry it took me so long to come here."

"It's okay. We know why you went there first. She's your lehti."

I shake my head as some of the lightness is replaced with the dark anger I've held toward Ivy. "I should have come here first. I should have come home. I just needed her to see what she'd done, but it wasn't worth it. She took enough from me. She took *everything*. Going there only gave her more to take. I should have come home."

My father frowns, his eyes shifting beyond to my Ap'ha, but then he smiles brightly, gripping my arms. "You're so much bigger than when you left, but still not filled out enough. Let us feed you."

***

"I cannot eat another thing."

Beside me, Ap'ha chuckles and squeezes my shoulder. He's kept his hand there in a comforting grip.

"We'll save it. If you get hungry later, it's here." My Ap'hati seals the lids on the bowls and platters, still piled high with all my favorite foods, and puts them away before coming back to sit across from me.

My fathers exchange a look similar to the one they shared in the hall when I mentioned Ivy's betrayal, and my Ap'ha clears his throat. "We'd like to talk to you about what happened to you with the Fein, why it took so long to get you out, and—about Ivy. Not now," he continues when I begin to tell him that I don't want to talk about her or think about her ever again. "Rest first. We'll take you to your rooms."

They lead me through our home, which hasn't changed much in the twenty rotations I was gone, and I start to tell them that I can find it myself, but the reason for their escort becomes clear when I enter the apartments I kept for my entire life before captivity.

These rooms are no longer mine.

The first giveaway is the smell. It's familiar and familial. But that's not all. The furnishings are different. There are still things that belonged to me, but they're mixed in with the possessions of another.

The thought that I was replaced feels bitter in my mind, and I fight back the saddening sensation that I'm standing in a home where I no longer belong.

"You were gone a long time. We'd like to tell you how it's been for us, too—what's changed." My Ap'ha places a hand on my shoulder and squeezes.

I nod without turning, not wanting to see their faces, to see if they, too, feel like I no longer have a place here.

Silently, they leave, and the moment they do, I go to the closet that holds the spare bedding and take a fresh blanket to the common room where I make a pallet on the floor and lie down. For a long time, I stare at the ceiling, remembering when I brought Ivy to Lyqa after we were first leht. She was so excited about being off-world that she couldn't sleep, so I carried her out to the common room and opened the balcony to see the stars. We joined for the first time on this very floor with the warm breeze blowing over our naked skin.

As I drift to sleep, I tell myself that those memories still live here. They're still mine. And I may not have the same place here anymore, but I'm home, and I can find a way to fit in.

***

"Do you still take roasted sawa for breakfast?"

Ap'hati turns from the cooking range as I pad into the

kitchen. His face brightens, but then falls as if he realizes there were no preferences where I came from.

I barely slept and awoke spans ago, but didn't leave my old apartments until I heard my parents leave theirs. I wanted to, but it felt intrusive. I imagined them waking to find me moving about the home and becoming uncomfortable. It was a silly thought, perhaps, but as my Ap'ha noted, things have changed.

I wave away my Ap'hati's guilt and drop heavily onto the seat at the island between us. "Anything you make is fine, but you don't have to cook for me. I was hoping I still had some credit left in my accounts. If there is enough, I can look for new apartments today."

My father smiles and plates the sawa before sliding the platter toward me. "Eat first. Then we can talk about credit and your apartments."

"Not mine anymore, it seems."

He chuckles lightly, turning back to the range. "No, not yours. They were needed, and we knew that if you were here, you would not mind."

"I understand." I'm glad he isn't attempting to spare me, though when I bite into the sawa, it's bland on my tongue. I force the swallow and push the other pieces around my plate. "I'd like to meet him, my brother. If he wants, and you and Ap'ha feel comfortable. At least to thank him for giving his rooms to me last night. I also understand if you'd like to wait. I wouldn't want to frighten him."

"Your son."

I blink at my father, my brow turning down.

His mouth tilts again in a sadder smile. "Your son stays in your rooms when he comes to visit us. He enjoys being close to your things. I think it made him feel close to you." He watches me closely. "Ivy commed last night. She was worried for you."

I blink again, confused. "My son?"

"Yes. BJ, Ba'ir Junior. The 'junior' is a human distinction given to males when they are named after their fathers. BJ's been coming here since he was born, first with Ivy and then on his own. He spends more time on Lyqa now that he's older and pursuing his educational interests. He and your Ap'ha enjoy going to see shows, as you did. He's also a fairly good cook, though he has his mother's tastes in that he prefers flesh. The rest of our family adores him. He's a good young man."

I take in all of these details, although I'm still too baffled to comprehend what my father is saying fully. I assumed Ivy went straight to Earth and had forgotten all about my fathers and our home on Lyqa.

I assumed she'd erased me from her life, but she hadn't. She had given birth to our son and named him after me. She brought him to my home so he could know his grandparents and the rest of his Lyqa family.

Until I saw BJ standing between us, I hadn't thought about her pregnancy, which was so new when I was taken.

I recall now what she yelled at me last night: that she didn't want to leave me. She looked so hurt, almost betrayed in the same way I've felt all these years.

"Does he know I'm here? My son—BJ?"

My father's head tilts. "Are you asking if Ivy told him that the male who threatened her enough to trigger the lehti'an was you? No, she didn't reveal your identity to him. As I said, she was more concerned for your well-being. Your behavior was very confusing for her. She is under the impression that you believe she left you with the Fein on purpose."

I don't want to have this discussion. Obviously, Ivy at least did right by our son in allowing him to come to Lyqa, but that doesn't change what I know to be true about the circumstances of my capture. "It doesn't matter anymore. I thought it mattered, but I realize now that anyone would have wanted to live. We were young, and she barely knew me. The leht isn't the same for her kind. She had no reason to sacrifice herself to try to save us both. If her betrayal meant my son was saved and born, then I'm prepared to leave it be."

If anything, my father looks more pensive. "Okay. Let's leave it for how."

"So what now? I mean, with BJ. How often does he come here? Will he come soon?" My heart races with a mix of unfamiliar excitement and apprehension at the thought of meeting my son.

"Lately, he has been busy with his studies. He comes to visit us and his mother when he has a break." Ap'hati offers a gentle smile. "You should meet him, but not like this. We love you however you are, but you don't have to wear that mask anymore."

I know what he means. As I rested on the floor in the apartments that my son now uses, it no longer felt necessary that I hold onto the reminder of what was done to me. As I pondered being Lyqa again and fitting back into the society that reared me, this part of my vengeance seemed petulant, silly even.

Tentatively, I reach up and trace the scars marking my cheek. Lines and grooves that act as a chronology of grievances against me. The conclusion I came to at the festival with Ivy returns, that maybe this is a new path for me. I was saved, something I never thought would happen, and life is still possible.

"Your Ap'ha made you an appointment at the healing center. You need this, not just so you can see yourself again, but I think there may be damage you cannot see—or feel even."

I think my father's right.

Since my confrontation with Ivy, there's been a throbbing hollow in my mind, a place where things seem to be missing or misaligned. I want to be whole again.

I want to be the Lyqa I know the Fein didn't destroy.

***

The walk to the healing center shows me, in the daylight, just how much things on Lyqa are the same yet so different.

The doors to the place where I was born and received all of my primary care as a child open to a soft-spoken Lyqa greeter who directs us to the correct floor.

We're met by the same healer who birthed me, and she is just as I remember: gentle and with a reassuring smile. She is round with a child, and when my eyes widen upon seeing her belly, she laughs.

"These two were a surprise. The look you have is the same as my lehti when the conception sickness came upon me." She smooths a hand over the swell. "My eldest daughter is your age. Do you remember her?"

My memory flashes with the image of a lanky young Lyqa who would never quite meet my gaze when we spoke.

"She was very taken with you." The healer offers an amused smirk. "She was sure you would be her lehti."

I think about the woman who was eventually given that distinction. Would I have been happier if I had been leht to someone else? If my lehti had been Lyqa, I never would have

114

felt compelled to accommodate Ivy's mating custom of presenting a ring. I would never have ended up with the Fein.

"She's partnered now, to a Lyqa and a Pashtani, and happy. As I understand, a great deal of joy was stolen from you. Let's hope today that we can restore some of it." She takes my hand and squeezes before waving me toward the examination table. "Come; lie down."

I do as she says, settling on the healing table.

"Your injuries are extensive, particularly the interference with your brain, but we will have you set correctly in no time. Just relax."

The lights dim, and the soothing sound of a rushing river plays from somewhere. I close my eyes as the machine above whirs gently to life.

"The physical corrections to your face and body will barely be felt, but the brain repairs may trigger some memory stimulations that feel quite real. Your mind may feel muddled. You will be given a serum to counteract the Fein toxin that altered your brain. Your skull is full of it, so they must have been trying to suppress a significant memory. You will feel as if your sense of reality is shifting. Don't be alarmed."

Her words trigger a sharp pain as if my brain is rebelling against what she's telling me. I hold still as the medical wand moves over my body, focusing instead on the obvious technological advancements.

Things have improved dramatically since I was taken. Back when I was a youngling, while they didn't hurt, medical procedures did sometimes have a tingling sensation. The want tracks across my body with feather-light touches that are almost a caress. It's not a span later that the tightness that's held my body hostage for twenty rotations is gone like it never was. It's a faraway sensation quickly fading as a memory.

Just as quickly as the remnants of my scars start to fade, pain lances through my skull, and I'm jerked into darkness…

Two Young Lehti in Love

BA'IR

"Morning."

The light filtering from my open balcony twinkles off the metal bars stuck across Ivy's teeth when she smiles brightly the moment her eyes open.

I have been staring at her as she slept, watching the slow rise and fall of her chest, skimming my fingers along the smooth skin of her breasts and belly.

"How are you feeling, my *lehti*? Are you sore?"

She blushes, an adorable flush of blood beneath her brown skin. "A little, and a little embarrassed."

"Why?" Is she ashamed of what we shared, or did I not turn things around as well as I thought I did?

Since it was my first time joining as well, I was not as gentle as I should have been. When she permitted me between her legs, I thrust eagerly into her slick heat, bucking hard and fast as her knees gripped my hips. It wasn't until

117

she softly gasped my name that I opened my eyes from the rapture of being inside of her the first time and realized I was hurting her.

I'd been filled with guilt, pulling from her body, my skin pulsing with heat when I saw the blood marring both our sexes.

Still, my lehti had been kind, explaining that the blood was normal and calming me with petting strokes over my head and shoulders.

Then she'd kissed me, licking through my mouth, her braces clinking against my teeth as she took control of the moment until we were both once again surging with desire for one another.

When I'd entered her the second time, she'd opened for me, coaching my movements until the discomfort passed. Then she'd lifted her hips for my thrusts, urging me faster and harder before we both coasted to an end that neither of us could contain.

Stunned but full of energy, we lie beside each other, our hands clasped tightly. She'd turned her head to find me already looking at her—I couldn't look away—and grinned. "Again?"

Again had turned into a third time, until we both fell into an exhausted sleep. Now, she is beside me, the most beautiful being in the Universe, and she smells of shame.

"I was just so loud. I hope no one heard me." She ducks beneath the blanket, pulling it to cover her mouth, and relief makes me smile as I ease the covering away.

I won't tell her that it is likely that both of my fathers heard our pleasure, but I feel reassured that neither of them will think anything of it, beyond perhaps a warning that we share our passion responsibly since we are still young.

"You do not need to be embarrassed. No one will shame you. For my kind, pleasure is natural and nothing to speak about."

This seems to comfort her, and she sits up from under the cover of the blanket and clears her throat. "Last night was nice."

My smile is broad, and my chest lifts, my First heart thumping wildly as fresh lust has me growing hard. "Last night was better than anything I could have imagined. The way you felt, so wet and tight, so warm."

She squeaks, slapping her hands over her face. "Don't talk about it!"

My chuckle echoes through the room, and I take her wrists and try to pry them away, but she holds fast. "Why are you embarrassed? Did you not enjoy the feel of me? I did not even know I could get that hard. Did it not feel good when I stretched you—"

Ivy's hand claps over my mouth, her eyes wide. "Ba'ir, stop."

I laugh into her palm and nod my assent. Cautiously, she removes her hand and immediately focuses on the cover, flicking at the fabric.

"So what now? Are we dating or?" Her tone makes me frown, but she can't see it because she's not meeting my eyes.

"Dating? We are leht."

Her hands lift, the motion easy before they drop back to the bed. "So is that like dating?"

The cover flaps, sending a wave of her scent floating up, and I freeze.

"What's wrong?"

I blink, my mind shuffling with what I've just scented, and I meet her worried gaze, trying my best to school my features. "Nothing is wrong. I need to speak to my fathers. Can you wait here for a moment?"

"Uh, sure. Actually, I'm feeling a little strange. Can you show me to the bathroom? I really hope I'm not having a bad reaction to the food your dad made because it was *so* good."

I help her stand, pointing her toward the bathing room in the back of my apartments. I wait until she is inside, the door sliding shut behind her, before I leave, running through the halls until I get to the common room where my Ap'ha and Ap'hati sit sharing a morning meal.

They look up as I enter, having heard me rushing through the house. My father is already standing, his gaze panicked. "Is everything okay, dahni?"

I swallow, my heart thumping. "She's pregnant."

"You must tell her while there's time, and whatever she decides, you must accept it."

I sit on the couch between my fathers, my legs bouncing with nerves.

"Do not pressure her, and do not attempt to sway her. This is her choice."

They look at me earnestly, and I nod, my gaze swinging between them. "I love her. I would care for her."

They nod, always patient and kind.

"We know," Ap'hati covers my hand. "Still, whatever she wishes to do, that is what you will do."

I know they are right, and when I leave them, the entire way to my apartments, I tell myself they are right, but when I walk in and find Ivy pacing the common room, her hand pressed lightly to her lower belly as if she knows our young is there, I swallow the words I should say, and say what I feel.

"Stay with me."

***

"Are you sure?" Ivy's worried gaze looks out onto the large clay mountain.

I smile and take her hand, squeezing so she feels the strength that will protect her. She has nothing to fear. This planet is in such a secluded sector of the quadrant that it is doubtful any life inhabits it. "You are my *lehti*. I want to make you happy, and if this will make you happy, let me do it."

It's not just that I want to make her happy. I also want to secure her as mine before I tell her of her pregnancy.

I know it isn't what my fathers advised, but I want her, and I want our family. I believe that if Ivy knows I mean to honor her as she should be honored, she will want the same.

It's not what my fathers advised, but it is a good plan.

Ivy worries for nothing, but she still looks concerned as she surveys the landscape again. "When I said my people usually give rings, I didn't mean we had to go to a whole other planet to get one. We could just go to JCPenney or something. Honestly, I don't even really need a ring. I was just saying that's what some people do."

I don't know what JCPenney is, but I cradle her face, loving how soft she is. After the initial conception sickness passed, I eased her worries about the source of her illness without revealing her condition and fed her before joining with her again, unable to resist. "This is special, and you should have something special. I will let nothing happen to you. You should know this."

"I don't need special, and this looks dangerous. Are we supposed to go in there?"

I chuckle, too full of happiness at the life we will share to give her concerns any weight. This is the beginning of a beautiful future for us. She will see that soon. I'll mine the stone for her partnership ring with my bare hands to show her how capable I am as her lehti. And when I finally tell her about our child, she'll know the only choice is for us to stay together. There will be plenty of time for her to decide on termination if she wishes, but she won't want to. I am sure of it.

It's simple.

"There is nothing here to harm you, *lehti,* and if there is, I will protect you. I promise."

She sighs, her mouth twisting nervously. Her anxiety is so potent that it cuts through the thick dust like a blade. "Okay, but if some wild animal comes crawling out of that darkness, I'm running. You're just gonna have to keep up."

I smirk and press my mouth to hers in a hard kiss. It's a promise, like my words. "Everything will be fine."

I've nearly released the stone from the hard clay rock when a chitter sounds from the darkness to my left, so close that I startle back, knocking the stone loose to the floor.

Ivy steps closer and clings to my arm, her breath loud in the quiet that follows. "What was that?"

Heart thumping, I stare into the recesses of the cave, but nothing else happens. Regaining myself, I cover Ivy's hand with my own, giving her trembling fingers a squeeze. "It was nothing. I am here for you, my heart."

I bend to retrieve the glittering stone and close my hand over it. It will make a beautiful ring for my lehti. It will make a perfect ring to symbolize the start of our lives together.

I imagine presenting it to her, how her eyes will light with pleasure, and how once I have placed it on her finger, she will know she is mine.

"Can we get out of here now?" Ivy's voice trembles with fear. Her scent is tinged with it as well.

I could assure her again that she has nothing to worry about, but if leaving now will make her feel safe, then I won't delay any longer.

"Yes, my *lehti*. Let us—ah!" I jerk my hand back as something swipes out from the darkness, three sharp points dragging along my skin.

In the dim light, I look at my hand and find claw marks.

The chittering sounds out again, and when I look up, my breath stalls at the nearly three dozen sets of glowing eyes peering at me from the darkness.

I have made a mistake.

Despite what I told Ivy, I have not protected her. I have more than likely led her and our child to their deaths.

I don't turn. I keep my gaze on the threat, but the roar that erupts from me is nothing but desperation.

"RUN!"

14

BA'IR

"No!"

Hands press to my shoulders, forcing me back as the terror of the memory overtakes me.

I was wrong, so very wrong.

All of these rotations, I resented Ivy. I wanted to hurt her as she hurt me, and I was wrong.

"Dahni, you're safe." My Ap'ha's voice is gentle at my ear as he places a hand over my First heart and presses firmly. "Listen to your body. You're safe."

I do as he says and focus on the thump beneath his palm, the clean air of the healing center, and the turmoil brightening in my mind. If anything could engage me with the present, it's this last feeling, so clear now that the Fein's remaining hold releases.

In the moments as we ran for our lives toward my pod, Ivy was barely able to keep a pace quick enough to escape the clawing beasts at my back. As I urged her along, I'd felt my flesh open and knew I could not let them get to her.

The pod came into view, and with it, the realization that only one of us could make it.

It had to be her.

She carried our young, and even if she hadn't, I would not have been able to live with myself—literally and figuratively—if she died.

It wasn't a choice for me then, and knowing what I know now—that death would have been a mercy compared to what she would have gone through if she had been captured —it's a choice I would make again.

With no other options, I'd grabbed Ivy by the waist and, using the strength of my First heart, launched her across the remaining space into the open door of the pod. She'd hit the wall hard, and even this I'd felt in my heart and regretted as I tapped my band to close the door before she had even managed to stand.

My last view had been of Ivy's fists pounding the window as she screamed words I couldn't hear.

The Fein had descended on me as I gave the command for the pod to take her back to Lyqa, then succumbed to the pain of being torn apart.

"I'm sorry that was so startling for you. Mind mending can be traumatic, and I know you've already been through so much." The healer stands over me with a kind smile as she taps at her tablet. "We discovered some anomalies in your brain. I'd like to discuss them with you if you feel comfortable. We can wait until—"

"No, tell me. I need to know what was real."

The healer glances at my fathers before focusing back on

me. "It seems the Fein were very targeted when they altered your memories. It was not haphazard."

"How do you mean?" The strain of the procedure is still lifting from my subconscious, and I focus on the healer's words as she responds.

Again, she exchanges a glance with my parents. "The only physiology they altered was that associated with your leht. Without stopping your heartbeat altogether, they slowed it significantly. The toxin they flooded you with triggered aggression in response to the hormone that's released when a Lyqa responds to their lehti. Essentially, they turned the leht against you. You would have been unable to feel anything but anger and resentment when you thought of your lehti." Her expression is empathetic. When I glance at my fathers, they look pained, and I know it's for me, for what they know I did to Ivy.

"I know this feels terrible now, but—"

"But?" My eyes are hot as I meet the healer's gaze. "Is there anything good about me betraying the one true test of trust in my existence?"

She smiles, and I resent it. She should have no sympathy for me. "The Fein had you, and there was no reason for them to do anything to your mind. You were at their mercy. The only reason I can think of that they would attempt to disconnect you from your feelings toward your lehti is that those feelings somehow interfered with your captivity. There's something else."

Dread fills my belly as I anticipate some new evidence of my betrayal of Ivy.

"When correcting your physical form, we found something beneath your skin. It was wedged deeply, as if it had been put there on purpose. Scar tissue had long covered it, so you probably didn't even realize it was there. Do you know what it was?"

A sudden flash of memory has me bolting upright. "Where is it? Do you still have it?"

"Yes. We've put it away for safekeeping and will return it to you upon your release." She pats my leg and offers another gentle smile. "You need time to process. I'll leave you with your parents. You'll continue to have bursts of awareness for a period, but if you experience any discomfort, I should be alerted." With a nod, she leaves me with my mind mended and my existence once again shattered.

***

"How are you, dahni?"

I meet my ap'hati's concerned gaze and shake my head. There is no point in lying. I've been having jarring flashbacks, violent apparitions of my time with the Fein, and every part of my mind is raw with the truth. "I wish I had died there. I would be better off. She would be."

He sighs. "I cannot say that death would not have been a mercy to you, knowing what you endured, but I know that I can only be happy that you are here with us now. It may be selfish, but *we* are better off with you here. You have a son who would benefit from knowing his father, a son who thought he would never get that chance."

Shame makes me curl into myself, my shoulders hunching against the shadow of the first time I saw him. "Why would he want to see me now after what I did?"

My father smiles kindly. "BJ is you in many ways, in all the ways that matter. See him."

He nods to the door, and I follow his gaze, my own eyes widening as I sit up. "He's here?"

"He's in the corridor with your Ap'ha. He came as soon

as he heard you were returned. However, your father and I asked that he wait to meet you properly until you decided on reconstruction. When you didn't immediately make yourself known to us after your rescue, we suspected you may have been altered in ways that were more than physical over the past twenty rotations."

I stare at the door, my shame mixing with nerves to create a noxious rolling in my gut. However, hope also lingers at the thought that my son *wants* to see me.

"Okay, yes. I'll see him." I nod to my father, and he rises, going to the door and opening it to the tall figure standing just outside.

My son walks in, his expression warm with a guarded smile as he focuses on me. I stand, wanting to appear better than the last time he saw me, even if he did not know it was me at the time.

"*Dahni*, son—BJ. Ba'ir." The greeting fumbles from my lips, a need to acknowledge our connection in every way possible. My voice catches when I say his name, and as I really look at his face for the first time, I am overcome with the truth that *I know him.* I know him the way only a parent can know their child. My First heart beats as surely for him as it does for his mother.

Ba'ir Junior. A child named for me, a way for his mother to honor me even after she thought I was lost.

"I know this is an intense moment for you both. There is so much to say, so I will leave you to speak. We are just outside if you need us. Grandson." Ap'ha pulls BJ toward him by the head, placing a kiss on his temple, and my hands clench with the desire to do the same.

"Thanks, Grandad." BJ smiles at my father, who observes him for a moment before nodding and leaving.

I take a step forward, my First heart soaring with happiness for my child's existence, only to freeze when he focuses on me again.

The smile is gone.

The warmth, if it was ever truly there, is gone.

What's left is only what I deserve, and I know, without him having to say anything, he was not fooled by Ivy's excuses the other night. He realized who I was.

"Do you know what you looked like when I saw you with my mother?" He speaks Lyqa. His tone is light, but his chest heaves with the lehti'an, his deep brown skin vibrating.

I open my mouth to reply, but I can't find the courage to put into words what he saw.

His brows lift as if he expects an answer, and when I give none, he makes a soft "hmph." "My mother always talked about how handsome you were. She said I looked just like you. I think it was this she was remembering." He waves a hand over his face, and I listen. "A demon."

I frown, unfamiliar with the term.

"That's what you looked like, a demon. It doesn't matter if you know what it is, and it wasn't because of your scars. I knew who you were the second I laid eyes on you. To me, it was clear as day, and I want you to know that I would have loved you regardless." His gaze blazes with hurt. "But what you did to her, that you could blame and accuse her, *scare her*, after all she did, after all she's been through. You were supposed to be this man who was so honorable and so brave, so beautiful. That you could turn into what I saw means there is no place for you in my life." He swallows and continues. "I love my grandfathers. They have been the father you couldn't be, and I won't hurt them by telling them there is nothing within me for you. I plan to go forward as if you had died on that planet, and the only thing I'll thank you for is that the Lyqa you were was good enough to sacrifice himself so that my mother and I could live."

"I understand." The words are out before I can think about them. "I-I understand, *dahni*, BJ. What I did was unforgivable."

He holds my gaze for a long moment, then nods, briefly looking like Ivy. "Then we agree that no forgiveness will be given. I don't want to see you. I don't want you near my mother. You stay the fuck away from her. She's been through enough and doesn't need whatever bullshit apology you might want to give. You had *one fucking job,* to show up and be the fucking man we waited all this time for," his fists clench, and I wouldn't stop him if he wanted to strike me. Instead, he relaxes and holds my gaze with renewed calm. "Just do us both a favor and pretend like we're dead."

A sharp pain grips my First heart, like the claws of the Fein when they ripped out parts of me. I wince, but BJ ignores it and goes to the door. As he pulls it open, I glimpse my fathers waiting in the hall.

"Is everything well?" My Ap'ha sounds concerned.

"Of course." The lightness has returned to my son's voice. "I'll let him rest and call you in a few days."

"Are you sure?" Ap'hati's tone is suspicious. "We have plenty of room at home. You can share your apartments with your father, like you imagined when you were a youngling. You two can talk more—"

"Nah, it's cool." BJ's voice is strained. "I'll call you. Let him get settled first. It's been a lot for him. We have plenty of time."

"You're right," Ap'ha intervenes, silencing my Ap'hati's

concern. "Once your father is settled, we'll comm you. I'll make my stew for you both."

"Love you guys." I watch BJ embrace my parents through the open door and wonder what it feels like to hold him.

A moment later, when my fathers reenter my room, I turn away so they don't see the shame on my face.

They smell it. They must. It's choking me.

"Are you well?"

"Yes."

I hope they don't pry, and I'm relieved when they each place a hand on my back for a moment before leaving me alone.

***

Le'if, Fadi, Goan,…

"Come back, son." My father's hand on my shoulder warms the chill of memory holding me captive.

These episodes have been overtaking me with lessening frequency and degree since I left the healing center. As the healer warned, the revelations after my reconstruction have shown the lengths the Fein went to suppress and influence my memory of Ivy.

The flashback my father pulls me from is one where I'd managed to block the mental torment of my captors by constantly filling my thoughts with names for a child I wasn't sure I would meet. They'd always been boy names, I realize now, and wonder if I knew then that I was having a son.

I'd chanted the variations over and over until they were a shield in my mind.

It had worked for a while, keeping my head clear of the Fein's constant interference, which was used to control us.

When my captors finally figured out what I was doing, I'd paid for it with three fingers and an injection that made Ivy's pregnancy feel like an apparition in a corner of my mind until I barely remembered it.

"You need to eat. The healer said it's important to keep up your strength." Ap'ha helps me up, using a warm cloth to wipe the sweat from my brow, and when I'm seated in the kitchen with my fathers a short time later, I voice something weighing on my newly lucid mind. "I would like to find a way to generate credit. I was hoping you had some suggestions for work that I would be suitable for."

My Ap'ha makes a face and sets a bowl of stew, the one he offered to make for BJ, in front of me. "I'm sure you are suitable for any number of occupations. However, you have plenty of credit available in your accounts. We invested what you had at the time of your captivity and have let it accrue since then."

I frown. "You didn't use it to care for BJ? Anything I had should have gone to him."

My fathers both make faces.

"We were perfectly capable of providing for our grandson," Ap'hati supplies, almost offended.

"Your credit is yours to do with as you wish," Ap'ha adds, "but, of course, you should stay here. We will build an addition—"

"No. There's no need for that. I will find something close and visit often. I want BJ to feel free to visit as he has been."

"Why wouldn't he?"

I duck my head to escape Ap'ha's penetrative gaze and start eating. "I just mean, I missed so much of being an adult. I'd like to do this on my own."

He hums.

"Speaking of BJ, it has been a few turns. Have you spoken to him?" Ap'hati asks the question I know they've been avoiding.

I shift, clearing my throat as I spoon another helping of stew into my mouth. "He is probably busy. I remember how many things I wanted to do at that age." I pause, my mind fixated on some past before the Fein captured me. Another memory erased by the Fein materializes, transforming the kitchen into the dark shadows of the mines I was forced to work. Screams echo through the present, and I know they're mine.

"Dahni?"

Blinking back on my fathers, I eat another spoonful. "I wouldn't disrupt him too much."

"He's waited his entire life to see you free. I don't think he'll take it as a disruption," Ap'ha offers gently.

This is not the first time my fathers have questioned why I am not spending time with BJ. Over the past turns, since I have been recovering at their home, they have been confused by my reluctance to visit my son. They've also been dismayed that whenever they attempt to comm him, he is unavailable.

I won't be able to hold off their questions much longer, and I don't have a good enough excuse for why he and I haven't been making up for lost time.

"You're right, of course. I will visit with him today. I'm feeling much better." I have never lied to my fathers; this first feels sour on my tongue, but I'd rather lie to them than tell them that I have dishonored myself so severely in my son's eyes that he doesn't wish to see me.

They look relieved, and Ap'hati gifts me a bright smile. "Good, good. Maybe now that you are back, Ivy will take the help."

"What do you mean?" My meal is forgotten as I focus on them. I've tried to distract myself from thoughts of Ivy, but every renewed memory lifts my First heart to near soaring.

It wants her. I want her.

"We have done what we can for BJ, but Ivy would never accept our assistance."

My First heart thumps. "What does that mean that she hasn't accepted your help?"

Ap'ha sighs. "It means there is a reason she is not the tooth healer she wished to be when you both were younger."

I wondered about this as well, but at the time, I was spitefully glad she had also not had the life she wanted. "Her life has been difficult?"

My fathers exchange a glance before my Ap'ha sighs. "For most of the time that you were captive, Ivy spent the majority of her days and nights working to provide for your son beyond what she allowed us to contribute and hiring mercenaries to rescue you."

My heart lurches. "What?"

Ap'ha shrugs. "Earth credit does not go far in the Universe, so beyond the essentials for herself, she's taken on multiple employments at a time to fund attempted rescue missions."

I don't understand. My fathers were more than capable of supporting any efforts to retrieve me. Did they not wish to try?

"She wouldn't let us pay on her behalf," Ap'ha responds to my unspoken question. "Of course, we hired our own contractors and implored various agencies to help rescue you from the Fein, but for every being we hired, Ivy hired ten."

"Her funds were never great, which means she was unable to secure help that was worth much in skill or honor, but she never stopped trying. She was relentless, and it made a hard time for her. Not every being she negotiated with was good. In fact, most were not. She was tricked many times and cheated—attacked."

The thump of my heart is painful now, and my stomach twists with nausea. "She was harmed trying to save me?"

Ap'ha looks sorrowfully to the side. "Several times, when the beings she attempted to hire only wanted the credit and realized she was vulnerable and desperate. She'd have bruises where she had been struck. But once," he pauses and looks at my Ap'hati.

"Stop looking at him, Ap'ha, and tell me!" I almost don't want to know, but after what I've done, I can't hide from the reality of what Ivy's been through.

Ap'ha sighs. "Once, it was bad. Very bad. After that, we made her promise not to attempt to find contractors without our help."

"What happened to her?" My voice is quiet, but my skin vibrates with the agitation of the leht. Not a span ago, I thought I wanted to see Ivy hurt, but now, imagining her harmed and alone in a universe she barely understands makes me want to break something.

Again, my father seems reluctant to share. "She was beaten, Ba'ir—almost fatally, and left in a filthy alley at a port station to die. Some kind Somii were able to get her to healers in time. In many ways, it was fortunate. She stayed with us while she healed and was able to rest. I think the realization that she could have left BJ without both of his parents is what opened her eyes to the dangers of what she was doing. Still..."

"She never rests. She does nothing kind for herself. She eats plainly, dresses plainly." Ap'hati shakes his head, his mouth turning down before he meets my gaze. "Maybe you can help her with that. She deserves it. The last twenty rotations were unimaginable for you, but they were also terrible for her. When she returned home carrying BJ, her family distanced themselves from her, and she couldn't safely reveal the truth of BJ's parentage, so she went off on her own. She felt too guilty to stay with us beyond BJ's birth and visits, so we could spend time with him, even though we begged her to. She was alone."

Alone.

In all the time I spent with the Fein, I imagined Ivy enjoying her life without me, enjoying her youth as my body was being torn apart over and over. I imagined her smiling and laughing as claws and teeth ripped my cheeks.

I remember now that thoughts of her joy sustained me before the Fein manipulated them, but still...what I've just learned makes sense of things I didn't want to acknowledge on Earth.

The entire time, Ivy was either at work or at home. She had no friends and visited no family. She made no comms and received no guests.

I think of the stack of missives on the table in her home and how she dismissed them when she saw me looking. Were those her creditors, creditors she has because she tried to save me?

"You should go to her." Ap'ha's pulls me from my thoughts before I can fall into another memory lapse. "You owe her an apology at least, dahni."

***

I'm nervous.

My fists clench and unclench as I stand at Ivy's front door. I've been standing here for a long while, trying to gather the courage to press the bell that will alert her to my presence.

I shift from one foot to the other, going over in my mind the speech I've prepared, my attempt at righting a wrong that I know can't be undone.

I even went over what I was going to say with my fathers, and though they had assured me that Ivy would be receptive to my heartfelt words, their expressions told me that they were only saying this because they felt they had to.

"What part of there's nothing here for you didn't you get? What the hell are you doing here?"

I turn from where I've been cowering on the steps to find my son standing at the base. I was so caught in my mind that I didn't hear him approach. "Dahni—"

He snorts, cutting me off, and starts up the steps, his shoulder colliding with mine. "Shit!" Hissing, he grabs his arm only to release it just as quickly.

"Son, are you okay?" I reach for him, thinking that perhaps he has not inherited my more resilient form, but he knocks my hand away, his mouth curling into a snarl.

"Don't touch me! And I'm not your son. What do you want?"

I am having a moment of intense memory, recalling the time I barked the same admonishment at Ivy when we first met at her place of employment. I'd sounded just as full of contempt, just as hateful.

This rejection hurts, and knowing I made Ivy feel this way only hardens my resolve to see her. I may have been captured when I was barely an adult, but I have lived more lives and died more deaths since then to feel solid in my place.

I take the steps, broadening to my full height so that I stand a head above my son. "If you are hurt, you should not feel ashamed to ask for help. It is a luxury I didn't have for a long time that I wish I had."

The indignation on his face shifts a bit before hardening again. "And I'm supposed to feel sorry for you?"

"Maybe," I tilt my head to observe him. "Maybe you think I don't deserve it. There was a time when I believed I had suffered enough and help was due to me, but now I know that what I suffered is what I suffered, and perhaps the real mercy is that I suffer no longer. A fact that would not be possible without help."

BJ stares hard at me, and I think for a moment he will open up, but he blinks and looks away, clearing his throat. "My mother isn't here, and she doesn't want to see you. If it makes you feel any better, she's spent the past twenty years blaming herself for what happened. There's nothing about her life that's been easy or joyful. She did her best to make it happy for me. She gave it to me if she had any joy, but she's been sad, overwhelmed, and overworked, everything you hoped she would be. So, don't worry about trying to apologize for your behavior. What you don't realize about my mother is that knowing you hate her as much as she hates herself for what happened to you has been something of a relief." He meets my gaze, and there's sadness behind his eyes. "You may only think you deserve pity, but she wholeheartedly believes she deserves her misery. Leave, dude, and don't come back."

He turns away, his steps heavy as he climbs the porch, and I can't help but think he's too young to be this weary.

"I can't leave. You know my heart won't let me." Saying

it, finally, acknowledging the resurgence of the muscle in my chest and its attachment to my lehti feels like breathing again.

I tried to ignore it, but pretending it's not there and not longing to be close to Ivy again has become a different kind of torment.

He smiles, but it's not true. "I may have your face and your name, but thankfully, I was relieved of inheriting your First heart. So, no, I don't know what that feels like. Thank god." He turns away again and unlocks the door, disappearing into the house without another word.

I stand for a long while, thinking over what he's said. The sky changes color as people move around me, grumbling their annoyance as I block the walkway, until a familiar voice shakes me from my thoughts.

"I'm sorry about BJ." Ivy stands behind me. "He texted me and said you were still out here."

Her mouth is pulled into the tight smile I've noticed on her before, which felt mocking and malicious, a figment of my warped mind. With a clear memory, I realize now what's wrong with it. "Your smile. You're stopping it. Why?"

She frowns, then realization lifts her brows, and she chuckles, shrugging before pulling her mouth wide to show her teeth, which are once again dissected with uneven spaces. "When my mom took me off her insurance, I couldn't afford the braces anymore. Had to get them removed, and you know I hated my teeth. Then I lost one here," she pulls her cheek wide, showing a gap between two of her side teeth, and shrugs, "so I try not to show them too much."

"They're beautiful. They've always been beautiful."

She laughs fully this time, and my eyes are drawn to the

arch of her neck and the crinkle at the corner of her eyes. "Wow, they must have patched you up good, huh? Got that First heart leading you around again?"

She shakes her head and starts past me, and when I take her arm to stop her, she looks at where we touch, her expression unreadable.

I should release her, but instead, I pull her close, instinct making me lean in to kiss her temple, at the same time inhaling the sweet scent of her hair. "*Ma'h qitah, lehti.* I'm sorry—for everything." It's not the apology I planned, but now that she's here, everything I've wanted to say feels jumbled in my mind.

She sighs, a slight sound I could have missed, her body pressing into mine for the briefest moment before she eases from my gasp. "It's okay. I just don't want you to feel confused. What happened between us was wrong. I knew you were vulnerable. I never should have taken advantage of that to try and make up for what happened. That wasn't right, and you responded exactly how you should have." She swallows, looking away. "I'm glad you're better—whole. I missed hearing that, you know." She nods to my chest, where my First heart beats a furious rhythm. "I hope it leads you somewhere better this time."

"Ivy—"

"I have to go, Ba'ir. I have to get ready for work."

I frown. "Are you not coming from your shift?"

Her shoulder lifts with a heavy shrug. "Going back to close. Now that you're free, I have some things to take care of. I'm going to try and sleep a little bit."

I swallow around the regret that's blocking my airways. "Is this your life? Has there been nothing else?"

This time, her smile shows me everything BJ said she

believes to be true about her worth. "It's been a life, at least. I can't complain about it. There are worse fates, but you know that. Take care, Ba'ir."

She climbs the steps, and the new mission that's been slowly replacing the revenge that consumed me for so many rotations solidifies in my mind.

15

IVY

"Hey, baby boy. I made breakfast."

BJ pauses on his way to the door and turns, confusion marring his features. He stares, then casts his eyes around the kitchen like he's expecting someone to jump out. I laugh, but it's tight with guilt.

Yeah, I'm hardly ever home.

When BJ was young, I wanted to be there for him, so I used the excuse of taking him to Lyqa, where we could be with his family, and also have a place to stay when things on Earth got rough. I knew Ba'ir's parents didn't mind; they probably preferred it. Still, I couldn't sleep in Ba'ir's rooms without smelling him and thinking about the short time we had together. Before I made him believe he had to get me a stupid engagement ring. To this day, I wish I had just kept my mouth shut.

Even though all I wanted was to spend my time trying to

free Ba'ir, I didn't want me being gone to be what BJ remembered from his childhood, so I leaned on his grandfathers as much as I could, despite my guilt. As BJ got older and more self-sufficient and started spending more and more time off-world on his own, I used that as an excuse to find jobs to pay for mercenaries and a lot of swindlers in my attempt to get Ba'ir rescued.

BJ took over the household expenses a few years ago against my wishes. Since he's better at alien tech than I am, things were being paid, and I couldn't stop it.

I know he did it with the hope I wouldn't feel the need to work so much, but it just meant I had even more of my limited resources to dedicate to freeing Ba'ir. Since then, we've been like leaves passing in the wind, a quick kiss here, a short but tight hug there. I can't even remember the last time I made him breakfast, so his shock is warranted.

"I didn't get fired if that's what you're thinking. Just thought I'd take a day off."

His shock is replaced by a hardening of his features, which makes him look so much like his father that if he knew it, he'd probably fix his face. "Like I would be mad if you got fired. I told you a long time ago that I could take care of you."

"Yeah, but I'm the mama, and you're the kid. It's kind of my job to take care of *you*."

"I'm a grown-up now, Mom, and I think we can agree there's no reason to work yourself to death anymore."

"BJ—"

"Nah, it's fine." He shakes his head, avoiding my gaze. "I don't know what I was expecting, but I shouldn't have gotten my hopes up."

"He's been through a lot."

"And?" His eyes meet mine with barely restrained

disgust. "I've been through a lot. Grandpa and Grandad have been through a lot. *You've* been through the most, and he had the nerve to come here with that bullshit? *To you?*" He shakes his head again. "I know you'll probably forgive him because you're the best person I know, but I can't. I won't. You do what makes you happy, though. You deserve it."

I sigh because I can see he's speaking from hurt. My baby spent his whole life waiting for his daddy, and unfortunately, there's no memory to contradict the Lyqa he confronted the other night. "I understand, and thank you for saying that. What about breakfast?" I raise my brows and do a little dance, waving him over to the food like the squiggly lines of cartoon aroma.

The mask of resentment slips as he grins and comes to drop into one of the seats at the kitchen table. His eyes widen on the spread. "Oh snap, blueberry pancakes from scratch, turkey bacon, eggs, *and* homemade hash browns?" He chuckles, shaking his head. "Only you would take a leisurely day off for the first time in a decade and spend the morning making an elaborate breakfast for your kid. Best damn person I know," he mumbles the last part and picks up his fork to eat, so he doesn't see how my eyes well up, but since he's got his father's senses, he sniffs and pauses, twisting in his chair to fix his deep brown eyes on me. "There hasn't been a day that I thought you didn't love me, and there hasn't been a day that I haven't been proud of you for working as hard as you do, even if I hated that you thought you had to. You were always there for me. You gave me everything. Please, don't ever doubt that. I just hope you realize you can rest now. I can't make you, but *Am'ha*, I wish you would."

He hasn't called me that since he was a little boy. My son may look Lyqa, but he's culturally Black in more ways than not. I've been Mama, Ma, and Mom. Sometimes, when we visit his grandfathers' home, and he breaks out his fluent Lyqa, I have to do a double-take and remember that my child is half-alien.

Wiping my eyes, I nod and lean in to kiss his forehead, rubbing my fingers through the part-lines of the cornrows that hang around his shoulders as he returns to his meal.

"If you're bored, you could braid me up. These are looking a little old." He looks back with a playful smirk. "Can't be all up in the Universe and not have the best braids."

I chuckle and kiss the top of his head. "Sure. Bring your breakfast to the living room. You can eat while I do it."

As BJ gathers his food, I get the hair care basket from the hall closet and meet him at the couch, where he's already seated on the floor. He's refilled his plate and is focused on sawing off large triangles of pancakes to shovel into his mouth.

Settling behind him and noting how I'm level with his head, I start to undo the braids he currently has. "These are nice. Who did them?"

When he sputters and clears his throat, I smirk and wait. "Uh, um, a friend I made in one of the quadrants."

My brows raise. "And does this friend have a name?"

"Uh, it's kind of hard to say. You know, lots of consonants and throat sounds, a few trills—real *alien*," BJ mumbles before shoveling a forkful of food into his mouth.

"Mm hm. I bet. Well, whenever you're ready to introduce me to whoever it is, I'd love to meet them. I feel like I haven't met any of your friends since you were in high school."

BJ shrugs. "I mean, I don't really hang with anyone like that. Mostly just on Lyqa with the granddads and maybe chilling in some of the quadrants that have good nightlife."

"And beings with unpronounceable names who can cornrow?"

He laughs. "Yeah, I guess. But if there's ever anyone serious like that, you'll be the first to know."

"I better be."

We lapse into silence as I detangle and moisturize his curls, taking care with the six even parts down his head.

"I know I've already asked, but how are you doing?"

My fingers pause at his softly spoken question. "How do you mean?"

He twists, forcing my hands out of his hair, and meets my gaze. "I mean, since my father, who was enslaved for the past two decades, showed back up being a dick."

Sighing, I take his head and twist it back to the front. "So you want to talk about it now?"

"I don't want to talk about *him.* But I want to make sure you're okay."

I take time to consider his question. I don't want to lie. "I think I am. I won't say I've always been, but I think I can start to be. Is that good enough for now?"

His head dips, and after another lapse, his hushed voice breaks the silence again. "I'm not mad about it, you know."

"Me only being kinda okay?"

"Him being free. I don't want to mess with him like that, but I'm glad he's not there anymore. I'm glad Grandpa and Granddad aren't sad."

Wrapping my arms around him, I press my cheek to his. "Oh, my sweet baby. I know you're not mad. I know."

"I'm happy he was rescued."

"I know."

I can tell the conversation is over for now, so I change the subject, asking questions about BJ's travels and his schoolwork. Lyqa college lets him study basically whatever he wants, and it's cool to hear about his life off-world.

He clears a third plate as I finish his hair, cleans the kitchen, then makes a sandwich to go. In the foyer, he gives me another quick kiss and a tight hug. "The word of the day is 'rest,' Mom. R-E-S-T."

I swipe at him as he opens the door. "Boy, bye. You weren't even alive when that movie came out. Go, but be back tonight if you can. I miss you."

"Actually, Ma, I have this thing. I'll be back in a couple of weeks, then we can do anything you want." He smiles, and something there makes me want to ask more questions, but I hesitate.

"Lyqa?"

He smiles again in response, and I nod.

This is his lie smile, and he knows I know, so he doesn't answer because my baby doesn't lie to me. He just gives me another kiss on the cheek. "See you when I'm back. Anything you want. I promise." He jogs down the steps toward the pod parked in the yard, his cloaking mechanism activating before he clears the porch, and then he's gone.

I stare at the spot where he disappeared, wondering when he got so tall, so broad, and so much like his father.

Back in the house, I wander around looking for things to do that my son hasn't taken care of already, and find none.

Damn, he's a good kid, and despite his encouragement before he left, I end up falling back on old habits. I find my phone and pull up a meal delivery app to see if there are any orders nearby. Just to give myself something to do.

***

"Sir, if you relax, I can call the restaurant and see what

happened."

I sigh and take out my phone, turning my back on the guy holding the Chinese takeout bag like it's full of shit and not his chicken fried rice, but missing his order of egg rolls.

Since BJ left, my mind has been all over the place, and it's very likely I left the bag with the egg rolls on the restaurant counter.

"Yeah, and now I have to wait for my food. You drivers suck."

I sigh again, trying to suppress my annoyance because I don't need this shit.

I'm not even sure why I decided to do these stupid deliveries. Before, I only did it to hire contractors, but now that Ba'ir's free, it's not like I need the money. Well, I do need the money. I always need the money, but it's not like Ba'ir is going to continue to waste away on some torture planet, and BJ was right. I could rest now if I wanted to.

A crystal blue beach fills my mind, the sand rippled and warm, the sun bright above.

I haven't been to the beach since BJ was a kid, but I could lounge around in a bikini, now, right? Maybe do something really different, like go skiing or rent a cabin in the woods and hike every day. I could even go out for a drink or dancing. Have I ever even been to a concert?

Any of these options sounds better than getting yelled at over egg rolls.

Turning back to the man, I end the call with the restaurant and pocket my phone. "Sir, you're absolutely right. I am just the driver. I did not make your food. I did not pack your food. Once I get your food, I don't touch it except to bring it to your door. If there's a problem, call the restaurant. Bye."

Exhaling a breath that feels like it's been brewing for two decades, I start back to my car. I haven't taken two steps before something flies by my head, and the bag holding the food splats to the ground, spilling out the contents.

I turn, a gasp on my lips, but the man is advancing quickly, his finger stabbing in my direction.

"I want my money back."

"You have to call the restaurant!" I back away, stumbling over the food carton and falling back, hitting something hard. However, instead of looking up at the sky, I'm at an angle, leaning against whatever stopped me.

"I've got this, *lehti*. Sir," Ba'ir takes my shoulders and sets me upright before stepping in front of me. "I suggest you take your complaints up with the proper party."

Ba'ir.

His massive body blocks my view of the irate customer, and I peek around him in time to see the guy jump away, twisting to run to his house.

Ba'ir waits until the guy's back inside before shifting to face me, his eyes full of concern. "Are you okay?"

I step back, giving us some space. "I'm fine. What are you doing here? Have you been following me?"

"You still wear your resident marker, and yes."

He's so serious I could laugh, and I do. Not because of what he's said, but because it's just so good to see him. It's so good every time I see him.

"You know, there was a time when I thought I would never see you again, Ba'ir, and now that you're here, I'm almost disappointed that it feels so normal. Fireworks should go off every time you take a step." I avoid his gaze, instead looking down to shake my foot, trying to get as much of the mushed rice off the sole of my shoe as possible. When it's clean enough, I start toward my car. "Go home, Ba'ir."

"My fathers said you weren't okay." I feel him following behind me and quicken my steps.

"I'm fine. You can see that I'm fine. In fact, I just quit one of my jobs, so I'm even better. I wasn't the one being tortured for twenty years. Getting yelled at by some hangry dude who was craving egg rolls isn't the end of the world."

"There are many ways to be tortured, my *lehti*."

Pausing, I take a deep breath and turn to face him.

I almost screamed when I saw Ba'ir standing in front of my house the other day, looking as beautiful as he was the day we met. Older, yes, but no less fine. All of the scars were gone, but as I faced him on the sidewalk, I knew the ones that couldn't be seen were still mending.

"I haven't been tortured, Ba'ir. Just sad, regretful, worried about you. And now you're back. You can live your life and be happy. Find another *lehti*. Have other kids if you want, and a family. I know things with BJ are strange right now, but maybe in time, you two can have a relationship, too, if that's what you want. Just don't give up on him yet. He's still a kid."

Something changes on his face, and he steps closer. "He's a great kid, and he has every right to be disappointed in me." Tilting his head, he peers closely at me, making me shift under the intensity of his gaze. "My fathers didn't explain the *leht* to you?"

"What was there to explain?" I shrug. "And they kind of had more important things to do. Their only son had been kidnapped. What we had was a long time ago, and as you said before, all that's gone now."

"It's not gone."

I start to respond, then stop. Ba'ir opens his mouth and

closes it, his breath expelling in a frustrated puff.

I've spoken to his fathers, and I know that the Fein did some mental damage, and that's why he thought I had betrayed him, but that doesn't mean he was wrong.

The more I think about what he looked like when he returned and how confused and hurt he must have been for all of those years, not knowing why he wasn't being rescued, the more I realize my suffering at not having him was nothing compared to what he went through.

Now that he's back to normal, I know Ba'ir's nature is only going to lead him to guilt about how he exploded on me. And that's why he's here and why he's flustered.

When he continues to stare at me in frustration, I reach out and take his arm. "Hey." His eyes dart to where I touch him, and I pull my hand away. "I'm sorry." I back away, even when he starts to shake his head. "Listen, I'm good. I've been good. I'm just glad you're good now. I'm really glad you're good."

"You never used to lie to me, Ivy." His accusation makes me stop short in my retreat.

"I'm not lying."

He closes the distance between us again. "You are not good. You have not been good. You are tired and concerned about credit. You are sad. I can smell it on you. I smelled it before, and I wish I had told you then that you had no reason to despair any longer. I wish I had not done what I did. I could blame the Fein, but I was also resentful and angry. I wanted you to hurt, which is not the way of the *leht*."

"Well, thankfully, you don't have to worry about any of that *leht* stuff anymore."

He shakes his head, his expression one of disbelief. "My fathers really told you nothing of it?"

"What was there to tell?"

Given his reaction when I grabbed his arm, I don't expect him to touch me, but he cradles my cheek in his hand with such care that emotion immediately tightens my chest. "Only that there never has been and never will be another for me."

I sigh. I was prepared for this. I may not know everything about the leht, but I know enough to know that it's always been wrong about Ba'ir and me. If it were this great fated gift, it wouldn't have led him to a woman whose stupid mention of an engagement ring ruined his life.

"Ba'ir —"

"Ivy, please. I have no right to ask, but I'd like to show you what the *leht* means, what it should have meant for us."

My heart thumps; it's a painful, heavy contraction, and I'm reminded of those first days after we met, how right it felt, how connected I'd been to another being for the first time in my life.

Twenty years taught me that connection was misguided. But, still, I can't bring myself to tell him no.

I owe him so much.

"What can I do to make you feel like you can move on because this isn't why you fought so hard to get free, following some woman you barely know around Earth."

His face hardens, and I take an automatic step back, worried that I may have triggered him again. But it softens just as quickly. "I won't harm you, Ivy. I'll never harm you again. Allow me to do something for you."

"Something like what?" I don't mean to sound cautious. I believe he wouldn't harm me, but I still remember how he looked just days ago.

"Anything." His eyes sparkle with excitement. It draws

me in, this flare of life, and I chuckle.

"Well, I was thinking while that guy was yelling at me that I could use a vacation."

His grin widens. "Then let me take you on a vacation."

I chuckle again. "I was kidding."

"I do not kid. I would like to take you." This levity is so far from the void that was there when Ba'ir first appeared after his release and so unlike the searing hatred I saw in my bedroom that I move closer, examining the ochers and ambers in his eyes, following the tether to the restored part of his soul.

My breath catches at what I see because I recognize it. I'm carried back to that moment before we went into the mine: Ba'ir's boyishly open face, how excited he was to get the jewel for my ring.

Sadness trails the memory. Despite everything he's gone through—horrors I could never imagine based on what he looked like when he got back—Ba'ir is still that young Lyqa, hopeful and ready to live his best life.

Healing his wounds didn't bring him to reality. It regressed him to the time before the injuries were inflicted.

It breaks my heart. He really doesn't know, he can't know, how wrong this is. And it's my fault for being selfish enough to sleep with him because I missed him so much.

"Okay." It's an agreement only so that I can try to fix this. Maybe I can help him move past that part of his life and turn the corner on where he got stuck all those years ago.

"Yes?" He steps eagerly forward, seeming to forget the invisible wall that erects between us whenever we touch. His large hands close around mine, squeezing, and my body remembers how gentle he was with me back then. How carefully he touched my body. His nostrils flare, and he steps even closer. "All I ask is for one trip. After that, I will live the happy life I deserve, the life I should have had."

16

BA'IR

Ivy does not believe me and has every right to be suspicious.

I was in no way stable the last time she saw me, and there was nothing about my previous state that implied I was ready to look to the future.

But now that I am clear, at least in my mind, all I can see is what could be. What happened to me with the Fein feels so far away.

I need this time to reconnect with her, and then I will work on building a connection with my son. The leht demands that our hearts beat strongly together again.

"How long are you thinking for this trip?" Concern creases her brow, and I know where her worry lies.

"I will maintain your expenses while we are—"

She is already shaking her head. "No, no. I'll go somewhere with you, but you're not paying for anything. You've paid enough. I'll figure out things at home, and I'll pay for myself."

The set of her face lets me know it's pointless to argue. "Then I will allow you to pay for your transportation. If I choose to do something for you, you must accept."

She makes a face. "That's not fair. In that case, you could choose to do everything for me."

"Ivy, I was held captive for nearly twenty rotations. In that time, I can assure you I was not compensated for my labor. There is a limit to my credit. I only wish to offer you meals if you will accept them and a few excursions if you are willing."

The mention of my captivity changes her demeanor, as I knew it would, and I feel guilt at having used it to get what I want, but the truth is, I will if it means I can be close to her for a time.

She inhales, releasing it with a rush of air. "Okay, but please don't put yourself out. You don't owe me anything, Ba'ir. I just want you to be happy."

***

"Where will you take her?"

"Is BJ coming as well?"

"Lehti, of course, he isn't. This is a time for just them."

"Well, where will BJ be then? He can stay with us. Comm him and tell him to stay with us."

My fathers speak rapidly as I fill a pack for my trip with Ivy.

Not wanting to give her time to change her mind, I insisted we leave immediately. She requested a day to arrange her leave from work, so I have only returned to Lyqa to gather my possessions.

Secretly, I used a voice-altering device to call her employer and resign from her position. I also installed a block on that terrible food delivery service that nearly got her accosted, after I visited that customer again and had a very short but effective discussion with him about how he treats those who perform services on his behalf. Whether Ivy chooses me or not, she will never work another day. There is nothing that will stop me from ensuring she is secure and able to rest.

My life has become normal almost overnight. She deserves the same.

Since I returned, my fathers have been enthusiastically purchasing clothes and other essentials for me and leaving them in the new wing they had constructed, so I now have more possessions than I ever did before.

I didn't argue against them buying me things since I sensed it was more for them than me, but I did argue against the addition to the house. They were insistent, stating they were not ready to have me leave after so many rotations apart.

In the end, I agreed because I, too, missed being close to them, and while I know he doesn't wish to see me, knowing my son occasionally comes to visit gives me hope that our paths may cross and a bridge to peace can be constructed, whether or not I reconcile with his mother.

"BJ is an adult, my heart. He probably has other things to do." Ap'ha says this to Ap'hati as I move back and forth across the room.

"You're right. He is an adult now. Okay, Ba'ir, dahni, I know that before you left, you and Ivy had joined, but you were young, and if there is anything you wish to know about —"

I turn, my brows meeting in an amused frown. "Ap'hati, are you attempting to speak to me of sex?"

My father's cheeks flush a pulsing pink, and he looks to my Ap'ha for support, but my other father merely shrugs. "I am not touching this. I'm sure our son is more than capable of navigating a joining. We have a grandson, my heart, and you've scented him since his arrival. It's clear he and Ivy have rekindled their leht, at least in the carnal sense."

My face warms at the same time Ap'hati's expression turns sheepish. "Oh, yes. Of course. I just wasn't sure how, uh, thoroughly, he was able to enjoy his time with Ivy before he was taken or if he was properly satisfying her."

"Please, stop while you are ahead." Ap'ha chuckles, and I clap my flushed father on the shoulder.

"Thank you, Ap'hati. I appreciate you risking discomfort to advise me. I don't think your advice will be necessary, however. While the attraction of the leht did bring us together initially, I only wish to do something kind for her after everything."

I don't mention that when Ivy and I joined before I had revealed myself to her, it was spectacular.

My fathers exchange one of their looks, which means they know something I do not. This has happened many times since I've been home.

"What?"

"Well, your lehti is a beautiful woman," Ap'ha begins. "She is kind and generous. She is very intelligent. She is a wonderful mother. There were many males, human and other, who wished to court her."

"One of your cousins was quite persistent."

"Who?" My voice comes out as a growl, and my fathers smile.

"The point is, she rejected them all," Ap'hati offers instead of naming the kin who thought he could take what was mine. "She told them, she 'had a man.' Apparently, this is what one says when one is already committed."

A hot kind of possessiveness flares through my chest, speeding up my First heart. "And did she have a male?"

Ap'ha smiles. "She had you, dahni, and we believe that always meant something to her. She feels guilt, but there may still be regard there."

"Of course, if she rejects you, you must respect her." Ap'hati looks at me sternly, and I'm reminded of my youth and the similar instructions they would give me.

I nod. "This time, I will respect her wishes, whatever they are."

17

IVY

"You got BJ. Say what you need to say. Mom, if it's you, I'll call you back soon. Love you."

"You know, son. Your greeting says you'll call me back, but this is my fourth time calling you, and you have yet to return my call. Am I going to have to call you a fifth time? Get back to me, kid. Just to let me know you're okay." Sighing, I tap off my comm, which I only use to contact my son and his grandfathers, and return to doom-scrolling on my phone.

I may be trying to figure out the best way to style my hair for a month-long alien vacation.

After taking the day off to pack for my trip, I ended up with more time than I've ever had on my hands. Once or twice, I even pulled up the meal delivery app, just to see if there was something nearby to occupy me, but it hasn't shown any orders all day. Apparently, no one's hungry.

I resorted to calling BJ again to tell him I'm going on a

trip with his father. I don't want him to come home and find me gone, and I don't want him to hear about me taking a vacation with Ba'ir from his granddads.

I'm also a bit worried that he hasn't gotten back to me, but before I can call him again, the doorbell rings.

I know it's not BJ, since he has a key, and my heart quickens at the thought that it might be Ba'ir arriving early.

He could have changed his mind or realized that trying to relive the past isn't necessary. Either option should give me relief, but they don't.

Heart thumping, I go to the front and peek out the window. "Oh, god." Quickly, I close the curtain and step back into the shadow of the living room, but not before Vitem's head swings to where I was peeking.

I already know why they're here, and while I adore them, I am *not* opening the door.

"We see you, *dahnai*. Let us in."

I tiptoe around to the foyer, wincing when the old hardwood creaks. I know they hear it. Those Lyqa ears mean they can hear *everything*.

"We have plenty of time to wait, but why make this harder than it must be, daughter? Come now."

"Um, Ivy's not here." I make my voice deep, then frown, realizing how stupid I'm behaving, but unwilling to back out now. They'll have to break the door down if they want to get in here and—

"You are clearly here, *dahnai*."

"Ah!" I spin, my hands coming up in some useless gesture of defense. Tali, who's standing behind me with an exasperated look, shifts his eyes behind his lids and strolls past me, unlocking the door and letting his lehti in.

"We do not relish having to do this any more than you,

dahnai, but we cannot let this stand. It has been too long." Tali moves, allowing Vetim to come to his side and complete the Lyqa barricade, keeping me from running. I cut my eyes to the side, contemplating making a dash for the back, when Tali sighs. "Please do not make us chase you down, daughter. Just let this happen."

I pout, bouncing like a toddler as I take a step to my left. I'm going to run for it. "It's so unnecessary. You all have done enough. I'm fine like this. I promise, I'll bring something nice."

Vetim snorts. "You will bring one dress, most likely, the same dress you have worn to any important occasion for the past ten rotations. Everything else will be those leg tights. No. Come." He takes my arm and leads me toward the kitchen, forcing me down into a chair.

I don't argue because the open suitcase in my bedroom definitely only has a single item inside: the black smock dress he indicated.

Tali, who must have gone back to their pod, joins us a moment later with a hovercraft behind him loaded with cases and packages. When I make a face, he waves it off. "We've been to Earth before, *dahnai*. It was cloaked until I entered the house." Gesturing to the pad, his eyes light with excitement. "We have brought all of the things."

"I see." Undeterred by my stank face, he and Vetim begin opening the cases.

Piles of cloth spill out, along with several pairs of flats that are simple in design yet achingly beautiful. They're made of some material that looks like the softest leather I've ever seen, cut into delicate lace and floral patterns.

Secretly, I love nice things.

One of the few indulgences I allowed myself was to go downtown and window shop. I'd look, but I never let myself buy anything. I told myself that, one day, when Ba'ir was rescued, and everything was as it was supposed to be, I'd let myself indulge a little.

I lean over to get a better look.

Tali's brows lift when he sees me checking the shoes out. "These were crafted by *the* most renowned cobbler on Lyqa, possibly the galaxy. They are element-proof and will automatically adjust to the needed support of your foot. Here, try it."

He doesn't wait for me to comply but drops and grabs my foot, pulling off the ratty house slipper and sliding the flat over my toes and up my heel.

I jolt, my hands gripping the seat of the chair as the shoe tightens and then molds along my high arch in a way that I imagine a masseuse's thumb might feel working out a kink.

"Sweet Lord," my shoulders sag, and I sink into the chair as the shoe conforms perfectly around my sole. I don't even realize I've let out a sigh that sounds more like a moan until Tali chuckles.

"See? This is why it's important to listen to your Ap'hati. Other foot."

I willingly raise my leg, and by the time the other shoe is fitted to my foot, I collapse into the chair, my skeleton turned to jelly.

Was I really that tense?

I couldn't tell before, but there's a void inside me now, and it's released the perpetual knot in my belly and left me feeling almost serene.

From his perch at my feet, Tali's gaze goes soft. He pats my knee in fatherly affection. "It's okay to rest now, *dahnai.*"

I avert my gaze, twisting my toes in my new shoes. "Everyone keeps saying that."

"Because it's true. You did everything you could for a long time, more than anyone expected of you or was required. But Ba'ir's back where he should be, and you don't have to do any more. You've done enough."

"More than enough." Vetim's hands land on my shoulders, giving a light squeeze.

I've kept my distance from Ba'ir's fathers over the years, using BJ as the wall between us, keeping their focus on him as a way to distract them from whatever resentment they may have felt toward me.

It was difficult to see them, to know every brave face and smile was hiding a pain I wouldn't want to know. There was nothing that could make me forget the looks on their faces after I'd been transported back to Lyqa, arriving at the port, disheveled and without their son.

Lyqa Twenty Years Ago

IVY

"Ivy, can you hear me?"

Hands lift me from where I collapsed onto the floor of the pod, and I'm placed on a bed of some sort. A slight jolt indicates I'm moving, and I try to open my eyes, but it feels like my head is going to burst.

"Concussion, fractured ribs, several contusions." The accented English filters on the back of a melodic, breathy language I feel like I've heard before.

"Has her resident marker been activated?"

"We've reached her lehti's parents. They are on the way."

"Ivy, you are back on Lyqa. We are taking you to a healing center. You will be taken care of."

I moan as pain tears through my side but fight anyway to open my eyes.

I have to tell them about Ba'ir.

I don't know what happened or why the pod door closed

before he could make it, but someone has to save him. The image of him being dragged down by those things fills my mind, and I push it back, along with any idea that there may not be something to save.

He's alive.

I can feel it. I just have to *tell* them.

"Ba-Ba'ir." I force his name beyond the metallic taste of blood on my lips, even though the air it takes to make the sound sends a slash of pain through my entire body.

"Do not speak. Once we have you stable, we can understand what happened. Your fathers will be here soon."

My father? My dad died of a heart attack when I was ten. He can't be coming.

"Rest."

My eyes close on their own like I'm being forced into unconsciousness.

A gentle mechanical whir pulls me from sleep, and when I open my eyes this time, there's no pain, just a vague sense that there's something urgent I must do.

"Hello, Ivy. You are in a healing center and safe. We've corrected your concussion and your broken ribs. However, it is best to let the remainder of your healing take place during your next resting period. Your pregnancy is also progressing without concern, which is good. Human-Lyqa pregnancies can pose some risk."

"What?" I focus on the smiling Lyqa female standing at the foot of the bed holding a tablet. "Pregnancy?"

She frowns, and her smile falters a bit. "Did you not know you had conceived?"

I shake my head, trying to move. She comes over and helps me into a sitting position. "I can't be pregnant. I just did it. I mean, it hasn't been long enough to know. It was only a few times earlier today or yesterday."

She smiles again. "I understand that a longer period would be needed on Earth for confirmation of such things, but our technology allows us to verify immediately. You have conceived, and while it is still early, your pregnancy will progress quickly. Lyqa have a shorter gestation period, and from all the hybrid conceptions we've seen, human females follow the timeline of our kind. You will give birth in roughly two and a half months."

She says other things, but my eyes stray to the sheet covering my lower body and my belly, where I've just been told there's a life forming, a life Ba'ir and I made.

I stare until I hear her leave the room, and I keep staring, even when the door opens again, and two shadows fall over the bed.

"Ivy, *dahnai*, we're here. You're safe. Can you tell us what happened?"

"Where's Ba'ir?"

"My heart, please give her a moment. You heard the healer. She is in shock. Ivy, when you feel ready, can you tell us where you went and why you have returned without Ba'ir?"

Ba'ir.

I raise my gaze to Vetim and Tali. The latter looks near panic, his hands twisting as he waits for my response. Vetim leans over me, his face calm but his eyes tense with the anticipation of grief.

They're going to hate me, but I have to tell them. If only so that they can try to save their son. "They took him."

***

"Thank you, daughter. You've done well." Vetim kisses the top of my head, and he and Tali leave, speaking in hushed tones as they exit the healing center room.

I told them what I could.

It was a red planet, smoky with a lot of clay. Ba'ir was trying to get a diamond for a ring.

They'd been confused.

"A ring? A ring for what?"

I averted my gaze when I explained the human custom of giving rings as a sign of commitment and omitted the fact that I didn't want Ba'ir to get me one. They've lost their son. There's no way I'm going to make it seem like him doing something nice for me was the reason.

"Do not feel guilt, dahnai. *None of this is your fault."*

I don't believe that, and as they leave, I know that if they don't see their son again, I'll never forgive myself.

The room grows bright as the suffocating guilt makes it hard to breathe. How could everything go so wrong so fast? How could Ba'ir be gone?

The door opens, and the doctor returns. She's walking quickly. "You must calm yourself, Ivy."

"I-I can't. He's dead. I-I can't." She reaches me, and when she grabs my arms, I hold her back, my chest heaving, but none of the air seems to make it into my lungs. "He's gone."

"You cannot go on like this. It is not good for your youngling. I am going to induce a resting period. You will be safe." She releases one of my arms to tap on the tablet she dropped on the bed beside me. Like I've stepped into quicksand, my body goes limp, and I fall into an empty darkness.

***

"What the hell?" My mother's gaze travels down my body, stopping when it reaches my belly, which, even beneath my jacket, is noticeably rounded. "This is why you've been MIA for over a damn month?"

I open my mouth to explain, but I don't know how to explain what's become of my body, and I know "knocked up by an alien" isn't going to cut it.

My mother waits, her expression getting more and more irate as I stand in silence, until she finally kisses her teeth, steps back, and closes the door. I stare at the entrance to the place I've called home until the chill of the night air seeps through my light jacket.

"Come home with us, *dahnai*. We'll take care of you." Someone takes my arms and turns me toward the street. Vetim is there at the bottom of the steps, and beside me, Tali offers a reassuring smile. "Let's go home."

Home?

They take me back to Lyqa, and at the end of the first night, when they've coaxed some food into me and brought me to Ba'ir's room to sleep, they stand in his bedroom, their eyes fixed on me.

I wonder if this is the moment when they'll confront me about leaving Ba'ir, but then I realize they're only looking at me, so they don't look around the room where their son should be.

I start to say something, anything, but Vetim speaks before I can decide what would make any difference for them right now.

"We must apologize to you, Ivy."

I blink, my head already shaking. "No, I—"

"Please, listen. My *lehti* and I have done you a disservice, and we must correct it before you progress any further into your pregnancy. When you were put into stasis, we were told that you were unaware of your conception. We were unable to confirm your wishes regarding maintaining the pregnancy, and we were asked to decide on your behalf. We chose for you to keep the pregnancy until you could be removed from stasis, and we realize now that was a selfish decision and not truly ours to make."

I shift, the weight of my stomach still new and foreign. "So what does that mean?"

"It means," Tali moves closer, sitting on the edge of the bed and taking my hand, "the choice is still yours. While termination is not an option, we are happy to take responsibility for the child once it is born and provide you with ample resources to return to your life on Earth. No one will judge or fault you. However—"

"Tal," Vetim's interruption carries a warning.

Tali faces him, still holding my hand. "She should know she's wanted, too." He turns back to me. "However, if you wish to keep this child, we would love to support you, daughter, in every way we would have if Ba'ir were here."

It's the first time they've mentioned him, and I was too afraid to have my suspicions confirmed. "So, he's dead?"

Tali looks back at Vetim, and his expression tightens in pain before softening again. "He's not dead. He was captured by a race of beings called the Fein. Most likely, they are keeping him for forced labor."

I sit up, hope flaring through my chest and chasing away the disparity that's been living there. "So, you can get him back? Will your government or your military…" I trail off as neither of their expressions reflects the optimism I'm grasping for.

"The situation is—difficult. There are very few beings who can withstand Fein subjugation. We are doing what we can, but do not concern yourself with that now. Think on what we've said. Whatever you wish, we will do."

They leave me with the decision and the guilt, which slowly eats at me.

The days pass. I fall into resting periods, and first Vetim and then Tali try to get me to eat. I choke down what I can, avoiding the decision I have to make. I ask about Ba'ir, and it doesn't take me long to translate "we're doing our best" into parental grief for "there's nothing to be done." I let the weight of the answer push me back into the shelter of Ba'ir's bed. I succumb to his smell, still potent in the linens and throughout the room.

The shadows cast across the blanket become scenes from our short time together. Ba'ir's incredible face appearing out of nowhere at The Taste, his body shielding me when the stampede started, the way he held me close to his chest when he carried me to his pod, then sat with me on his lap as his fathers carefully explained that I was in an alien spacecraft, and they were from a planet called Lyqa.

I don't know that I would have accepted the news so easily if it weren't for Ba'ir's presence, grounding me, his eager smile letting me know I was okay.

A bug flies in from the open window. It's large, its webbed wings sinister. But I only see Ba'ir's wide grin when the bug's shadow hovers above the blanket.

The days pass. Vetim and Tali cook for me and take me to the healers to check on the progress of my pregnancy. I've given them no answer to their offer, but when I do occasionally wander the halls, mainly to stretch my body, which is tight with the load of my belly, I hear them quietly preparing for the baby I can barely wrap my head around.

Before I know it, I'm in a healing center, slapping the cup out of the healer's hand when she tries to give me a tea that will ease the pain. My eyes stay fixed on the bright white ceiling as I scream my child into the Universe—a child whose little cry triggers something profound and joyful in me. Something I thought died when I lost Ba'ir.

Vetim and Tali stay with me through it all, the former watching the healers to be sure my hybrid birth has no complications, and the latter smoothing a hand over my head as he speaks words of encouragement and praise.

He tells me how brave I am.

He tells me I can do it.

When they try to force the tea, he tells them to let me do it my way.

He holds my gaze, his Ba'ir-brown eyes full of something in my pain-filled delirium I want to believe is love.

And when they hand him my son, he looks at me and knows what my answer is without me having to say it. He settles the squirming bundle in my arms and kisses my temple. "He's yours, *dahnai*."

Everyone leaves to let me bond with my baby, but I felt the connection to him the moment he came from my body, and I also know it was always there, obscured by my heartbreak.

"Hey, little BJ." I don't have to think about a name. As I look into his beautiful brown eyes, eyes identical to those of his father and grandfather, I know he's not just mine. He also belongs to the Lyqa I love, and no matter what, I'm going to get him back.

Ten rotations later...

"You said ten thousand."

The being, some stocky, gray dude with warts and a very fishy smell, snorts. "Yes, universal. What am I supposed to do with this?"

I inhale, trying to find a calm I don't feel. I can already see this is going to be a waste of my time, like so many other pointless efforts I've been too desperate to pass up. "Listen, I made it clear that all I had was Earth money, and you said whatever I could get in Universal would be enough. Now, are you going to help me or not? If not, I can take my money and find someone who will."

I turn to leave the alley where the guy insisted I meet him. Apparently, he's a pretty nasty dude, who may or may not be wanted in a few quadrants, which seems to be precisely what I need to get to Ba'ir. All of the respectable mercenaries I've hired haven't done shit.

A meaty hand swallows my wrist as I'm jerked to a halt. "Or, I can take your credit, and you can go back to Earth with nothing."

I pull against his hold, my heart thumping when it doesn't budge. "Look, you don't want to help me? Fine. You want to take the money? Fine. It wouldn't be the first time someone ripped me off. Just let me leave."

His grip loosens, and I exhale, preparing to run as soon as he's let me go. The murmur of voices at the mouth of the alley draws his gaze, and his hold tightens again; the soulless void of his eyes goes even more opaque. "Not going to risk it."

"Ivy."

I blink and shy away from the bright overhead lights, turning my face into the pillow beneath my head.

I'm in a healing center.

Like hospitals on Earth, the equivalent on Lyqa has a distinct smell.

I keep my eyes pressed closed as the memory of my last conscious moments comes back, filling me with shame.

I should have known better. That guy was willing to help me for so much less than any other contractor I've worked with before. I should have realized he was just after the money.

"Is BJ okay?" I keep my face turned but can feel Vetim, the one who spoke my name, standing on my other side, close to the bed.

"Of course. I had Tal take him on *ta'ani maul* the moment we got the comm that you had been found. He's been on Qiton, enjoying the best month of his life."

I gasp and shift over, meeting his tired gaze. "A month? What happened? Was I taken? Did the guy put me in stasis or something?"

"Hm," Vetim's brows raise, his mouth pinching. "He almost put you in the ground, *dahnai*. If the Somii who found you hadn't heard the danger of his thoughts and scared him away, you would not be here talking to me," he holds my gaze, his worry shifting to censure, "and we would have to tell BJ that he no longer has a mother *or* a father."

His voice is tight, and the heat of shame washes over me again. I sit up, surprised that my body feels so normal despite what he's said I went through.

"I know I messed up. I usually meet people in highly visible places, but he changed it up on me last minute—"

"You think this is about *where you met him?*"

I meet the fury tensing Vetim's face. "It was a mistake, but I really thought he could help Ba'ir. It's been ten years, and I just don't understand why it's so hard to get to him. I don't get why someone isn't doing something."

"Do you think," I've looked away again, but the calm of Vetim's voice brings my eyes back to him, "that I've been merely enjoying my life while my *son*, my only child, is being held captive by one of the most ruthless races of beings in the Greater Universe?" His eyes shimmer with emotion—and offense. I couldn't keep eye contact with him if I tried.

"No. Of course not. That's not what I meant. I'm sorry."

"You're sorry that you nearly got killed trying to do something that in no way would lead to the rescue of my son, or you're sorry that you almost left your son without a mother?"

My fingers claw into the sheets as a twisting ache tears through my chest at the thought that I almost left BJ.

What the hell was I thinking?

I'm stewing in this gut-wrenching reality when Vetim's following words go off like the loudest bomb, even though he speaks them quietly. "And almost left me without a daughter."

My sob catches me off guard. I nearly choke on it as it bubbles up my throat. I cover my face, too ashamed to let Vetim see my disgrace.

He clicks his tongue and settles on the edge of the bed, pulling me against him. "It's difficult, dahnai. I know. Tali knows. But we are his fathers, we love him the way you do, and we've accepted it. You have to."

"I can't." I shake my head against his chest, and he squeezes tighter. "I never should have said it. All I had to do was not say anything about that fucking ring, and he would be here now."

Vetim sighs. "Maybe, but he's not, and you are. Your life is tied to his in more ways than you know, so you have to protect yourself and take care of yourself, or if there is a chance, he won't make it out of there alive anyway. Promise me."

A promise feels like giving up. It feels like saying I'm

going to go on with my life, having fun and trying to find joy, when Ba'ir is wasting away somewhere.

"If you can't do it for me, do it for BJ. He deserves to be raised by the person who loves his father the most."

My son's beautiful, bright face flashes in my mind. He really is the spitting image of his father and already taller than me at ten. I imagine him laughing with Tali as they explore Qiton, collecting stories to tell me when he's home. Then I imagine how life-altering it would have been for him to return only to find out that I was never coming back.

"I promise. I promise. I promise." I nod my head frantically, a vain attempt at dispelling the look of utter destruction on BJ's face that my mind has conjured.

"Good." Vetim rubs my back, his relief a deep exhale. "We won't give up. We've accepted the reality, but we will never give up. No matter how long it takes."

19

IVY

It took twenty years.

Vetim and Tali are still fussing through the crates, pulling out clothes, devices, and other gifts, and the same way Ba'ir's sudden freedom feels unjustly unremarkable, having them here like this, attempting to stage some alien fashion intervention, feels grossly undeserved.

"Can we stop for a second?"

The two Lyqa, whom I have come to love and respect more than my own family, pause and face me, their expressions resigned.

Tali speaks first. "Would it help if we told you that we've resented you this entire time for what happened to Ba'ir?"

My eyes widen, but then I'm filled with a longed-for relief. I close my eyes and nod. "Yes. Thank you."

"No."

My eyes snap open to find them scowling at me.

"Why would we tell you that when it is stupid and untrue?" Vetim's brows lift as he waits for an answer.

I frown, fumbling for something to say, until in perfect unison, they kiss their teeth and turn back to the cases. I sit like a chastened child instead of a nearly forty-year-old woman until Tali's voice brings me from my brooding.

"You've never been less than a daughter to us, Ivy, from the day our son's heart beat for you. You may not realize it, but the only relief for us when Ba'ir was taken was that you had not been taken too. We hoped eventually you would believe that."

I want to believe it.

We leave it at that, and I don't fight when they stand me up and start to hold clothes to my body. At some point, they comm a human woman who introduces herself as Crissette. She looks me over from her digital projection and tells them which pieces to have me try on.

The sun's setting by the time they've packed my bags for the trip and primped me within an inch of my life. One of their gadgets installed loose, knotless braids that fall down my back. Another permanently removes the hair from my underarms, bikini line, and legs. When it gets close to dinner time, Vetim takes over my kitchen to cook, and we sit down to eat.

I push my newly installed braids over my shoulder to hang down my back and taste some of the stew. "It's really good."

"Thank you. I missed cooking for you. There haven't been many opportunities over the years, but there will be more now." Vetim gives me a pointed look.

I eat another spoonful and try to think of the best way to address this. "I don't know how you all feel about me going on this trip with your son, except that apparently my wardrobe wasn't good enough."

"It was terrible. You would have worn those leg things the entire time."

"Leggings," I remind Tali, who waves his hand like that will also banish the clothing from my wardrobe.

"We are grateful Crissette was able to consult with us because we were tempted to attempt your making over ourselves, and that would have been disastrous, but still better."

"Wow, shade. Okay. Either way, I don't want you to think I'm trying to pull Ba'ir back into something with me. I'm only going so he can get closure."

"And what do you think closure would look like for him?" Vetim's gaze is genuinely curious. It catches me off guard because, although I've reiterated my motives to myself several times, I've never examined what it would mean for either of us to finally put a period on this chapter of our lives.

I shrug. "I don't know. Maybe he realizes he doesn't have to pick up where he left off. I hope that along the way, we can build a new kind of relationship—a friendship. I just don't want to be the thing that holds him back from moving on with his life."

Vetim hums. "And BJ?"

I groan and shake my head. "That kid. He just needs time. He's waited his whole life to meet Ba'ir. He'll realize soon that the Lyqa he met that first night wasn't really his father. Have you seen him?"

They exchange a look, and Tali frowns. "No. He said he was staying here."

"Oh. He said he had a thing and he'd be gone for a few weeks. I just assumed it was on Lyqa. Maybe it's a school thing."

"Maybe. We're sure he'll come around. Especially once you and his father are back together."

I make a face that Tali ignores, turning his attention to his bowl. "Yeah, I feel like you just ignored everything I said."

"We did," Vetim smirks, and he and Tali share another look that makes me deep sigh.

***

"Do not unpack your bag." Tali hugs me at the door.

"I won't. I promise."

"Well, even if you do, we've sent along another case of clothing to meet you for the trip so that you will have something either way."

I laugh and shake my head. "Of course, you did."

"We love you, *dahnai*." Vetim leans in to kiss my forehead in the fatherly way he does.

They turn, taking the steps together, their hands finding each other's as they make their way to the pod camouflaged in my yard.

"Hey!" I call out before they step beyond the concealment barrier, and they turn back. "Thank you. I love you, too!"

I've never said it back to them. Not because I didn't feel it, but because acknowledging how they treated me as their own felt too much like I was enjoying something Ba'ir never would again. Now, it feels selfish not to acknowledge how much they poured into me, even though they'd lost their son. I really do think of them as fathers.

Vetim presses his fingers to his lips and lifts the kiss toward me. Then, in a blink, that would seem like a trick in the light, were anyone to see it, they're gone.

I close the door and turn into my home.

The constant quiet is even more pronounced, and I

wander over to the sealed pack. It's locked with some sort of biometric feature that beeps but doesn't open when I pass my hand over it. Vetim and Tali probably rigged it so it doesn't open until I get on the ship, assuming I'd try to sneak some leggings in, which would be correct.

Going to my room with the express intention of packing a few pairs in another bag, I pull open my dresser drawer and gasp.

"Those fuckers."

***

"I told you I love you, and this is how you do me?"

Tali snorts, failing to hide is smirk. "It was necessary. It was beyond time for you to give up that uniform of efficiency."

"It was comfortable! And you couldn't have left me with one pair?"

"We saw no need. We provided you with more than enough comfortable garments for you to wear. Now, Vetim and I have some work on the house to oversee. Ba'ir left not long ago to retrieve you. He should be there soon. Have fun."

The comm disconnects, and I stare at the place where Tali's annoyingly cheerful face was a moment ago.

I was actually starting to feel really good about my little makeover until I pulled open that drawer and realized Ba'ir's fathers had completely cleaned out my whole wardrobe and replaced it with an entirely new one. They must have snuck and done it while I was showering before getting my hair braided.

Pushing through the hangers, I find a jumper made of soft, jersey-like material, which I will admit is pretty comfortable when I put it on. It's a shade of teal that I probably would have admired in a store but never bought.

The asymmetrical ruched bodice bands over one shoulder, and the pleated legs drape wide to the ankle.

It's cute and simple, and I will only begrudgingly admit this to Vetim and Tali when I speak to them next.

I gather the one bag I'm carrying and leave my house to wait. As I stand on the porch, fidgeting with my braids and smoothing down the legs of the jumper, I think about what Ba'ir's parents said and hope this trip isn't a mistake.

20

BA'IR

The ride to Earth takes moments, but feels like an eternity.

As I descend onto the front yard of Ivy's house, my gut dances with nerves.

Has she changed her mind?

I wanted to comm her as we prepared for our departure, but I didn't want her to feel pressured if she had resolved not to come. I also did not want to annoy her into deciding against going.

So when I see her standing on the porch with her back to me and a small pack by her side, I shout, my rejoice echoing through the pod. By the time the pod door opens, I have contained my grin as I exit to meet her at the steps, stopping at the bottom.

She is beautiful in a shade of green that complements her brown coloring. Her hair has been styled into braids that hang down her back, grazing the curve of her bottom.

It is so different from what I've seen her wear during our time together, yet perfect for where we're going. Her choice of outfit is fortunate since I kept our destination a secret. I wish to surprise her.

I'm afforded several seconds to admire her before Ivy turns and sees me. We stand silently. Ivy fidgets with the keys in her hands, and while I can't see my face, I imagine every part of my excitement shows.

My eyes trace over her body, liking even more her choice of attire, particularly the single shoulder bared above the bodice. I meet her gaze again, and she shifts nervously. "You look perfect."

She looks down at herself, plucking at her pant leg. "Your dads got to me."

I chuckle, unsurprised that my fathers could not resist meddling, but I know it's because they love her.

She breaks eye contact, turning to close her door and lock it. When she faces me again, we stand quietly for another long moment before she gestures toward my concealed pod. "Ready to go?"

"Yes, my *lehti*, I am."

She bends to grab the pack at her feet, and I rush forward, tripping in my haste. Our heads collide, and she cries out, slapping a hand over one side of her face and stumbling back.

"*Hu'l*. Ivy, I'm sorry. Are you okay?"

Her laughter cuts through my concern as she peeks at me with the uncovered eye. "Dude, your head is super hard."

That is not all that is hard. The sound of her laughter rolled through me like a wave, sending blood rushing straight to my crotch.

Shifting to the side to hide my reaction, I reach for her

hand. "Are you sure you're okay?"

She angles out of reach, but the heat from her skin radiates against my palm.

I want to feel her again.

I did not touch Ivy as I wanted to before, and now all I want is to show her the gentleness she deserves as we both find pleasure.

"I'm fine." This time, she doesn't remove her hand, and when she bends to grab her bag, I stop her before she can take it.

"Let me." I make sure she is out of the way and lift it, immediately surprised by its lightness. "Is this all you will bring?"

"I wish, but your dads also arranged for things to be sent wherever we're going."

I chuckle again and hold my hand out. "Then I am sure you have everything you need." She stares at my outstretched palm and hesitates, so I redirect my arm to wave toward the pod instead, nodding her forward. "After you."

Ivy enters the pod with ease, and I can't help but compare it to the only other times I've accompanied her in a spacecraft.

"Do you remember the first time you brought me on one of these, and I almost passed out?" She laughs, looking around the pod with the kind of comfort that can only come from familiarity. My heart warms that she was also thinking of our past times together.

"I do. That first time, and the other, you were so filled with awe. I found it amusing but also enjoyed knowing I had impressed you."

"I *was* impressed," she laughs outright. "I thought I was

about to have this crazy, great adventure." The excitement of that time lights her eyes, but just as quickly, it dims as the reality of how things turned out sours the moment.

"Ivy, *lehti*, there is plenty of life left to have adventures. This can be the first of new ones."

She smiles and holds out her hand.

I take it, squeezing her fingers before bringing them to my lips. "I know things did not happen how we imagined, but I am coming to realize that is life. It would be terrible of me to wish that it had happened to another, even if I know that it should happen to no one. Still, the most important thing is that you are here. You survived. Our son survived, and I, despite never believing it possible, also survived. We won't dwell on the past. We are going to enjoy the present because I, more than most, know that is all that really exists. Yes?"

Her mouth folds, but she affirms with a dip of her head before twisting her lips to the side. "I was, actually, reaching for my bag."

"I know what you were reaching for." Pressing a final kiss to her palm, I release her and hand over her bag, stepping toward the command panel. "We should secure ourselves. It won't take long to reach Qiton."

She drops into her seat, her brows rising in surprise as she hurriedly pulls her safety harness across her chest. "We're going to Qiton?"

"You've been?" I pause in strapping myself in. I'd hoped to experience this planet with her for the first time together.

She shakes her head, and a tinge of shame enters her scent. "No, but your Ap'hati took BJ once, and BJ said it was amazing. He had such a good time."

I secure my strap and try to sound casual. "You did not

go?"

I keep my eyes forward, but I can feel her unease. "I had something else to do, something important, and then it got a little complicated, and I was away for a while."

"Something like trying to find mercenaries to rescue me?" I meet her gaze then, and she looks away. The cabin fills with the scent of her shame—and guilt.

"It was the least I could do. I couldn't give up trying."

"You should have. You should have enjoyed your life. But," I continue when she would argue, "I also never went to Qiton. My fathers planned to take me, and I am glad Ap'hati was able to take BJ. It means we can experience the wonders of the planet for the first time together." I hit the command for transport, and the pod rises quickly into the atmosphere.

The moment we clear orbit, space opens up faster than we can comprehend, and we are launched into orbit above the ocean planet.

"That's it?" Ivy leans forward to stare at Qiton's undulating surface. "It looks like it's alive."

"It is." I activate a comm announcing our arrival to guest services and steer the pod toward the receiving portal. A floating receiver scans the travel documentation stored in the pod and grants us access.

"How is it alive? Is it sentient?" Ivy looks at me as we enter the transport center, and I concentrate on docking while I answer.

"It is a kind of sentient, more like an omniscient presence than a self-serving being. It will not harm you if you are worried about that. Either way, we won't be traversing the surface. It is the planet's long season, so there won't be land for turns yet."

"BJ said that he and his granddad camped on a tree. Is

that what we're doing?"

Joy fills me at the image of my son enjoying a traditional Qitoni holiday with my father. "Not quite. I thought we deserved something a little more luxurious." I point ahead, and she focuses forward only to gasp.

"What the hell? Is that a—"

"Boat. Well, a luxury watercraft. The best they have to offer. I have booked us passage to enjoy our month aboard. There are many things to do, and we will dock to take part in excursions along the way."

"So it's a cruise?"

My translator gives me an understanding that matches what I've described, and I nod. "It is. Is this to your liking? When I saw this trip, I thought it would be perfect, but perhaps the idea of spending so much time on the water is not appealing to you?"

"No, it seems great. It's just—is it expensive?" She glances worriedly at her comm, which my fathers informed me she has insisted remains connected only to her universal accounts. I'm already working with the Threshers who rescued me to hack into her accounts so I can fill them with funds. However, I will entertain her need to pay her own way—for now.

"It is feasible, Ivy. I made sure it was something we could both afford. However, since I arranged this excursion without knowing for sure what your budget was, if anything is in excess of reason, I will cover it."

"Well, okay." She still seems uneasy, but we gather our bags and exit the pod to meet the Qitoni standing at the base of the ramp.

The Qitoni's garbled language filters through my translator. "What are you doing here?"

I frown at the curt inquiry but offer a smile. "We have passage for this trip."

The Qitoni's expression shifts, but it's hard to tell what she's expressing. "You're boarding this ship?"

"We are." I smile again and remind myself that they are not known for their amiability. "I have our passes."

The Qitoni stares at us for a long moment before waving a hand at our packs. "Are these your only bags? This hardly seems enough. You're not prepared for this trip. Perhaps you should delay your travel and board the next craft."

I frown as I hand over my boarding pass. "We have several more bags that were sent ahead and are already on board." I push the electronic ticket out again, and she glances at it but makes no move to check us in. "Is there a problem?"

The Qitoni meets my gaze, the swirling void of her eyes narrowing. "We've had issues with counterfeit tickets."

"Well, if you would bother to check mine, you would see that they are in order." I again raise my travel pass, which she glances at dismissively before holding out her data pad.

"Tap for payment. Universal credit only."

"We were told Qitoni credit."

"Universal credit only." There is no room for argument, and the Qitoni's tone is not at all kind.

"I only have Earth credit." Ivy sounds worried. "Maybe we should wait. I'll exchange my money—"

"Yes, do that." The Qitoni rushes to agree, reaching out to usher us around. It's strange. Qitoni adults are not very fond of physical contact.

Cautiously, I ease out of her grip, setting Ivy behind me. "Do not worry. I have the correct currency." I tap my band, and the Qitoni's mouth tilts into a tight smile.

I did not think they did that either.

"It seems everything is in order then." She turns her back on us, leaving us to invite ourselves onto the ship.

"I'm supposed to be paying for myself," Ivy hisses as I take her arm and lead her forward.

"You can repay me." Glancing back, I eye the Qitoni, who's glaring after us. Her body is tense as she watches us approach the ship's entrance, her milky gaze unflinching. "She must not be having the best day. Qitoni can be temperamental."

Ivy snorts. "Tell me about it. I accidentally stepped on the skirt of one when I was in the Fourth Quadrant, and I thought she was going to bite my head off."

I hum an acknowledgment and turn my gaze forward.

"Welcome!" A cheery greeting draws my attention.

A bright blue Aemu male waits at the dock with a tray of libations. He uses one of his free hands to pass one to Ivy, who accepts it with a smile. I refuse the drink with a shake of my head and urge Ivy aboard with a hand to her back.

"You're not going to have one?" She takes a sip, tilting her head in approval. "It's good."

"I am not fond of mind-altering substances just yet." My reply is absent as I look around the large main entrance, which is teeming with beings from all across the galaxies.

I lock eyes with several Lyqa who nod respectfully.

"Wait, is this free? The drink, I mean. Do I need to pay for this?" Between her barrage of questions, Ivy continues to sip her drink.

"I forbid you to worry about credit, my heart. Here, this way." Having located the corridor leading to our rooms, I point us in that direction.

We move through the throng, weaving around more beings than I've seen in a very long time. It's overwhelming, but I take steadying breaths, not wanting to alert Ivy to my distress, even as a familiar tingling starts in my head, slowing my steps as I instinctively begin to track the forms around me, looking for what? I don't know.

Ahead, a pair of Hosa females separate, and I go still.

I may have had my mind repaired, but no mind-mend could erase the image seared into my psyche of razor-sharp teeth and narrow nasal slits in an otherwise blank face.

"Oh god. Ba'ir?" Ivy's voice sounds far away. "Ba'ir?"

I blink. She's looking at me with worry. Turning back, I seek out the being I just saw, but instead of a snarl, there's a smile that confuses me. Their features are similar to those of the Fein, but there is no mistaking the amusement pulling their mouth wide as they speak to another passenger.

They catch me watching and tilt their head. The slit of their mouth relaxes into a smirk that sends a chill through my body.

How did they find me? Will they take me now?

Does no one else realize the danger we are in? If there is one, then the hive is not far away.

"Ba'ir." Ivy's voice triggers images of her body, torn and bleeding, her spirit broken as mine was for all of those rotations.

I will die first.

I turn back, my body rigid, ready to defend my lehti, but the place where the Fein stood is empty. I frantically scan the atrium. I know it was here. I didn't imagine it.

My mind is sound. It has to be.

"Hey. Look at me." Ivy takes my arm, stepping in front of me and snapping me from my spell.

"We must leave this ship." I grip her hand and start toward the entrance, only to be blocked by the Aemu who greeted us.

"Accommodations are that way." He smiles, his face blooming a cheery, kind color. He has no idea the danger we are in.

"This ship is not safe. We would like to disembark. You are all in danger. We should abandon this trip at once."

"Disembark?" The Aemu's smile does not falter, but he is clearly confused. "We have already departed. There will be no exiting the ship until we have reached our first entertainment port. Did you forget something? We have several replication pods where you can replace the item, for a small fee, of course."

My hold on Ivy tightens, and I can feel her growing concern as she looks from me to the Aemu. "Did you not hear me? We are in danger. I *need to leave* this ship. Please open the doors."

"*Sa'qi,* we are already out to sea."

"Then I will swim. Now, let me out!" My voice booms through the atrium, echoing off the tall ceilings, and at once, all chatter ceases.

"Hey. How about we take a deep breath?" Ivy gives our hands a shake before turning her attention to the attendant. "I think my, uh, friend," she stutters around how to describe our relationship, "is concerned that you seem to have a Fein on board. Did you know that?"

My stunned gaze swings to my lehti, but she remains calmly focused on the Aemu. I thought I was losing my mind again. Lyqa science is exceptional, but perhaps I was too damaged. If that is the case, I would only be a danger to Ivy if I devolved further. Trying to leave was as much for her as for me.

But she saw it. She saw it, too.

The Aemu's skin shifts to yellow, a color indicating that he is hiding something. "I am not sure what you mean. There are no Fein in our record logs."

Ivy's eyes narrow, but her lips pull into a smile. "Okay. Perhaps, we were mistaken then. Come on. Let's go to our room." She tugs me away, and I let her, regaining my bearings the further away we get from what I saw.

My chest thumps, and I look down, realizing that both of our hearts are beating in quick rhythm.

"These symbols match our ticket. Here." Ivy scans her wrist across the entrance pad, and a door slides open to a large suite glowing with soft pink light from the wading pool in the middle.

"Perfect. Come on." Ivy tugs me inside, guiding me to the center of the room, where a deep bowl swirls gently with sparkling water. "Just what we need."

We need to leave. That is the only rational action to take. I need to get her away from here before the past repeats itself, before I fail her again.

Ivy releases me and pulls her shirt over her head, tossing it aside.

I stare in mute captivation as she peels off her bottoms and kicks them away with her shoes, leaving her only in her undergarments, which are dark blue and designed with finely knit material that shows an enticing hint of dark nipple. A glance lower reveals the perfect slit of her pussy outlined against the net.

Despite my worry, my dick responds, tightening to its full length almost immediately.

"Lift." Ivy pulls my shirt up, revealing my stomach, and I instinctively raise my arms.

She gets it to my shoulders and goes on her toes,

struggling to pull it over my head. I help her, lowering my torso and pulling my arms free.

Her hands go to my waistband at the same time she notices my erection. "Oh." She pauses for only a second before continuing, methodically pushing my pants down so I can step out of them.

"I am sorry."

"No, it's okay. I know it's automatic."

Once we're both undressed, me naked, her still in the enticing undergarments, she leads me to the pool and steps in.

"My heart's racing. We need to calm down." She brings me with her, and I follow until we're both chest-deep. Only then does she release me and move to lean back against the opposite side of the pool.

We're quiet while the water does its work, settling the nervous energy in our bodies. My First heart slowly eases into a regular rhythm, and across from me, Ivy sighs.

"You saw the Fein." She said it to the Aemu, but I need to confirm it again.

Ivy holds my gaze, hers steady. "Of course I did."

"If they're here, that means—"

"For now, it just means that one is here, and that gives us time to figure out what to do."

I shake my head. "I thought my mind was broken. I thought maybe none of this was real. That I was still with them—"

"You're not." She pushes through the water until she reaches me, straddling my waist and cupping my face with both hands. "Ba'ir, baby, you're not there." Her head lowers until our foreheads press hard together. The pain is grounding, and I hold her hips tight, pulling her against me.

"You're here, and you're free. Whatever this is, we'll figure it out together."

21

BA'IR

Our lips tremble as they touch.

I didn't kiss her the times we were together before. I was still bitter then. I desired her, but it was a spiteful lust, devoid of all the tenderness we once shared.

But when Ivy presses forward, molding her lips to mine, the pull of the leht, that unshakable urge, has me crushing her to my chest.

She isn't naked, but it's nothing to push aside the scrap of lace covering her cunt and thrust inside of her wet heat. She gasps, and I make a sound that's almost painful before freezing in horror.

"I am sorry. I did not ask your permission." I lift her, but her knees clamp onto my hips.

"You have it. Don't stop." Her amber gaze stares apprehensively into mine. "I mean, if you don't want to, don't stop."

I shake my head, holding her gaze. "I do not want to."

Still, I don't move. Instead, I kiss her again, more surely this time, slanting to slide my tongue between her lips.

"Ba'ir."

I swallow her moan and deepen the kiss, stroking along the soft parts of her mouth, using the restored length of my Lyqa tongue to reach every corner.

I'd nearly forgotten it was back to normal.

Suddenly, my mind is filled with all of the things I never got to do with my tongue, highest on this list of regrets, using it to give Ivy pleasure.

Breaking away, both of our chests heaving, I meet her dazed gaze. "Can I taste you?"

She frowns, then her face lights with understanding. Her skin warms with embarrassment. "Oh, yeah, sure."

Her smile is shy but excited as I shift her onto the pool ledge so that her lower body is level with my face. Pulling her panties down her legs, I discard them somewhere behind me.

The heady, sweet scent of her arousal fills my nose, and I lean in, inhaling deeply.

It's instinct, the primal need to bring her to my senses, but she recoils, her hands clenching on the rim. "Ba'ir."

My eyes lift to hers as I move closer. "There is nothing about you that you need to hide."

"It's not that. I've never, um, done this. Just a little nervous I'm going to come all over your face, to be honest." She makes an expression of horror, and I laugh.

I'm still not used to it, but the sound rumbles pleasantly through my chest, not at all distracting me from the feast before me. Holding her gaze, I lower my face to hover over the slick seam. "While I have never done this either, I am fairly certain the objective is for you to do exactly that. Let us see how successful we can be."

The first taste of her nearly has me going over my own edge. The second has me gripping her hips to yank her into my mouth, my tongue unfurling to its full length as I drag it between her lips.

"Oh god!" Ivy pants, her head falling back only to straighten again so she can watch as I lap through her silken folds, twisting along the sides, sucking the plump flesh while she jerks and gasps.

She grows wetter as I persist, teasing the flaps and folds before closing my mouth over the tight bud nestled above them and sucking hard.

"Ba'ir!" She bucks, chasing the pleasure as I let her slip from my lips with a wet suction.

"You taste, mm," I close my eyes, rolling my tongue, savoring the sweet tang. "I wish I could have spent the last twenty rotations tasting you. Can I have more?" Pressing a kiss to her lips, one then the other, I wait.

Her face is flushed and damp with sweat. Her chest rises heavily, and her legs shake where I'm nestled between them. "Yes."

I perch my chin over her, pressing down until she whimpers from the pressure. "Can I have it all, Ivy?"

She sucks in a breath, her head starting to shake, but I cut off her refusal, dropping my chin to latch onto her clit again, sucking until she screams, her entire body jerking as her release steals over us both.

I groan into it, working my tongue lower to push inside of her and tunneling through the clenched heat of her core as she whines a staccato echo through the room.

I drink her down, my hands getting tighter and tighter

on her thighs until my face is wedged so hard against her that I can't breathe.

Only when she stills do I ease away, flicking over her clit one last time and sending a tremor through her body.

Flipping my tongue around my lips, I stand, rising tall, my length straining from my pelvis.

Her gaze is hazy as she drags in a deep breath, staring down the length of her beautiful, lush torso to watch me watch her.

I want her so badly, but I could also gladly look at her like this for the rest of my time in the Universe. "Can I have it all, Ivy?"

Maybe I don't have the right to ask, but I also know that so much was taken from us that we deserve all that is left for us to have.

Her eyes focus, but she still doesn't answer. Instead, she lurches upright, gripping my dick and pulling me down with her as she guides me between her legs. I follow as she presses me to her opening, sinking into her in a hard, deep thrust that has us both crying out.

She's splayed beneath me, her thighs spread to reveal her dripping core wedged tight with my cock. Tingles spread through my pelvis at the sight of her so vulnerable and open, taking so much of me inside of her.

The feel of my bare skin gliding along hers as I sink deeper makes a groan rumble through my chest. "*Hu'l.*"

"Ba'ir." She keeps saying my name, and I want to hear it more.

Her brows pinch in plea, and her hands grip my forearms, the pointed tips of her nails pinching the skin.

I hate pain.

After experiencing so much, I am both numb to and

abhorred by the sensation.

But this pain, this slight tinge, lets me know she feels me, that she is taking me in and experiencing every point of the stretch that could bring me to my knees.

My eyes fix on that place, mesmerized, and she lifts just enough to see where she's so full of me. Her eyes blow wide.

"Do you see, my *lehti*, how we fit? This is the *leht*. This is a match that is greater than fate, greater than captivity and revenge, greater than all that has kept us apart. It is what brings us together, despite the winding circumstances of this existence, to find each other. You are mine. *Look at me*, Ivy." I jerk her hips, forcing more of my length inside of her and making her moan as her eyes fly to mine. "You are my *lehti*. Mine. *Mine*. Can I have you? Can I have it all?"

Her lips part, but nothing comes out.

Is it that she still sees me as broken, or did I change her view of me with my anger so much that what I'm saying can no longer ring true?

If that is the case, then it only means I have work yet to show her.

Slowly, so slowly that I vibrate with the effort, I withdraw against the clinging tug of her passage, easing until just the tip pulses at her entrance. Beneath me, she pants, her gaze locked on mine, as I ease back in, feeding her my cock span by span until I'm seated again.

She gasps, her hips twitching as I repeat this motion. With every drawn-out stroke, she grows more impatient, lifting her hips against my easy rhythm, trying to increase the pace, but I resist, halting the sharp snap of her hips.

"Not yet, *lehti*. We have time." I don't know this. No one can know this, and there is a Fein on board, but whatever time we have is enough.

I continue rocking, the tension winding tighter and tighter.

Ivy's gaze glazes over as she takes me. Her hands go limp, her body falling into the pace I've set.

"Ba'ir." This time, my name is a sigh, and that is all it takes to snap the control that a moment ago felt so completely tethered.

I fall over her, hooking behind her knees and pushing them up along her ribs, my hips snapping between her thighs as I shatter into the chasm of release.

I slam my pelvis into hers, grinding onto her clit until she jolts and goes with me, the wet squelch of her cunt clenching around the pulse of my shaft.

***

"Are you well?"

We've moved to the large bed.

Until I voice the question that's been tossing through my mind, Ivy hasn't said anything, and neither have I, but she allows me to hold her as we both linger in a state of contentment.

Qitoni mechanics are elite in the known Universes, but they've engineered this ship to allow for the lulling rock of ocean travel. I focus on the gentle sway, my breaths matching its soothing tempo as I await her answer.

"Ba'ir, I—" The sound indicating someone is at the door interrupts whatever Ivy is going to say.

I sit up, easing her from my chest, loving the feel of her beaded nipples grazing across my skin as I rise from the bed. I'm nearly to the door when Ivy's amused voice sounds out. "You going to put on some clothes?"

I turn back, relishing the sight of her satisfied and lying in the place I just abandoned. The air smells of our joining, of her pleasure, and what I left inside of her. The scents mingle together to make my First heart flutter with rapture. I am going to keep her in this room for the remainder of the trip. "Nudity is nothing in these places, and I'd like to save time on removing them once I have dispatched whoever is at the door. I'm not quite done with you if that is acceptable."

"Oh." She blushes in the discreet, beautiful way her skin does and smiles shyly. "Yeah, that's okay."

I nod, the heat rising through my pelvis nearly putting me in a state that, while it wouldn't necessarily be unacceptable, would make it awkward for whoever has come to call. What I want is to leave them outside the door and go back to her, but reluctantly, I turn and pass my hand over the sensor to open it.

It slides open, and what is on the other side is such a contrast to the bliss I experienced moments ago that my brain spasms between the present and the horrors of my mind. I fall back, darkness pulling me into the nightmare of the past.

My only thought as I sink beneath the abyss of memory is that I have once again failed Ivy because the Fein walking into our room will show no mercy.

***

"Ba'ir, baby. Listen to my voice. Just my voice. Don't worry about what you see when you open your eyes. Please, just listen to my voice."

Ivy's appeal pulls me from the emptiness I fell into, and my mind scrambles to follow her words as I come to. I blink, the soft lighting of the stateroom obscuring the image above me, but it slowly comes into focus as the gentle smile of my lehti.

"Hey. It's me. You're okay." Ivy strokes over my face,

crowding me as much as she can so that she fills my entire line of sight. She's in a robe, the ends wrapped tightly about her torso.

"Why are you dressed, *lehti*? I want you naked."

"I know, baby, but did you hear me? You're okay."

I'm not okay. Ivy is dressed, and I am not done tasting her body or feeling her clench around me as she comes apart in my arms, my name a caress on her lips.

My brain is still sorting itself, but it knows that Ivy's reassurance is something I need to hear. Still, there's something more pressing I need to be sure of, and I find my voice, which, to my ears, sounds like it remains in the void. "Are you?"

Her smile widens. "I am. I'm okay. I'm here. No one is going to hurt me. You passed out. Well, you were kind of knocked out from shock, but it's okay. You're okay. I'm okay. We're okay, baby."

I relax, taking hold of her waist for assurance, but just then, my mind configures all of the pieces, and the moments before I lost consciousness come back to me.

Arriving on the ship with Ivy.

Seeing the Fein, only to be told I was mistaken.

But Ivy saw it.

She saw it and brought me to our rooms, where we would be safe, and then gave herself to me, so sweetly if not completely, helping me forget. A stupid thing to do when we were in danger, but felt a worthy risk at the time.

A knock at the door, and the same Fein standing on the other side.

As I recall all of this, a soft sound passes through the room.

When I was captive, I never heard the Fein speak. They

commanded in mental control and violence, slashing and cutting until I figured out what they wanted. I learned quickly, but that didn't stop them from exacting their demented torment despite my compliance. And yet, the entire time I was held, there was a low hiss that rumbled through the compound.

During captivity, my translator had been disabled, torn from behind my ear where it had been placed when I was a youngling, so I only ever registered the constant hum on the compound as a product of outdated mechanics.

Now, with my translator restored, the hiss filters through. "If he is settled, I'd like to speak with him."

"Shit. Ba'ir, wait!"

I roar upright, ignoring Ivy's plea as I stand and wrench her behind me, my teeth bared. I have no weapon but my hands; this time, they will do.

"You will have to kill me. Do you hear, Fein? YOU. WILL. HAVE. TO. KILL. ME!" My roar bounces off the wall, making Ivy grab me, though the Fein doesn't react.

Why would they? These beings have no feelings except for a thirst to destroy the lives of others.

"I have no wish to harm you, friend." Their tall, pale form goes blurry as my eye twitches.

I start forward, my body going numb as the single determination to rip this being apart with my bare hands overcomes me. It settles as a satisfying blood lust in my gut, a *need* replacing every other.

"Oh god, Ba'ir. You, leave!" Ivy stabs a finger at the Fein and steps in front of me, but I can barely see her. All I can see is the soulless being too close to my lehti, staring calmly back. "I'll try to explain to him when you're gone. Ba'ir, just wait." Ivy stumbles back as she tries to head me off, but I persist, my hands folding into claws.

I want to see their blood.

Suddenly, she jumps, wrapping her body around mine, her legs clamping at my flanks, her arms locking around my shoulders as she presses her cheek to my neck.

"I'm not letting you go, so you'll have to kill him while holding me." She turns her face, her voice going low as she whispers near my ear, and I freeze.

In a rush, things expand from my narrowed intent toward the Fein into the vast universe, encompassing everything beyond this moment and what she has just revealed. I take several steps back, clutching Ivy to my chest, even though she hasn't lessened her hold.

Keeping my eyes on the Fein, who has not moved, I take another step back. "Leave here, or I will kill you."

"I will honor your wish, but I implore that you allow me to speak first."

"Ba'ir, listen to him. Please." My heart beats painfully against my sternum, but my First heart has an easy rhythm that mirrors Ivy's composure. "Trust me."

I do trust her, so although it goes against every instinct I have, I meet the blank face of the Fein. "Say what you have to say."

They begin by raising their arms, and I tense again. "I only wish to show you that I am unarmed, but if your reaction to me is any indication, I imagine even my hands are a threat." Their shoulders drop, and it looks like defeat. "I can only imagine the harm my kind has done to you. I will spare you providing me any details."

"You'll *spare* me?" My muscles vibrate, and Ivy rubs over my back.

"Ba'ir, just listen."

Pressing my lips together, I give silent consent that they continue.

The Fein nods. "I will say many things that are inadequate and insensitive, but that is not my intent. I know what my people are known for, but what many do not know is that there are Fein, such as myself, who despise how our people have chosen to move within the Universe. We know that they have abandoned the honor of our collective and turned it into something vile. I am not here to harm you, but I am sorry for the harm my presence has caused. I have requested to disembark at the first safe port along our voyage. I will do my best to stay out of your way until then. Please, enjoy the rest of your trip." With another dip of their head, they turn and leave.

The moment the door slides shut, I urge Ivy away from me, setting her on her feet as I run my hands down her body. "Are you hurt? Did they touch you?"

"Ba'ir, I'm fine." She takes my face in her hands to still my roving gaze. "Did you hear what they said?"

"They lie." My nose curls in disgust at the obviousness of the tactic. "If they are here, their swarm is not far behind. We must warn those we can and find a way off this ship. I will swim us out of here if I have to."

Ivy takes my hands and squeezes. "Ba'ir, I don't think they're lying. I think they're telling the truth."

I step away, the chill of betrayal curling in my gut. "You believe them?"

"Ba'ir, I'm here for you, and if you want to find a way off this ship, I'll go with you, no questions asked. But you're the one who said that you wanted to let go of the past and move forward, find a life. You'll never be able to do that if you believe you aren't truly free of the Fein. So much of why you suffered for so long is unknown. I think you deserve answers."

I don't want to admit she could be right, but I know the Fein. After twenty years of subjugation, I've seen the worst of what they can do, and they don't—reason.

Or apologize. They certainly don't leave other beings unharmed. They cannot resist the opportunity to destroy, so the mere fact that the Fein left us means that I may be incorrect.

But is it even possible?

"He gave me something," Ivy continues carefully. "I think we should look at it." She takes my hand and pulls me over to the comms station set against the far wall. When she tries to urge me toward the seat facing the windows, I move to the one facing the door.

She takes the other seat and taps her comm, syncing a file to the display screen. The image of a planet emerges, rotating as a 4D replica. I blink back, shocked because it is, by the translation of the symbols hovering above it, the home planet of the Fein.

The planet where I was kept was a toxic mining planet on the edges of a vacant quadrant. The air tasted of metal, and everything was covered in rust.

This globe from which my tormentors originate is awash with lush greens and blues, indicators of life sustainment, and not what I would expect in a thousand lifetimes.

"Wow," Ivy exhales. "That's—"

"Beautiful." And even this word I've supplied feels inadequate.

Ivy hums and swipes at the image, moving to the next file, which is a historical summary. The recording details the origins of the Fein, a reclusive but peaceful people who spent thousands of generations to themselves, harming no one in the Universe.

It wasn't until an evolutionary jump triggered the emergence of a latent hive mind that a single Fein was given the ability to control large swarms of their kind. Unfortunately, this leader was not a being of peace, and since then, the Fein have become known as vicious savages who overtake unprotected beings without remorse.

However, a smaller population still exists, disconnected from the horde due to the absence of the hive trait, and that appears to be what the Fein who just left belongs to. This small part of the population has tried to halt the crimes of their kind to no avail. They are fewer in number, and the Fein's reputation makes other societies hesitant to associate with them. After all, it would only take one hive leader to overthrow a society. There is only one society that has risked welcoming lone Fein, and that is Qiton, which has become a haven for the outcasts of Fein's hive societies.

As an aquatic species, the Qitoni possess exceptionally sophisticated brain functions, which render them immune to the influence of the Fein. There are only three other beings that can withstand the mental subjugation of the Fein — Somii, slpoi, and Thresher multiples, whose psychic connection creates a closed mental network which cannot be penetrated without allowance.

Ivy and I read the rest of the account in silence, and when the final slide collapses, I sit back with a sigh. "He was telling the truth."

She rubs my arm, her expression gentle. "I think so. I don't think he's going to hurt us, but we can still leave if it's too much for you. I mean, in light of everything else, maybe we should leave anyway. I'm so sorry I had to tell you that way."

She smells of guilt, and it occurs to me that she always smells so strongly of this emotion.

"Are you sure about what you revealed?"

She nods. "You can check, but I think so. It was the same as—before."

I inhale, and my heart thumps. My anxiety has subsided so that I can see things clearly after the shock of the Fein. "Let's stay. I will need to process what I've learned, but I want to stay."

"You sure?" There's hope in her eyes, and it's so much better than the sadness that was there before that I latch onto it, letting it give me a strength I don't feel.

"Seeing the Fein was unsettling, but if my restoration showed me anything, it was that my perception of my experience before and after the Fein didn't always reflect reality. If I let the past dictate this moment of happiness, it will never end. I will always find a way to be too afraid to move forward." Holding Ivy's gaze, I lift her hand to my lips and press a kiss to her palm. "Let's stay."

22

IVY

If I weren't a mother, I don't think I could have stayed as calm as I did when that Fein showed up at the door.

The experience of being a terrified young parent leaning into a sweet but mischievous toddler who was just as exuberantly naive as his father means I'm well-versed in being the voice of reason in the middle of what could easily become a shit-show.

I'd frozen in fear when Ba'ir fell back, his eyes rolling into his head. There was no mistaking the terror twisting his features. His fists pounded the floor as if fighting off an unseen enemy. Watching him convulse, my belly had twisted, bile rising in my throat as I scrambled from the bed.

The Fein had rushed forward, crouching beside Ba'ir's head. I'd felt helpless, watching them touch Ba'ir's head and face, until I could finally crawl over to shove them away. Subconsciously, I registered the soft give of its chest, the fragility unexpected for a species so vicious.

"I only mean to check that he didn't injure himself." The Fein had moved away, allowing me to pull Ba'ir's head into my lap and check for myself that he was okay.

"What did you do to him?" My scream reflected the fear consuming me as I bent over Ba'ir to be sure he was breathing.

He was, though it was fast and erratic. It was shock. Coming face-to-face with his nightmare of the past twenty years had reasonably sent him into a state of disassociation.

After seeing the Fein on our arrival, I'd hoped to make Ba'ir forget, if only for a while. I may have told Ba'ir that we would find a way out of this, but there was likely no hope. The best we could have done was enjoy ourselves before everything was ripped away again.

"I have not harmed him. I believe he is merely startled. That was not my intention, but I sense there may be a misunderstanding concerning my presence here."

"Are you going to try to convince me you aren't Fein?" I'd used my body as a shield, keeping it huddled over Ba'ir, ready to defend him the way I hadn't all of those years ago.

"No, I am Fein. But it is more complicated than that. I believe this may help explain." They'd held their arm out, indicating they wished to transfer something to my comm, and I'd hesitated until they'd nodded. "I promise I will not harm you."

"And I'm supposed to believe that?"

They'd smiled then, a strange lift of the slit of their mouth that didn't feel as sinister as it should have. It had felt almost friendly. "If anything, you would believe that the Fein you mistake me for does not make promises. They do not speak to their prey. They only hunt and devour, neither of which I am doing."

He'd had me there.

Hesitantly, I'd raised my arm and waited on guard as he took only enough steps necessary to tap his band to mine before backing up. Ba'ir had come to, ready to fight to the death for his life, and I'd been forced to tell him something I'd never meant to say.

"You should eat."

I blink from where I'm pulling a dress up my body to find Ba'ir watching me.

"I'm not sure I can eat. My stomach is in knots." The adrenaline of the past hour is catching up to me.

"We have not eaten all day. Let me feed you." He moves to the door as I slip on a pair of sandals.

I may have been reluctant to come on this trip, but I got excited as we boarded. Ba'ir's fathers' gifts of clothing also helped build my anticipation, despite my initial protests.

I'm wearing one of the dresses Crissette designed —a flowing, pleated magenta that shifts around my softly curved body in ways that make me feel fancier than I have in my entire life. However, it feels weird to be so dressed up after being in battle mode not an hour ago. My heart's still thumping, and I wasn't lying when I said I doubt I could eat.

But we're here, and despite the hiccup of a Fein on board, I know that this trip is going to, in many ways, define whether Ba'ir believes he has a shot at a new life. And that means this trip has to be great. It has to make him laugh and have fun. It has to make him finally feel free.

We're off to a terrible start.

I swallow down the guilt of having already thrown a wrench in that future. We'll have to talk about it, but I hope that by the end of this trip, Ba'ir will also be okay with being free of me.

I make my way over to him, smoothing my hands down the dress. Over the past twenty years, I have only thought about freeing Ba'ir and taking care of my son. There was no time to worry about what I looked like or what anyone thought of me. Now, wearing this beautiful dress, nervousness makes my steps wobble as Ba'ir watches me approach.

"What is wrong?" His eyes roam over my body, and I tense even more.

"Nothing. We can go."

He frowns but turns to wave his hand over the door sensor. When it slides open, I stop him, rushing to step ahead.

"I'll go first, just in case."

He grabs my arm, halting me. "Ivy," his gaze is troubled, "do you believe I am unable to protect you?"

"What? No. I just," I maneuver so I can take the hand holding my wrist. "I know this is hard for you, and I don't think you can handle any more surprises."

I squeeze his hand, but he gently eases it from my grip.

"I suppose I have not been of much help in moments of crisis. Even when the Fein came earlier, I—"

"Ba'ir, no." I get into the space to halt the path his mind is trying to wander. "You've been through something terrible. I don't expect you to jump in front of danger for me. No one would expect that."

He nods and takes a step back. "Understood. You should eat. Come."

I follow him down the hall, noting the tense set of his shoulders.

When we reach the central atrium, he pauses, allowing

me to catch up. "Do you have any particular craving?"

He waves a hand to the dozen or so restaurants lining this level of the ship, and I scan them, but nothing triggers even the faintest stirring of an appetite.

"How about there?" I put to one of the storefronts, and Ba'ir makes a face but starts toward it without comment.

Inside, an Aemu host leads us to a table where the menu and ordering process is automated. Ba'ir pulls up the projection, which lists the available dishes. "I can go through the options for you."

"No need. Just choose something you think I'd like." I'm probably not going to eat anyway, so after Ba'ir squints and taps at a few things before dismissing the order projection, we sit in silence until I can't take it anymore. "Do you want to talk about it?"

His gaze shifts to mine. "Not at the moment."

"Oh." I blink, and we descend into an even more uncomfortable silence.

A moment later, the middle of the table parts, and four dishes rise from wherever the hell the dishes come from in this world of technology beyond anything on Earth.

My eyes widen, my stomach clenching as I stare at the plates piled high with *wiggling* tentacles and other things. I meet Ba'ir's equally confounded gaze. "So...sushi?"

He's still frowning, his head tilting as if that's going to help him understand what's happening with our food. "I merely selected something. I assumed it would be vegetation."

"Yeah," I reach into the pile and pluck one of the squirming tentacles, watching as it curls around my fingers, the suckers tickling as they stick to my skin, "this thing definitely had parents. I'll go first."

I move to put it in my mouth, but before I can, Ba'ir reaches across the table and grabs my hand, pulling it so he can close his lips over my finger and tug the stubborn meat off.

I sputter a laugh and watch as he chews, his jaw working hard and fast before he swallows dramatically. When he clears his throat and smacks his lips, I raise my brows. "Well?"

He shrugs, straight-faced, glancing cavalierly around the room. "It is terrible."

I crack up. "Really?"

He finally looks at me, his mouth quirking. "Ivy, I barely had food for twenty rotations, and what I did have was absolutely not fit for consumption. That," he gestures to the plate, "is terrible."

I want to laugh, but I end up twisting my mouth in awkward silence.

"It is okay, *lehti.*"

I blink. "What?"

"You can feel joy, even at the expense of what I have been through. I am not there anymore, and I do not want to live my life jumping at phantoms believing I am. There are many things we need to speak about, but for now, I would only have you tell me one thing—are you sure?"

I nod. I don't need to think about it. "I'm sure, and I know you just got free—"

"If you are sure, then there is nothing left to say for now. Let us have fun, starting with going to another restaurant." He stands and holds out his hand. I take it, letting him help me as I round the table.

When we start to walk away, I pause. "Don't we need to pay?"

"Our meals are included in the cost of our board. Come." He pulls me along, and we exit the restaurant. He turns right on the landing and heads toward a storefront at the far end of the deck. "Lyqa fare is always safest."

We enter the restaurant, and familiar scents envelop me, instantly invoking a sense of home I've missed for the past twenty years. The truth is, even before my mom kicked me out for being pregnant, and I didn't fight it because I knew the dangers of the baby I was carrying, I'd always felt a little on the outside of my family.

It wasn't anything mom did. We'd just never been close. She used to say she was a boy-mom, like my two brothers were the only ones who existed.

Still, not her fault. We can't control who we bond with, just like I can admit that I never cared that we weren't close, especially after I met Ba'ir. He could have told me he was from Mars, and I would have followed him to that rusty-ass planet, so Lyqa wasn't so much of a stretch.

The first meal I had there was made by Vetim, and it was the best thing I'd ever eaten. If I hadn't wanted to stay for Ba'ir, I would have stayed for the food. This sentiment is shared across galaxies because when we enter, the place is packed.

Beings of all kinds, many I've seen and many new, sit around tables talking and laughing. Noises and sounds, from chirps to drawn-out syllables, filter through my translator, giving me a glimpse of the conversations happening throughout the space. The general air is one of excitement, which infiltrates my lingering tension.

"There is an unoccupied table there." Ba'ir points to a single empty table in the far corner, and we make our way there.

Once seated, we go through the whole automated ordering routine again, but this time, when the table opens, the plates that rise are filled with beautiful Lyqa vegetables, covered in sauces and glazes that have me shimmying in my seat.

I reach for one of the platters with the tongs provided and start piling my plate. "Oh my god, it's been so long since I had this food."

Ba'ir, who is also filling his plate, frowns. "Did my fathers never cook for you?"

I pause in the middle of the first bite of a long, asparagus-like stalk before folding it into my mouth and chewing slowly. "No, they did. I stayed with them while I was pregnant with BJ, just because things went so quickly, and they wanted to make sure I was safe. However, after that, I usually just let them spend time with their grandson. I didn't want to intrude."

"Intrude how?" He seems genuinely confused, and I'm back to feeling like everything we talk about is going to sour the mood.

"Just, you know. They missed you. They were really happy about BJ. That was the one silver lining since no one expected me to be pregnant after I escaped and got back to Lyqa, but it didn't change the fact that I got you kidnapped and tortured for two decades. I wasn't going to keep showing up and throwing it in their faces." I shrug and shovel food into my mouth, keeping my eyes averted.

"Ivy, you did not get me kidnapped. But also," Ba'ir's voice draws my gaze after he's silent for several long moments. "I knew you were pregnant. My fathers did as well."

I make a face. "What do you mean?"

His face pulses a dull mauve beneath his brown skin, but he doesn't shy away. "That morning before we went to look for the stone for your ring, I scented your pregnancy and told my fathers. They—" he swallows, looking away briefly as his face flares more.

"They what?"

"They advised me to tell you so that you could have the option to terminate if you wished, since we were so young, but I decided not to tell you. I had not taken care of you; it was my duty to care for you once you were carrying my young, so I said nothing. And when you told me about the engagement ring, I knew it was not that important to you, but I wanted you to stay," he shrugs, a sad smile lifting his lips. "So I ignored you when you said you were afraid. I ignored you when you asked to turn back. All I could think about was what I wanted, and *that's* why I was taken by the Fein. It was not you. The torment I suffered for those rotations was my doing. I have had to accept that, and I need you to as well."

My heart's beating fast, and the food I was so excited to eat feels like it's swimming in bile.

Ba'ir leans forward, concern creasing his forehead. "Are you well, *lehti*? *Hu'l*, come."

He pulls up the pad beside the table and taps something in. The table opens and lowers the barely touched dishes back into its depths.

Ba'ir grabs my hand again and pulls me from the table, leading me out onto the deck, where the salty ocean air helps me breathe again.

"Keep breathing. I am sorry I upset you." Ba'ir moves to stand in front of me, bending down to look into my face, but I just shake my head and step back, pulling my hands from his.

"I won't have it."

He frowns and steps close again. "How do you mean?"

"This baby. I won't have it."

I've finally spoken out loud what I told Ba'ir when the Fein showed up at our stateroom. It was the only thing I could think of to keep him from attacking the other being, and desperation had made me put my lips to his ear to whisper, *"I'm not letting you go, Ba'ir. When you passed out, I threw up, and the Fein said he could smell my pregnancy. So if you want to get to him, you'll have to do it while I'm carrying our baby inside me."*

It snapped Ba'ir out of his murderous rage, but now it feels like I doused fuel on some honor fire that I didn't know was burning.

"Oh, my god, I'm about to ruin your life again. That's why you don't want to talk about it." I feel panicked, and I turn to my right, then my left, looking for some escape.

"Ivy!" Ba'ir's hands are on my shoulders, and he jerks them, snapping me out of my flight mode. "Calm down. It is not good for you or our child for you to be this excited."

I shake my head again. "Why am I here? Why are we doing this all over again when we know how it turns out?"

His grip tightens enough to command my attention again. "How does it turn out, Ivy? With me caring for you? With me being present to see you bring a life we've created into the world? With our family and *leht* whole? What is wrong with that? Why should we not be allowed to do it again, together with BJ? Why should I not get to love you as my First heart and my soul aches to?"

Sighing, he lessens his hold and leads me to a seat in the atrium. I drop in a daze as he settles beside me. He's quiet, his gaze tracking my face for a long while before he speaks. "I don't know why my fathers didn't explain the *leht* to you, but I will explain it to you now. The *leht* isn't merely an attraction. It is how fate brings me to the one meant for me. The *only* one."

I listen, my stomach a jumble of knots. Over the years, Vetim and Tali hinted at something more profound in my connection to their son, but it felt like too much to acknowledge it, even as I felt it anyway.

"Additionally, the *leht* is a physical connection. When I tell you my First heart is bound to yours, that is literal. It's bound to you, Ivy. Only you. No one else, ever. This heart beats because your heart beats, and if yours stops, so does mine."

The jumble turns to dread, making my heart speed up.

Ba'ir presses a hand to his chest. "I feel that. Your fear, your anxiety, but also your joy, and that is what tells me that this is worth it because you deserve to feel joy all of the time, and I deserve to give it to you."

Everything disappears as he kisses me. His hold is urgent as he strokes through my mouth, coaxing me into compliance until I have to tear myself away to breathe.

He keeps me close so I'm pressed against the hard planes of his chest. "When I was freed, I wanted my life to be different. But that life, despite my torment, gave us our son. I would suffer that torment a thousand times over to ensure his survival. Now, I want our future together to be whatever we desire. So, no, I did not want to talk about this child in the way you most likely thought I did. I do not want to talk about this child as if it is a mistake we must remedy or a disruption to the life I would have." He points to my belly. "That is my child. BJ is my son. You are my *lehti*. I want you in my life more than anything else. I only forgot that for a while. We can have a different ending, Ivy."

I'm still unsure, but his words give me hope. "Okay."

"Yes?" He's smiling again, and that's almost enough to make me agree to anything.

"We can try."

"Good, then let me start by feeding you."

23

BA'IR

"So, what is this again?"

I help Ivy into her seat and take mine before answering. "A performance. The artists are highly skilled, and their talent is sought after. We should enjoy this."

As the other patrons take their seats, the hair at the back of my neck stands on end, and I get the impression that I am being watched. Turning, I scan the room behind me, but there is only one of our Qitoni hosts standing at the entrance, and while her gaze is focused in our direction, the milky whites of her eyes make it impossible to know if she is looking at Ivy and me.

"You good?" Ivy peers at me with concern, looking past me toward the entrance. "Did you see someone?"

"No, I," I look back and pause when the space where the Qitoni stood is empty. I smile and take her hand, bringing it to my lips. "I am sorry if I am behaving strangely still. I am not completely used to being among other beings."

"No, of course. If it gets to be too much, just let me know, okay?"

"I will be fine. I have to adjust."

The lights dim as I deliver this reassurance. The stage illuminates a short distance from where we sit.

"Presenting Florsten Padei, the humor technician."

Ivy frowns, a confused smile playing about her mouth. "Humor technician?"

I grunt. "This must be a new development while I was away. I have not heard of this before."

A Phleban appears on the stage, his affect unenthusiastic as he stares out at the crowd. "Greetings, passengers. As you may know, on these voyages, we strive to include aspects of all our guests' cultures. We are fortunate to have a human on board, so this presentation is in honor of her cultural traditions." Ivy looks around when he says human, her perplexed gaze meeting mine as he continues. "Tonight, I will relay anecdotes meant to humor you." Clearing his throat, spreads his arms wide. "How has everyone's first rotation on the ship been?"

No one answers. A glance around the room shows that everyone is just as confused as we are. The Phleban is undaunted, striding across the stage to speak directly to a couple seated near the stage.

"Ah, yes. While the gentle lull of the boat's movement may feel like a mother's embrace, do not let it put you to sleep, or you will miss all the festivities!" He chuckles loudly, and Ivy makes a choked sound.

Focusing on her, I see her lips folded in, her eyes narrowed as if she's attempting not to laugh.

At this? I am not even sure what is happening.

Leaning sideways, I whisper. "But he is not funny."

Ivy meets my gaze and loses her battle to remain silent. Her cackle echoes through the room, drawing the attention of the other patrons.

"Oh, my god. He's supposed to be a comic!" She leans over, nearly falling out of her chair, and the Phleban grins widely, obviously pleased that he's gotten the desired result.

Ivy continues to laugh, her entire body folding in on itself as she jerks with amusement. Tears spring to her eyes, and I start, rising to lift her into my arms, which only makes her laugh harder as she buries her face into my neck.

Addressing the Phleban, I nod. "My apologies. We enjoyed your show."

"No, please." He looks genuinely despondent at our departure. "If you leave, no one will understand my delivery."

This causes Ivy to wheeze, and I rush her from the room, my heart thumping when she strangles that she's "dying."

I carry her to one of the seats along the atrium wall and settle her down. She's relaxed, but her expression is tight, her gaze wet.

"Are you well? Should I get a healer?"

She chuckles slightly and sits up, prompting me to help her. "I'm sorry. I didn't mean to embarrass you. It's just that he was terrible, and that was hilarious." She hums, swiping at her eyes with the back of her hand. Her sight is focused on nothing in particular. "It's been a long time since I laughed like that. It felt good." Smiling, she rubs a hand over her belly, then peeks at me. "That's actually not a bad idea. Do you want to go laugh together?"

Though I was initially alarmed, the echo of Ivy's laughter has left a warmth that I yearn for more of. "Of course, I will laugh with you."

This is how we end up over the next few spans watching streamed videos of human comedy shows in our stateroom.

I barely understand much of what is said, but I get the sentiment, which is much more practiced than the Phleban's, and find myself chuckling. Mostly, I relish in the rumble of Ivy's laughter.

She lies along my side, her arm and leg curled over my torso as she watches with her head resting on my chest. The current show ends with the male on stage dropping the amplifying bar and walking off.

Ivy sighs and perches her chin on her hand. Her eyes shine with mirth. "That one was pretty good."

"You seemed to enjoy it." I stroke beside her lip, where her smile is on full display, no hiding.

"You probably didn't get a lot of that, huh?"

I shrug. "It doesn't matter. You enjoyed it, so I enjoyed it."

She hums, and a sudden change in her mood stings my nose. I tense but wait for her to speak again. "I almost died once."

Shifting, I get a better view of her face. The mirth is gone, replaced by an intense sadness.

"One of the shady guys I hired to rescue you took the money, and I guess he was worried I would get him caught, but it was bad. BJ was young. If I had died," in her eyes, there's guilt when she mentions our son, but also a desperate hope that unsettles me, "would you have been in that place so long?"

I level my gaze with hers, making sure she doesn't look away. "If you had died, I would have been granted a mercy that would not have been worth the price. Whether you knew it or not, you kept me strong, so there was something left to make it back to you. I would not have taken death over that."

As we stare at each other, I'm acutely aware of how much has changed from what I envisioned of our interactions after being freed. This is what I needed to feel whole again—my lehti, the mother of my children, my heart.

"I love you, Ivy."

She starts, the smile dropping as she attempts to lift from my chest.

I wrap my arms around her, keeping her close. "Please, do not deny me." When she looks away, I squeeze her to return her eyes to me. "Is it that you stopped loving me in that way while I was gone? It was a long time. I would understand if that were the case."

I expect her to either confess that I am correct or not respond out of fear of hurting me, but I am not prepared for the sharp tang of anger that fills my nose as she glares at me. "You can't ever say that to me, ever, Ba'ir." Her voice catches, and I feel both thrilled and chastened by her response.

"Then we agree that there is something still between us, yes?" I shift our bodies so that she's on her back and I'm resting in the cradle of her thighs. "The only thing to sort out is that you are clear that I loved you the moment I met you, and I have loved you ever since. Even the Fein could not take that from me. Even when my mind wasn't my own, my hate was fueled by the fact that I didn't hate you at all. May I?"

I've eased my hand between us against the slick heat of her cunt. Pushing aside the panties she left on with one of my tunics to feel more comfortable as we watched the film, I rest my fingers at her core.

Ivy sighs. Her troubled eyes remain fixed on me as I rub between her legs. The silky flesh slips between my fingers with her growing arousal, even as her brow remains pinched.

"What are you thinking, my heart?" Her expression falls even more, and I pause. "I won't continue if you truly don't wish to join with me again. If you are consenting out of pity or guilt—"

"No," her head shakes. "It's not that. This just feels so much like when we first met."

"And that makes you sad?"

She looks away, her scent ripe with her discomfort. "We aren't those people anymore. We were barely grownups, and we've changed so much."

I lower my mouth to hers, unable to stop myself from sucking her pouty bottom lip. "I don't know, *lehti*. This," I move my fingers again, coating them in her wetness, "feels very familiar, or did you forget how wet you got back then —"

"Don't talk about it!" Ivy's hand slaps over my mouth, and a deep chuckle rumbles in my chest. I flick my tongue at her hand, making her pull it away.

"You cannot still be shy. Did your other lovers not speak of how good you feel?" My expression is teasing, and she makes a face and rolls her eyes.

"You know, there wasn't anyone else. There's no way your dads didn't jump through hoops to tell you that."

I smile at her assessment of my parents. "They told me. I hope that your decision to remain unpartnered wasn't driven by guilt. You deserved to be happy and to have pleasure."

"I deserved to have you." Her declaration hangs in the air between us, the heaviest of truths. Then, nothing needs to be said as I lift and pull my shirt off.

Her eyes roam across my chest, and belatedly, I remember that I'm healed, while at the same time recognizing that I would have let her see me maimed and scarred. There's no part of me I want to hide anymore.

I fall forward, my lips crashing into hers. Her arms come around my back, pressing me into the soft swell of her breasts as she opens for my tongue.

Almost as fiercely as it begins, our kiss slows to a languid teasing. Our fingers skim gently along each other's bodies, and when I pull back, Ivy sighs, her eyes opening to a hazy droop.

"That was nice."

"Mm hm." I dip into her neck, inhaling deeply of her conception and tasting the sweetness there. Her moans are soft and only add to the nearly overwhelming desire to be inside of her. Still, I take my time licking across her chest until I get to her breasts. Pulling back, I eye them. "They're bigger."

Ivy chuckles. "Yeah, motherhood and pregnancy will do that–ah!"

I close my mouth over a straining tip, suckling tenderly until she squirms beneath me. Her hand tangles tightly against my scalp as she holds me steady to her breast.

"Ba'ir," I know what her urgent whine asks of me, but I take my time moving to the other nipple, administering the same laggard attention until she's moaning, her hips rocking up into the hard bar of my length in an effort to sate her need.

"The moment you permit me, I am glad to give you the entire span of what you ask for," pulling back, I meet her gaze, "but it cannot be just this. Tell me you understand and that you want more as well."

She's quiet for a long moment, her eyes glossy with hesitant longing. "I do want more. I want it all."

"And you will." Pushing my pants down my hips, I fit myself to her warm, slick center and press forward, easing slowly, ensuring she feels every part of me as I come to rest deep, our bodies fused so firmly that we both exhale in a rush.

"You are perfect." Pressing a soft kiss to her lips, I lift my hips, dragging through her tight grip until I nearly leave her body. In a firm hinge of my hips, I press back in a smooth, firm stroke. Ivy mewls, her back arching when I reach her womb. Her skin flushes beneath the brown, and just knowing I'm giving her this pleasure brings me to the edge.

The first time we joined, we were both inexperienced, and what we lacked in skill and patience, we made up for with unabashed exuberance. Now, though Ivy is still the only lover I've had, and I am hers, we pay closer attention, our bodies rolling until we find the rhythm that satisfies us both.

I keep my strokes deliberate, drawing out each measure of pleasure. The way her flesh clings to me as I slide free sends a shiver through my body. I move faster, building pace and force until our bodies slap together in desperate urgency. "You feel so good, *lehti*. So perfect."

Ivy clutches at my back, her nails leaving tingling trails over my skin as she lifts her hips for my thrusts. Her breathy moans fill my ears until they ring with the sound, and when I hinge deep, grinding our pelvises together, she cries my name, her passage clenching and pulling me into a release that leaves me shaking and sated.

I fall limply onto Ivy's sweat-slicked body, our breaths exchanging in rhythmic puffs, our hearts perfectly in sync.

Pushing back her soft hair, I kiss her cheeks, then her nose, and when I press my lips to her forehead, she huffs out a breathless laugh. "That was nicer."

I laugh, too. "Yes, it was."

***

Ivy stands at the window looking over the expanse of gently swaying waters. She wears one of my tunics, and I admire the sight of her toned, brown legs as she does on her toes to look out onto the deck. "So, what should we do today? I think I see something like a pool down there."

"I think we would enjoy the pools. If I remember correctly from the details of the ship, there are several to make use of."

"Alright, cool. Gimme a few minutes to get changed." Ivy grins and grabs one of her bags before disappearing into the bathing room.

After a quick rinse in the bathing pool, I dress and wait by the door. A short time later, Ivy steps out in an outfit that has my tongue staling in my mouth.

She looks up from where she's adjusting the hip straps on the bright red scrap of cloth covering her pelvis to find me staring. "Is this okay?"

"How-how to you mean?" The words catch in my throat, which has gone dry.

"I'm showing a lot of skin. It's a bikini, a human style." Her hands skim the soft swell of her bare belly, and I imagine, as I have before, our child growing there, filling out her flesh until it's taut and round.

The lingering desire of how things could have been rises in me again, but this time it's full of promise. I've been thinking about all of the things we've shared since learning the truth about the Fein on board, and an idea comes to me that even a turn ago would have seemed ridiculous. "Before we swim, I would like to try something if you're willing."

A playful smirk lifts her lips as she starts to shimmy her bottoms down. "I didn't think I had to say it at this point, but I'm always down to try something with you."

I chuckle and go to her, halting her hands just as she's about to reveal the tempting juncture of her thighs. "While I would gladly spend the remainder of this trip doing all of the somethings, this something requires us to leave the room."

"Oh," Ivy adjusts the garment again, and when I hold out my hand, she takes it, entwining her fingers with mine.

As we reach the door, the lock disengages, sliding open to reveal an Aemu female on the other side. She startles back, her face blooming a deep shade of pink.

"I apologize. I forgot to check if the room was occupied. I am here to service your lodgings." She looks kindly between Ivy and me, and I nod, stepping aside to allow her entry.

"If it is not an inconvenience," I turn as we pass each other, and the Aemu faces us, her expression eager. "My *lehti* has recently conceived. The room's motion may be too much during sleep hours. Please adjust it so she can sleep comfortably."

"Of course." The Aemu nods, her gaze tracking warmly over Ivy. "I will also notify the kitchen so they may have suitable foods ready for her hunger periods."

"Thank you." I lead Ivy away, and as we make our way down the hall, she squeezes my hand.

"You didn't have to do that. I feel fine."

"It is my responsibility to attend to you during this time. If you do not mind indulging me, I would like to take full advantage since I was unable to the first time."

Her scent turns sweet as she smiles. "Of course. So where are we going anyway?"

I swallow, gathering my resolve as I lead her to the ship's central atrium. "We're going to find the Fein."

"You don't think it's too soon? I'm all for you facing your healing head-on, but maybe you should give yourself time to adjust. Your reaction to them scared me last time."

"I can do this." I silence Ivy's protests and persist until I have located the Aemu from our departure. He is still stationed in the main reception area, which has been converted into a relaxation room for the remainder of the trip. The previously open space is now filled with seating, and several beings mingle, sipping libations from the roaming attendees.

When he sees me approach, panic colors his skin, and I silence him with a hand. "I am not here to complain. I now understand why you denied the presence of the Fein on board, and I do not fault you for it. However, I need to speak with them, and I would like you to arrange a meeting."

The Aemu looks nervously at Ivy before meeting my gaze again. "The passenger you speak of will be disembarking at the earliest convenience. We assure you they have no desire to cause you distress."

"I know. I was mistaken about them. I know that now, but there is something urgent they may be able to help me with, and if they are willing, I would be grateful."

"We aren't trying to cause trouble. We promise." Ivy offers the attendant a reassuring smile and squeezes my hand in a gesture of support. "We just want to talk. The Fein provided us with some information about their people. It helped us understand them. We know they are not like the ones who wronged us."

Though still unsure, the Aemu nods before turning away to speak discreetly into his comm. A moment later, he faces us again. "The Fein is willing to meet. This way, please."

We're led to an excluded part of the ship into a room that, while spacious, lacks the luxury of the state room where we are housed. It is functional, with a bed and a lounge area. On the sofa, the being that haunted my existence for twenty rotations waits.

They rise when we enter, their hands open at their sides, their lips pressed tight. I realize the effort behind the gesture. They know that claws and teeth are the weapons of choice for the evil of their kind. I acknowledge the attempt at tempering their sinister appearance with a nod. "I apologize for not inquiring before, but may I know your name? In my time with the Fein, I never saw them behave in a way that suggested the capacity for individual thought, but I would like to recognize yours if you will allow me."

The careful tension in the Fein's face relaxes. "My name is Ylt'r."

I nod. "Ylt'r. I will preface this by saying that I do not believe you owe me anything despite what I suffered at the hands of other Fein." Ylt'r's blank visage prevents me from reading their expression, but when they do not interject, I continue. "You can see into minds, to access memories and experiences, to make one relive them if you wish."

I don't need this confirmed. I experienced this during my captivity, in what, at times, felt like a never-ending loop. Those Fein would conjure my most treasured memories only to corrupt them with the reality of my torment.

Ylt'r shifts uncomfortably. "I can do this, yes, but—"

I hold up a hand at the wariness in their tone. "It is not for vengeful purposes. I was denied an experience with my *lehti,* and I would like the opportunity to share it. It would mean a lot to me."

Ylt'r considers my request, their gaze shifting to Ivy briefly before they nod and wave a hand to the seating bench they occupied a moment ago.

I lead Ivy to the bench and settle her down, pressing a kiss to her lips.

It isn't lost on me that she has not questioned my motives, and the fact that she seems to trust me unfailingly, even after everything I've done, only strengthens my love for her. "There was so much taken from us, and while I no longer wish things were different, there is one thing I would have knowledge of if you will let me."

"Okay." Her response is immediate, and I kiss her again, more deeply this time, cupping her face and stroking through the soft warmth of her mouth, uncaring that we're being watched.

When I lift away, her eyes are heavy, her skin warm beneath the surface.

Turning to Ylt'r, I take a steadying breath and close the distance between us, clenching my hands against the anxiety of being so close.

They remain still as I lean in and whisper my request, and when I step back, I think I can almost see joy on their face. "It would be my pleasure."

Lying down opposite Ivy, with my head beside hers, I close my eyes and force myself to relax as I do what I thought I would never do again: allow the Fein into my mind.

Ivy's lying in my bed in my fathers' home. I recognize the room as it was when I was taken.

The shades are drawn, and the room is cast in shadow. I can feel the weight of her body, her belly heavy beside her, and my heart thumps with the knowledge that our son is in there.

The door slides open a moment later, and my Ap'ha walks in with a tray of food. "You should eat, my dahnai."

Ivy does not stir at first, but then a rolling flutter moves through her belly, and slowly, she rises to a sitting position.

My Ap'ha settles the tray below the bulge of Ivy's belly, and I wait in anticipation to see her indulge in the array of Lyqa dishes he's prepared, except...

She picks up a stalk of root vegetable and takes an unenthusiastic bite before dropping it back to the plate. Sorrow is a weighted blanket around her shoulders. "I can't eat. I can't stop thinking about what could be happening to Ba'ir."

"Dahnai," my Ap'ha sighs. "We are doing what we can, but you have to take care of yourself. He would want you and your son to be well."

She stares at the plate, trying to find the will before pushing the tray away and lying back beneath the covers. "I'm not hungry."

Through the periphery of Ivy's gaze, which is blankly fixed on the wall, I see my Ap'ha sigh and rise. At the door, he pauses. His expression is filled with grief. "I know this is hard for you. I can smell what you feel, and I know there is nothing I can say that will convince you that your guilt is misplaced, but there will soon be a youngling who will not care that you are sad. He will need you to be your most capable self if he is to come into this world."

He leaves, and the memory blanks to Ivy standing in my bathing room. She's staring at herself. Her eyes are rimmed in shadows. She frowns and lowers her head to stare at her belly, which is even larger than before.

Suddenly, I think I have made a mistake. I'd hoped to share the joy of our son's birth, but it seems that much of

Ivy's pregnancy was spent in misery.

I pull my mind away, reaching out to the Fein to stop the share, but a hand grabs mine, squeezing tight, and I feel Ivy pulling me back in just as a sharp pain radiates through her abdomen in the memory, and she looks down at the fetus of our son rolling beneath her skin.

"Oh, no. Oh, no. No, no, no, no." Another sharp pain has her doubling over, and she cries out just as a flood of bloody liquid spills from between her legs.

The bathing room door bursts open, and my fathers are there as Ivy stares in shock at the puddle at her feet.

"He's coming, dahnai."

"I can't."

My Ap'ha, ever the practical one, takes her arm and leads her from the room. "You do not have a choice. We're calling the healers."

The memory is fuzzy from there, a confusion of delirium and fear, until a newborn's soft, high-pitched wail fills the air.

I realize now why Ivy urged me to stay. In this moment of the memory, her chest warms with a love so pure that she feels it through every cell in her body.

The lehti'an—a bond shared between mother and child that, from the intensity of the memory, rivals that of the leht by a span.

Someone lays BJ on Ivy's chest, and I look down as she does for the first time to see his little face, and my body jerks as I choke on a sob.

He is so beautiful, his round eyes gaze at his mother, the trust reflected absolute.

"He looks like him."

My Ap'hati offers a watery chuckle and leans in to kiss the top of her head, then our son's. "He does. I can't say what will happen with my son, but your son is the gift in this tragedy. Let him lead you to the happiness you deserve."

My fathers leave Ivy as is customary while she familiarizes herself with the bond between her and the baby.

When they are alone, Ivy leans in to whisper in our son's ear. "You have a daddy who loves you even though he doesn't know you exist, and I'm going to bring him back to you if it kills me."

"I'm sorry. I should have warned you—" I halt Ivy's apology as I pull her against me and sear my lips to hers.

I kiss her deeply, stroking through her mouth to swallow her regret and then her moans, only releasing her when she is breathless and clutching at me as if I am the lifeline I wish to be for her.

Holding her face between my hands, I press our foreheads together and release a ragged sigh. "You are the bravest being I have ever met, and I am sorry I was not there to let you know you had nothing to fear. As much as I love you for wanting to free me, you have to know that I was trying just as fiercely to get back to you. That is why my captors ruined my mind. I would not stop fighting them, no matter how much they harmed me. I only knew that I wanted to be where you and our son were."

Ivy sniffles and nods, pressing her lips to mine. I hold her to me, looking over her head to Ylt'r, who watches us with what I can clearly see is joy.

"Thank you," I mouth, and they dip their head and sigh, their body relaxing. This is as much a moment of relief for them as for us. This Fein is a good being, and it must be its own torture to know that your very existence is connected to such atrocities.

Ivy pulls away, her expression bright. She turns in my arms and addresses Ylt'r. "If you have the time, I'd like to share a few other things with him."

Ylt'r spreads their arms wide, their mouth pulling into a grin that no longer feels sinister. "I am at your disposal for as long as you wish."

We lie down again, and Ylt'r creates a bridge between my mind and Ivy's as she shares precious moments from the life we missed together.

BJ clings to a chair in my fathers' house, his chubby face cheerful. Ivy and my fathers watch in anticipation before he releases the chair and begins to toddle across the floor. Ivy lets out a hoot, startling the youngling, who drops to his bottom, making my fathers laugh. Undeterred, BJ's little face bunches, and he pushes up to his feet and takes one measured step after another until he has crossed the entire room. Emotion shines in my fathers' eyes.

"Your Ap'ha did the same thing when he was learning to walk," Ap'hati says. "He never gave up."

The scene changes. *BJ, now perhaps five or six rotations old, is perched on some contraption with two wheels attached to a metal frame with handles. Ivy stands behind him, holding the seat.*

"Okay, baby. You've got this. Just keep the handlebars straight and don't stop pedaling."

BJ nods, his eyes fixed resolutely forward.

"Go!" Ivy urges him into motion, holding the seat as his legs pump with furious determination. She runs alongside him and then suddenly lets go, allowing him to continue on his own, his arms wobbling to keep the handlebars straight. As he comes to a precarious stop several spans away, Ivy jogs to meet him, pulling him off the bike and squeezing him to her chest. "You did it! BJ, I'm so proud of you!"

There are more of these scenes, BJ reading his first words —in English and Lyqa; BJ attending a learning institute for the first time as a youngling, the space where his front teeth should be empty as he smiles widely; BJ taking a human girl named Ty'Asia out for something called "prom." Ivy also shares less humorous moments in her journey as BJ's parent, such as the first time he left their home without permission, only to attempt to sneak back in and cause such a commotion by knocking things over that he was caught. I chuckle at the look on his face in her memory. He appears very much like me when I was that age and causing mischief.

I don't know how long passes, but as Ivy ends the share of her memories, it almost feels like I lived a different twenty rotations. Much of the pain of my time with the Fein has been replaced with the support, patience, and love with which Ivy raised our son. Still, there is one more memory we need to reconcile.

She tenses when the scene from our last moments together before the Fein captured me flows between us. From my perspective, she witnesses my fear and regret, my love for her and our child, and the resolution that she had to survive. At the moment when I lift her, using all of my remaining strength to propel her through the pod door before sealing it and commanding it away, her soft gasp turns into an even softer sob.

Opening my eyes, I shift and pull her into my arms, holding her close as she buries her face into my chest. "It was always me. You never left me. I wanted you to live, and I'm glad I did it."

She nods, sniffling and lifting her face to kiss me. "Thank you."

"I hope you are not offended. I embedded as many of her memories in your mind as I could without completely altering your experiences." Ylt'r's softly spoken admission draws our attention. They have not moved since we entered, instead giving us space to experience the exchange.

I nod, my heart lighter than it's ever been. "I do not

mind."

"Thank you so much!" Ivy surprises me, releasing me and rushing to them to throw her arms around their waist.

They smile again and lean down to embrace her back. "I am glad I was able to do this for you. You both deserve it. Before we believed ourselves gods, my people worshiped a deity. I still whisper my hopes to it, and I believe they brought you two back together because a love like yours deserves the chance to flourish."

We thank them one more time, the Fein shocking me again by blushing when Ivy places a kiss on their cheek before we leave.

As we walk the halls, our hands swing between us.

"You are a great mother. And it seems our son is also very well turned out. You should be proud."

She makes a sound of acknowledgment, and her mouth turns up, but not enough to reach her eyes. "BJ is the best. I still worry about him, though."

"Why? Because my presence has upset him?"

"No," she shakes her head. "Believe it or not, he was drifting away from everyone before that. As he got older, I think some of the injustice of what happened to you really bothered him. He used to open up to me, and then suddenly he didn't. He spends more time with his friends these days. But also," she shrugs, "he's my baby, and I'm not all the way ready for him to grow up."

"I understand this, but our children always come home."

"I know. I'm sorry, by the way, that your introduction to him was so chaotic."

Stopping, I turn her to face me in the hall. "Why do you keep apologizing to me?"

Her skin flushes with heat, and she looks at her bare feet

as if they hold the answer. "I just feel like things could have been better for you when you got back."

"Then apologize correctly."

Her head snaps up, her brow furrowing in confusion.

I raise my brows. "Lyqa apologize in a specific way. It is vital to our culture, so if you insist on apologizing to me, I would like you to honor that."

She looks to the side and back. "Oh, okay. Uh, *ma'h qitah*, Ba'ir. I—"

I snatch her up, sealing my lips to hers. Backing her against the wall, I urge her lips apart, licking through her mouth to tangle with her tongue.

She's flushed and flustered when I'm done.

Giving her another smacking kiss, I step back. "That is the only way I will accept your apology. Otherwise, keep them. You owe me nothing, Ivy, and you've given me everything. I look forward to making sure you remember that."

I start down the hall again, noting that the patrons coming toward us watch our interaction with amused smirks. I don't check, but the sweet scent of her bashfulness mixed with her arousal is enough to let me know I've made my point.

We tumble into our stateroom, our hands tugging at each other's clothes. Neither of us is paying attention, so when I trip backward and fall into the relaxation pool with one leg caught in my pants, my head goes under, and I resurface to find Ivy doubled over laughing.

Lowering my face into the swirling, purple water, I fill my mouth and squirt it at her, catching her on the chest.

She gasps and looks down at her skin, then back at me.

I hitch a shoulder. "I guess you will have to remove it."

"It's a swimsuit, so it's made to get wet."

"And yet," I prowl forward, "you will have to remove it."

She smirks and peels the top off, tossing it aside. The tips of her bare breasts tighten as she steps slowly into the water. Lowering again, I open my mouth, letting the water flow between my lips, and Ivy pauses, narrowing her eyes.

"Don't you dare."

I release the water in an arc that lands just short of where she stands. "And if I do?"

"You're gonna regret it, trust me."

Levity fills me, and I hold her gaze, letting my mouth fill once more.

When the water lands with perfect aim on one of her breasts, she lets out a startled gasp. "I know you didn't."

"I did."

Her lips compress as she smothers a smirk, and then she drops down, disappearing beneath the water.

A graceful flutter of her feet propels her toward me, but instead of rising to confront me when she's close, she pauses, her expression mischievous.

The properties in the water allow her to breathe beneath the surface, so when she takes my cock in hand, stroking firmly from base to tip, I suck in a breath, holding it as I tense against the wall of the pool.

Even beneath the warm water, her mouth is hot. She exhales as she takes me in, easing me to the back of her throat before sucking back off.

"*Hul!*" I jerk, my arms grabbing the pool's edge as Ivy slowly bobs on and off my length. "Ivy…"

I know she can hear me. The water carries sound remarkably, even for human hearing. Still, she ignores me and takes me deeper, her torso jerking when she lodges me deep, and my mind blanks, release rushing over me so quickly that I can only hold on to keep from sinking as she swallows me down.

The swish of water signals Ivy rising, and I open my eyes to find her smirking. "I'm not sure that was the punishment it was meant to be."

Chuckling, I pull her close. "It was not, *lehti*. But I will take it as such if it means I can retaliate."

Her cackling laugh fills the room as I fuse my lips to hers and drag us both underwater.

24

IVY

"Baby, this is insane."

"Or fun?" Ba'ir has a twinkle in his eyes that's infectious as I fit the small breather over my nose. I've also been outfitted with a predator-deterrent wet suit and a special pair of goggles that allow me to see in the depths of the ocean.

We've reached our first docking station, which isn't a station at all. It's just a spot in the middle of the water where passengers can get off if they want to *swim to the "entertainment venue" at the bottom of the ocean.*

A bit of clarification let me know that "entertainment venue" was just alien for "club."

A club at the bottom of the ocean.

When Ba'ir first excitedly suggested the excursion, I didn't have the heart to tell him hell no, but now that I'm looking at the thick, murky waters below where I sit on the edge of the jumping platform of the ship, I'm definitely thinking hell no.

I pull my lips in. "Or sharks or whatever Qitoni version of sharks requires a predator-deterrent wet suit?"

Beside me, Ba'ir smirks, probably because he knows I'm ready to back out. "Come, *lehti*. There is nothing here to harm you, and if there is, I will protect you. I promise."

The moment the words are spoken, we both freeze, our minds traveling in tandem to that moment twenty years ago when we were torn from each other.

His excitement falters, and he looks stricken like he knows what I'm thinking. The same way, I know what's on his mind. He's thinking that I'm thinking that he wasn't able to protect me then, so he isn't able to protect me now. He's thinking that our life together will be great as long as we avoid any risk or stray too far from what's prudent. He's thinking I may want to be with him, but I'll never believe he can keep me safe.

I could reassure him or remind him again that what happened wasn't his fault, but there's only one way he'll ever believe I trusted him then and now.

So, I let his hand go and dive over the side of the boat.

"You're a good dancer."

"As are you, *lehti*." Ba'ir twirls me in a smooth rotation of his wrist before bringing us back together.

He's incredibly tipsy, having drunk at least a dozen of the all-inclusive drinks being offered. To my surprise, Ba'ir grabbed us each a drink as soon as we got here, chugging his back, and when I reminded him that I couldn't drink, he chugged mine, too.

I was able to get a nonintoxicating version of the neon pink cocktail and was delighted to find it tasted like plum lemonade. The surface swirled with green smoke that, when we licked at it, turned into sugary crystals in our mouths. After the first sip, I knew the only purpose of a drink like that was to get folks messed up.

It didn't matter that mine was missing that element. Ba'ir's so damn happy that it's contagious, lulling me into my own blissful haze.

"It's so beautiful in here." For the thousandth time, I look up at the clear dome overhead, watching the chemiluminescent creatures swim above us. Their fan-like fins, twirling tentacles, and arching antennae are a disco of nature's choreography. Colorful strobe lights play around the room, drawing the attention of the circling sea life.

"You are beautiful." Ba'ir's fingers skim up my bare back, and a shiver rushes over me.

After we reached the club and pierced the dome to be lowered to the main level, we shed our body-hugging wet suits and took a turn in a large cube that smoothed out our clothes, leaving our party outfits wrinkle-free. My dress is a daring look for me in the sense that I haven't worn something like this in *ever*.

The bottom half is a bowing bloom of petal-shaped panels that stop just at the tops of my thighs. The intricate Qitoni beadwork is a eddy of furls and swoops, giving the impression of rolling waves as I shimmy my hips. The bodice hugs my torso, pinning in at my ribs, only to gape in a diamond-shaped cut-out that leaves the space beneath my heart bare. It's another of Crissette's pieces.

Ba'ir's eyes stray to this patch of skin over and over as we dance.

"*Have I* told you how beautiful you look?"

"You have," I smile and clasp my hands behind his neck.

When he first appeared in the break room at my job, despite the deep gouges, tears, and haphazard repair jobs evident across his skin, he always looked like the boy who swept me into his arms in the middle of the food festival and asked me with the most soulful brown eyes I'd ever seen to let him take me away.

Now, looking at him, his skin repaired so that one couldn't even tell there was ever a scratch on him, I'm left to marvel at how beautiful he still is.

"You look really good, too."

He's wearing a dark shirt, not quite a t-shirt or a sweater, but something soft and form-fitting that settles over his muscular frame with a casual luxury. His slacks are also black. The relaxed fit isn't as stiff as a human design, which has the effect of accentuating the bulge in his crotch.

My eyes have strayed to that part of him over and over.

"*Lehti,*" he grumbles in warning, but there's no bite to it. "I am ready to swim back to the surface whenever you are, and if you continue to look at me in that way, we will have to."

I smirk and look away, letting him shift us around in a circle. Clearing my throat, I glance at the other beings in the room. I haven't had a chance to get a good look at anyone. I haven't been able to keep my eyes off of Ba'ir. "This new look is good on you." I flinch, my gaze flying to his as I fumble to apologize. "I didn't mean it like that. I never cared what you looked like."

He smiles, and there's no offense, only joy. It spreads between our beating hearts, casting aside my guilt. "I know how you meant, *lehti.*"

As for my skill at dancing, thankfully, there are some things one never forgets." He spins us around, expertly avoiding a drunk green dude with horns. The guy is massive, bigger even than Ba'ir, who towers over most of the beings in the room.

Green dude wobbles to the side, the frail neck of a drink glass gripped in his meaty hand as he sloppily sways to the music. My brows raise as I watch the lazy two-step. He may be drunk off his ass, but he can still keep the beat.

His eyes are closed, and he's narrowly avoiding colliding with the other dancers. When he stumbles in our direction again, Ba'ir shifts in front of me and grabs the man when he would bump into us, holding the dude's bare, muscular shoulders in a firm grip.

Now that he's still, I recognize the guy as Hosa. They're from a planet in the Seventeenth Quadrant. Most of their higher-ups are ambassadors. Their king and his brother, in particular, are known for their work in conflict resolution. Before Ba'ir's fathers' plea to Thresh, they were my next hope in getting him freed. I'd been on a wait list to meet with them for years. I'd only received the chance for an audience because their princess married a human man. He came across the request and bumped me up the list for a meeting with King Sekh just when I got word of Ba'ir's rescue.

After years of failed attempts, getting ripped off, and worse, I did my homework on the Hosa, which makes the sight of the unsteady alien even more shocking.

Hosa are big on decorum and honor. Getting wasted and nearly mowing down a bunch of strangers with sloppy but on-beat dance moves doesn't seem like their thing.

"I think, perhaps, you should sit, friend."

The Hosa blinks his glossy gaze on Ba'ir a second before his expression crumbles, and he begins to cry. Except, there are no tears, just angry grunt-like noises that I can only tell are sorrow because his expression is pinched in anguish. "She just chose another as if our commitment meant nothing! As if I were just something to *discard*." His head falls back, exposing a thick, corded neck, which is playing trumpet to a deep, ruckling sob.

I stare, unsure of what to do. A glance around the room. Luckily, this isn't Earth, or every person would have their phone out ready to blast this poor guy's meltdown all over the Internet. Most of the beings around us cast glances of curiosity and concern at the Hosa's display.

"I am sorry for that." Ba'ir pulls the Hosa into a hug, squeezing him tight, ignoring the poke of the other male's massive horns into his neck as the Hosa blubbers over Ba'ir's shoulder. "It is always difficult when things do not go as we wish. I understand." Ba'ir pats the Hosa's shoulder mountains like one would a baby, and they look so ridiculous that the urge to laugh bubbles in my throat, forcing me to turn my back so I can cover it with a strangled cough.

"See? Even your female—who is beautiful by the way—believes me to be a joke."

"She is beautiful, and no, *sa'qi*, she does not believe this. Do you, *lehti*."

"Hm?" I spin back, my brows high as I fight a losing battle against cracking the hell up.

"You do not find humor in this male's misfortune, do you?" Ba'ir gives me a pointed look, which only makes things worse when his lips twitch, too.

Breathing deeply through my nose, I narrow my eyes and chew the mirth into a small enough ball to swallow. "No, I don't find your situation funny. I'm really sorry that happened to you, but honestly, if she threw what you had away that easily, she didn't deserve it anyway."

Seeing the genuine agony in the Hosa's eyes, I step forward and place a comforting hand on his arm. He's warm, almost too warm, and his skin is velvety smooth. Up close, even with his tortured expression, he's stunning—all sharp planes and shining angles. The light bounces off the green of his skin, turning his face into a work of art.

"Do you truly believe that?" He smiles weepily, flashing sharp fangs.

Patting the rock-hard muscles in his forearm, I nod. "I do. When someone is for you, you'll know. There won't be anything that can keep you apart."

"Do you truly believe *that?*" The Hosa's drunken skepticism makes me chuckle.

"I assure you, sa'qi, we have tested the theory." Ba'ir smiles, and my heart stutters.

Shifting my attention back to the Hosa, I reach for the glass he's raising to his lips. "Maybe you've had enough. How-how long have you been drinking?" I stutter as I struggle to pry the glass from his grip, half expecting it to break the way he has a death hold on it, but it stays intact as I wrench it free.

"Four spans." He sniffles and swipes a hand down his face.

"Four spans?" I must look confused because he makes a face like he's confused too.

"You asked how long I've been drinking. It has been four spans."

I exchange a glance with Ba'ir, who's tilting his head at the Hosa. "You have been *here* in this place for four spans?" Ba'ir's tone suggests this can't be true, but when the Hosa only nods and reaches out to retake the glass, Ba'ir retrieves it from me and holds it out of reach. "I believe my *lehti* is correct, and you have imbibed enough. Why don't you sit with us? We will request some hydration packets for you. What is your name?"

Sniffle. "Qlai."

"Qlai," Ba'ir smiles, back to using his coaxing voice as he leads Qlai to a table. This time, it doesn't make me laugh to see him comforting the other male. My heart fills with a gentle warmth that he's still able to offer empathy after all he's been through. I catch up, sliding my arms around Ba'ir's waist. He turns, his gaze full of love—and winks.

"I love you." I blurt, unable to hold it back anymore. As much as I've felt it, I haven't been able to bring myself to repeat it after the night he blew up at me at my house. Until now, the words felt like an indictment, a shameful reflection of how I'd failed him for all of these years. It felt like I was asking for a deference I didn't deserve, but in this moment of watching Ba'ir continue to fall into the male he always was, it's just as important that I recognize it with my love for him.

He and Qlai halt and shift to face me. They wear identical expressions of shock that almost make me laugh again.

"Is this the first time she has said these words to you?" Qlai's voice is steady, the misery vanquished from his face.

Ba'ir shakes his head, slowly, his gaze burrowing into mine. "No, but events have transpired between us, and I was not sure I would hear it again. I was not sure I was worthy."

I throw my arms around his waist, pressing my face into the hard planes of his chest. "I love you, Ba'ir. I've loved you since the day I met you, and I'm going to love you for the rest of my life."

"She's a good female." Qlai is sober, and sober Qlai is *way* different than drunk for four days Qlai. All it took was a hydration packet of a special Qitoni water to flush the intoxicant from his system, and gone was the melancholy, heartbroken green giant. What we've been left with could better be classified as something of an ogre. "I *never* should have trusted her. She was superficial and duplicitous from the beginning. Females only care about one thing," he snorts in disgust, talking more to himself than Ba'ir and me.

I'm a little horrified. I keep trying to catch Ba'ir's gaze so we can find an excuse to leave, but I get the impression he's ignoring me on purpose.

Ba'ir listens without comment as Qlai details how his mate, which apparently is a very final decision in his culture, found a way to effectively divorce him and mate with another guy while he was on an ambassador assignment. They were newly official, and he returned home eager to begin a family, only to find himself dumped and embarrassed in front of his peers.

For his kind, arranged marriages are a thing, and while Qlai had been content with the choice made for him by his parents, the female had not. She took advantage of an old and rarely used law that required her to argue its validity before applying it to select someone else.

Clearing his throat and looking away, Qlai's expression shuts down before evening into an alarming apathy. "It matters not. I have no need for a mate anyway." He regards me for a long moment, and I see a flash of the Hosa who stumbled into us on the dance floor, vulnerable and hurt. "Thank you for preventing me from shaming myself further. Had one of my kind witnessed my behavior, I would be more humiliated than I already am." Standing, he quickly drops to a knee with his head bowed before rising. "Take care, Ba'ir," his eyes flicker to me, again betraying the vulnerability he's failing to hide, "and Ivy."

He marches off, and I watch as he makes his way across the room, his broad, muscular form parting the crowd with its sheer impressiveness.

"You said you love me."

I hinge my attention from Qlai's retreating back to find Ba'ir staring at me with sappy, soft eyes. "I do."

"Good. I'd like to return to the surface and explore this love."

I laugh as he helps me up and leads me to the gateway for the surface.

***

"Was there an issue below?" We're met by the same Aemu host who took us to the Fein as we arrive at the side of the boat's deck.

"There was not. We only wished to enjoy time on the ship. As I understand it, we are allowed to come and go."

The Aemu looks nervously to the side. When we attempt to pass him, he shifts, blocking our way. "Nearly all of the other passengers have chosen to remain below water. There are many excursions to partake in, a true Qitoni cultural experience! Please, return there." He waves both sets of his arms, trying to urge us back to the deck's edge. His voice is unnaturally jubilant.

"Thank you, friend. However, if the ship is empty, that is even better. We would like privacy." Ba'ir takes my hand and attempts to side-step the Aemu, but we're stopped again.

The Aemu's face has lost its joviality and is tense with panic. "Please. There is nothing to do on the ship. We—we are actually in the process of completing a very complicated maintenance check. It is critical that all passengers remain below surface." He shoves, his four hands ushering us around, but Ba'ir moves out of reach, pushing me behind him.

"Your display is purple. What has happened?" His voice is low, but it's obvious something is wrong.

"Do not attempt to move! Keep your hands where they can be seen." A tall but thin being with grayish-lavender speckled skin rushes from around one of the large pillars on deck, a weapon leveled at his bulbous eye.

The first thing I notice is how beautiful his eyes are. They're light brown, speckled with violet and yellow, like a little universe held in his gaze.

They're also filled with malice so potent that I immediately raise my hands, even though Ba'ir is blocking my body.

Ba'ir does the same. Moving with care, his hands lift to his shoulders, palms facing outward. "I am not sure what is happening, but we mean you no harm."

The guy's eyes, which are partly covered by thick, flat petal-shaped tendrils that hang over his forehead, narrow. His lips curl around thick lower tusks. "You should have stayed below sea, like the Aemu suggested. Now, you're going to stay here. Come! No, wait," he nudges with the gun when Ba'ir starts to move. "Send her first."

Ba'ir shifts even more, blocking more of my view, so I can only see the top half of the guy's torso and his face. "She is fine with me. We will follow any directives you have, but my *lehti* isn't going anywhere with you." Lowering his voice, he speaks out of the side of his mouth. "*Lehti*, when he fires, jump over the side of this ship. The suit will protect you from the fall. Secure your breathing apparatus underwater."

I sputter, glaring at the side of Ba'ir's face. "What do you mean, 'when he fires'? We don't want him to fire."

"It's the only way to allow your escape. Just do it!"

We're loud. Our voices rise as we argue in earshot of the guy. His nostrils flare, and his hands tense around the gun. "You must want to die."

Ba'ir's body braces as he waits for the blast, and panic rushes through me. Time halts as the guy sneers and aims.

"*Lehti*, jump!"

I grab the back of Ba'ir's shirt, unwilling to leave him again, just before my ears fill with the wavy boom of a sonic pulse as the guy pulls the trigger. The force of the blast collides with Ba'ir's chest, knocking us both back.

I cry out when my back collides with the guardrail, rolling to the side to catch my breath as the wind is knocked out of me.

Ba'ir is on his back, clutching at his chest, and I scramble to him, trying to see if he's hurt.

"Go, *lehti*. GO!" His shout comes through gritted teeth as he clutches at the front of his wet suit. He pushes at my hands, shoving me back.

"No," I crowd over him, using my body as a shield as the guy advances, leveling the weapon again. "I know why you're asking me to, but I can't leave you again. I'm sorry. I love you, and I can't."

"I love you too, *lehti*." He grips my head and pulls me down, smashing my lips to his. He holds me there, and everything else ceases to exist. As he kisses me while we wait to die, my mind flashes with a different life than the one we've suffered through for the past twenty years.

In that life, we never went to that terrible planet. Instead, Ba'ir woke me up that fateful morning with gentle kisses and the news that we were expecting a child.

From there, the time fills in itself: Ba'ir caring for me

while I was pregnant. Disagreeing over names, but finally settling on Ba'ir Junior to honor both of our cultures. BJ's first steps, his first day of school, his first Little League game, his first track meet, his high school graduation. The memories of this other life fill up the doom of the unknown, until I can almost hear my son's voice.

It isn't until Ba'ir breaks away from the kiss and looks to the side in shock that reality comes catapulting back, along with the realization that I am, in fact, hearing my son's voice.

"What the hell, Yemor! You said you weren't going to harm anyone. That we were just here for them." I follow Ba'ir's gaze to an unknown Qitoni standing chest to chest with the guy, her face tense with anger. She looks vaguely like one of the Qitoni I've seen around the boat, but her voice is unmistakably my child's.

"BJ?"

The Qitoni's eyes close, her shoulders, which, now that I look at them, seem wider and more masculine than other Qitoni's, drop. Slowly, she faces me, meeting my gaze for only a moment before reaching to pull at her face. My eyes widen when the Qitoni's skin detaches, and BJ's is revealed, his eyes lowered. "I can explain, *Am'ha.*"

"Mother? This human is your *mother*?" The guy, Yemor, shoves BJ, knocking my son off balance, and BJ surges forward to push back, sending Yemor sprawling.

"You're going to let her go. That is not a question." BJ stabs a finger, his voice hard and steady, adult in a way that I've only heard once before, when Ba'ir lashed out at me in my home. Until that moment, he was just—my baby.

Despite the shock of finding my son in disguise running with a group of murderous pirates, I'm proud of him. I've felt like I failed him in a billion ways since before he was born, but I raised him with love and made sure the people around him loved him too. And I know he loves me back.

Definitely gonna knock him upside his head when this is over, but proud.

Yemor scrambles to his feet and trains the weapon on BJ, his snarl so vicious that thick saliva drips from his jowls. "Are you trying to double-cross us? You know these people?" He whistles, and the rest of his gang rounds the corner where they must have been waiting for his signal.

"I'm not double-crossing anyone. You can still get what you want, but we said we weren't hurting anyone. You're letting my mother go."

"You don't issue the orders. We do as *I* say." Yemor steps away from BJ and nudges his head at the group.

They circle BJ, and I start to rise, only to be held back by Ba'ir, who is already struggling to his feet.

"If you put your hands on my son—" he begins, only for BJ to whirl around. Our son's gaze is hard.

"I don't need your help!" BJ faces the group and tackles one of the closest beings, punching the yellow, horned guy in the face. BJ's fists swing with sharp precision as he pummels the much larger male. Like a swarm, the others descend, punching and kicking my son so fast that I don't have time to blink.

"No!" Ba'ir rushes forward, but Yemor turns his blaster on me, halting Ba'ir's steps.

"I will shoot her in the face. Her suit won't protect that."

Ba'ir's tormented gaze swings between me and the grunting scuffle of his son being jumped. I try to meet his eyes to silently urge him to save our son, but he focuses on Yemor. "Do not kill my son, please. But know if you do, there is not enough space between us to escape me before you can fire that weapon again."

Yemor stares Ba'ir down for a long moment. BJ is curled into a ball on the ground, doing his best to protect his head and body. Finally, Yemor whistles, and the assault stops just as quickly as it began. The group steps away from my son's still form.

"*Lehti,* he lives. Stop screaming."

I blink. My ears are ringing, and my throat is raw. Was I screaming?

Ba'ir stands in front of me. He takes my arms, snapping my gaze from BJ to his calm, brown eyes. "They have promised not to harm you. Go with them. Once they have what they want, I will find you. You will be fine, *lehti.*"

My eyes stray to BJ again, and Ba'ir takes my chin, bringing our gazes together. "He will be with me. I will look after him. You will feel my heart, and I will feel yours."

He turns me to Yemor, who steps forward and takes my arm, pulling me away.

"No!" My son struggles to stand, his arm outstretched.

"Take them to the storage room." Yemor jerks me in the opposite direction, and I look back, holding Ba'ir's gaze until they're out of sight.

25

BA'IR

"WHY *THE FUCK* WAS SHE EVEN HERE?" My son's hands connect with my chest, shoving me back.

I stumble but catch my footing, pulling myself up straight. My heart thumps wildly, an echo of Ivy's fear from wherever they've taken her, and it makes my body vibrate with barely restrained tension.

BJ doesn't have a First heart. He has no way of knowing how fragile my temper is at the moment, but he is my son, so I try to calm myself as I respond.

"I think the more appropriate question is, why are you here associating with a band of murdering pirates, *dahni*?" I ask him in Lyqa. His nostrils flare, and he takes a step toward me, his intent clear by the clench of his fists. That my son wishes to throw fists with me stings, but I am too tense to wallow in it. I step forward, too; my height advantage deflates some of his hostility. "I understand that you are upset, but do not put your hands on me again, BJ. It would not be wise. My *lehti* is in danger, and I am not with her. Even without a First heart, you should know what that means. Do. Not. Touch. Me." This I say in English, nodding to the space between us. "Sit."

He huffs, wavering like he may still attempt to attack me. In the end, he drops and shoves back against the wall with his head between his legs. "Fuck, fuck, fuck! I can't believe this shit."

I sit, too, keeping space between us, and observe him. "You fought well, but still took quite a beating. Are you hurt badly?"

BJ cuts his eye to me, the one that isn't swollen shut, his jaw flexing. "I'm fine. I don't need you to check on me."

"You're my son. You can hate me, but it would be impossible for me not to care. I love you."

He snorts. His leg bounces quickly, the sole of his shoe squeaking against the floor. The scent pouring from him is a mixture of regret, fear, and anger.

I'm sure my scent carries the same.

I was just beginning to feel as if I could live a life without the worry of danger, and here I am again. Only this time, Ivy is the one captured. "Will they kill her?"

BJ stills, then shakes his head without looking up. "I don't think so. There was something on the ship they wanted. If they had gotten it, they would have gone before anyone came to the surface. That was the plan, in and out."

I narrow my eyes. "What did they want?"

He looks up, his lip curling. "It doesn't matter now. Because of you, they can't get it."

"How have I affected their mission? I don't know these beings."

"But you know the Fein, don't you? I saw you wishing them well, letting them walk away like their kind didn't ruin your life, ruin *our* lives! And now we can't find him. He's been hidden on the ship somewhere by you *sympathizers*."

As I look at the fury blazing in my son's eyes, the realization arrives to me that I've missed something.

Perhaps it's because, after twenty rotations, I am unused to deciphering people. Or maybe I was always naive, and despite what I thought, that was something the Fein didn't relieve me of.

I thought BJ's anger was merely directed at me for how I'd treated his mother, but it is not that exclusive. My son is angry in a way that has consumed him.

The irony does not escape me, but it still hurts. "My fathers said you were happy."

His mouth makes a sucking sound that can only be revulsion. "Who *the fuck* has time to think about happiness, *Dad?*" His nose curls with the snarled reply. I find myself studying the expression.

He looks much like me, but he has his mother's nose. I try not to think about what may be happening to Ivy, wherever she is, and focus on the beat of my heart.

"That shit is a fantasy," BJ continues. "There is no happiness. There's terrible people doing terrible shit, and everybody else is too fucking scared to *do* anything about it." The words strain from the tight line of his lips, and I wonder if this is what I looked like when I attacked his mother.

"Is that why you're with these pirates? You're doing something about it?"

"Maybe, I am. Maybe I'm not going to sit back like a coward and let someone rip my life away."

Twenty rotations is a long time. Every day of that time, I

wished I could have lived the life that was meant for me. Once I knew about BJ, I was glad that he'd been free of the residual captivity of the last twenty years. I'd imagined him as the young male I never got to be, but he isn't. He may have suffered more than any of us.

Even under the Fein, I had the memory of a life stolen, memories that were warm and filled with love. But all BJ has had is the knowledge that his father was helplessly under tormentors, and his mother was working her life away under the weight of guilt.

"I'm sorry you've had to live like this, with whatever emptiness you've filled with vengeance."

His expression shifts, going dark, even as shame fills the air between us. "You don't know what you're talking about." He stands and paces to the locked door, waving his arm in vain over the sensor. "I need to get out of here!"

"Stop. It's pointless to beat against a door that you know won't open." I stand, too, and go over to place a hand on his shoulder.

He flings it away, whirling on me with frantic eyes. "And what's your plan, to sit here and let them hold us captive? To do nothing to try and free ourselves? To let them kill mom?" He sneers. "I guess you have twenty years of practice doing that."

He bangs on the door again, leaving the words that were no doubt meant to cut hanging between us.

He really is just like me.

I lean against the wall, watching as he tries again and again to activate the sensor. "Five hundred and forty-two."

He pauses and glances at me in confusion.

I shrug. "Give or take."

When he continues to look perplexed, I lift my brows as if

the connection is obvious. "The number of times I tried to escape. In fact, I could show you a scar for—" I stop in raising my sleeve when I remember. "Well, I could have shown you a scar, or ten, for every time I tried to leave that place. You see, I had value to the Fein. I was a strong male, an asset to their mines. Their torture of me wasn't because I was there. It was because I kept trying to get away. And once I realized they were going to hurt me no matter what, I decided to make it worth my while. Perhaps I got free, but if I didn't, I knew I tried."

BJ swallows, his eyes shifting to the side before he faces me fully. I'd laugh at the disbelief on his face if I weren't using every part of my willpower to remain calm for my lehti.

"By the time I was rescued, they had done things to my mind, my memories, and I didn't remember how things really were. I blamed your mother, but the truth is, I spent most of the rotations under the Fein trying to get back to her. Even when they thought turning my mind against your mother would stop my attempts at escape, I still found a motivation back to her, even if it was vengeance. While I was captive, I watched, and I waited, plotting, planning, and I ran again and again. What I didn't do," I give him a pointed look, "is bang against a door that I knew wouldn't open."

BJ glances at the door he was just assaulting, and color creeps into his cheeks.

Standing, I go to him. "The cleaning service comes through twice a day, and to make it efficient, the biometrics are released on all of the doors at once. I noticed it on our first night on the ship. It should be any moment—" The short beep sounds from the door pad, and BJ's eyes widen.

I wave my hand over the sensor at the moment the lock releases, and the door slides open.

Grabbing BJ's arm, I pull him into the empty hall and immediately into the shadowed alcove across from us just before a pirate crosses at the end of the hall, his eyes scanning in our direction.

"Do you know where they're keeping the crew and your mother?"

BJ stares at me in astonishment, his guilt a heavy fragrance in the alcove.

Gripping the back of his head, I bring his forehead to mine. "You had every right to think what you did about me, but we don't have time to feel bad about things we've said. Once we're safe, we can show our love with words."

He nods tightly, taking hold of my arm. When I draw back, his eyes are moist. "I'm sorry."

"I know." I smile. "Where are they keeping the passengers—"

"Hey!"

We both spin to find the pirate who was patrolling the hall behind us with his weapon trained. I step in front of my son and start to raise my hands when BJ shoves me out of the way, at the same time, knocking the weapon from the pirate and delivering a round of strikes that leave the male sprawled on the floor.

I turn to face my son, and he shrugs. "One of Grandpa's cousins is married to a Yuk. He's been teaching me how to fight since I was like five."

"Tpicar?"

BJ nods with a grin.

Shaking my head, I bend to turn the pirate over so we can bind him. "He tried to teach me, too, when I was young, along with his sons. While Qil was more than eager and Qim reluctantly agreed, I held firm that 'violence wasn't the answer.'" I roll my eyes at how ridiculous I believe my younger self, and BJ chuckles as he secures the pirate's bindings and waves me down the corridor.

"Come. They're keeping the crew this way."

He leads me through the ship, avoiding the pirates guarding along the way, until we reach the area used as reception when we first boarded.

"They planned to put everyone in one of the restaurants on the second level."

"Well done, BJ." I clap his shoulder and point to a bench between us and the restaurant, where I can see someone patrolling the entrance. "You hide yourself there while I get closer to see inside."

"No, Dad. I can help."

We both freeze, our identical eyes staring into each other's. My throat tightens, and while I know this is not the time, I grab him and hug him to me, uncaring if he pushes me away. I still wouldn't blame him if he did.

Except he doesn't.

His arms come around my back, gripping tightly, and his shoulders begin to shake. I crowd over him, taking in his sorrow until he's ready to let go. "I wanted a dad so bad. It was so unfair that I didn't get to have you. I hated knowing you were somewhere hurting, and I couldn't save you." His voice is hushed but raw, and when he lifts his head, he doesn't shy away from me seeing his tears.

I press a kiss to his forehead. "You always had a father, *dahni*. I'm sorry I couldn't be there in the ways I should have been, but I thought of you every day. The only times I ever smiled in that place were when I thought of you and your mother. I would have let them tear me apart for the rest of eternity to make sure you made it into this Universe, and I'm thankful with every breath that you had such a strong, fearless woman to raise you. She gave you all of that and more, and now you have to let me save her. I can't do that if I'm worried about my son."

He holds my gaze for another moment, then nods before hugging me quickly again. Checking to ensure the atrium is still clear, he keeps low and runs across to crouch behind the bench I indicated. Once his back is pressed against the wall, he raises his thumb to me in an indication that he's okay.

Easing around my hiding spot, I make quick feet to the wall beside the restaurant where the pirates are holding the hostages. As I near, I can hear shouting from inside. My ears perk when Ivy's voice sounds out among the commotion.

"I don't know what you expect to get from this, but they don't know what you're talking about."

"I know they know where the Fein is being hidden. They will tell us. We want the Fein!" Something crashes, and someone screams. My heart lurches with Ivy's fear, and I look toward where my son is hiding. He's peeking through a space between the bench seat, and I meet his gaze and smile.

His eyes widen, and he starts to rise, but I move quicker, standing and holding my hands up as I round the front of the restaurant so I'm visible to those inside.

***

"Stop!" Ivy's cry is cut off when the pirate who's been ordered to torture me smashes his fist into my face again. "He's lying. He doesn't know where the Fein is."

"I do, but I'm not going to tell you anything until you release these beings onto a secure vessel and let them leave the ship."

The Borsk, Yemor, who seems to be the leader of this

group, snarls, his nose flaring as the tusks in his lower jaw jut forward. "If you do not tell me, I will begin to tear pieces from your flesh."

I shrug as much as I can with my arms bound to the seat where I was led after I walked into the restaurant and announced that I knew precisely where the Fein was hiding. "I would have called that a fourth day, not so long ago. Do your worst. However, if you wish to capture the Fein, you will have to meet my demands first."

Yemor's hands clench into claws, and I'm sure he's going to hit me again, but he only growls and flings himself away, rushing over to the nearest table to beat it with his fists.

His comrades watch him with wide, terrified eyes, and as I glance across the group, I realize they are mostly just out of adolescence. They are children.

Yemor's back heaves as he leans over the mangled table. Finally, he turns to glare at me. Like with my child, beyond the rage is hurt.

"I know the Fein has harmed you. So many have been harmed by the terrible among them, but this will bring you nothing. No satisfaction and no relief. If you know my son, you know I have every reason to despise them. When I was freed, I thought vengeance was all I had, but acting on it only made me closer to the ones who hurt me." I've said everything I wish someone had said to me when I thought revenge would give me deliverance from my anger.

Instead of my words extinguishing the fire that fuels Yemor's wrath, his expression hardens, and he turns on Ivy with violence in his eyes.

I jerk against my restraints, feeling my shoulder sockets pop, just as the door to the restaurant slides open and BJ walks in—with the Fein. My son has a weapon trained at their back, his face twisted in dangerous satisfaction.

"I told you all you could still trust me, Yemor. I found them." BJ shoves the Fein forward, and they fall, landing hard on their knees.

"BJ," Ivy's eyes are wide with disbelief, but when she starts to rise, I shake my head.

"*Lehti*, do not intervene." Keeping her safe remains my top priority. I nod to her lower body where our other child is nestled, and she reluctantly drops back to her heels. However, her gaze burns with disappointment at our son.

"Little boy," she admonishes, uncaring if it draws Yemor's ire.

"Mom, I can't just forgive and forget like you. They have to pay."

The Borsk grins, satisfaction replacing the glimmer of cruelty I glimpsed a moment ago. "BJ! Well done. Now we'll get everything we want and more."

My son nods, his grin just as wide but tight. His eyes flicker to his mother, who's silently shaking her head as she looks at him. "Great. Let's get these folks out of here."

Yemor follows BJ's gaze, his own narrowing for a moment before he shrugs. "Get your mother. I don't harm women, unlike this monster," he spits toward the Fein, whose head is bowed. They've said nothing since entering with BJ.

My son's steps are hurried as he moves away from the Fein toward Ivy, but when he would pass Yemor, the Borsk grabs him, clamping his thick arm about my son's neck and squeezing tight. "You must believe I am stupid. You reek of deception, but you've brought them to us either way, so I'll make your death quick."

BJ struggles, his mouth opening as he fights to breathe.

Suddenly, I am transported twenty rotations in the past, helpless, watching my life die a slow and scarred demise.

In the present, I probably could not stop Ivy if I were unrestrained. She is up before the Borsk has fully grabbed our son, rushing them both. In slowed time, I watch Yemor raise his weapon, even as BJ's eyes widen at the Borsk's intent. Ivy sees Yemor aim at her; she must, but she doesn't stop, and then a blast sounds, the force of it making everyone jerk in shock.

The past has finally caught up with me, and it pulls me into a darkness I willingly surrender to.

***

"Ba'ir."

"Dad?"

"What's wrong with him?"

"He is in shock, but that is better than the pain he would be experiencing otherwise."

"Ba'ir, baby. Come back. Please."

Slowly, Ivy's voice filters through the void where my mind plummeted when I heard the blast. In that dark place, I imagined thousands of scenarios that all ended with me losing Ivy, our son, and our unborn child.

I blink, and when my vision clears, Ivy is close enough that her face is nearly doubled, and I reach for her, grabbing her head and yanking her lips to mine.

She tastes of tears and life. She moans, a sound I pull into my soul, and leans into me, opening when I urge. It isn't until someone clears their throat that she pulls away with a light chuckle. "We might be embarrassing our son."

My gaze flies to the side where BJ stands. His face is still swollen, but he is alive and smiling, his cheeks pulsing a dull pink as he watches his mother and me.

"I don't mind. You two deserve it, and I always wanted more siblings. It's just that Dad's arm is kind of—broken."

The moment he says this, my memory snaps back, like a fog has been lifted:

The Borsk choking my son. My entire body revolting against my restraints as I ignore the sharp tearing of dislocation.

Ivy running to BJ's rescue.

The Borsk aiming his weapon and warning her back.

The crack of my arm as I finally ripped myself from my bindings before leaping to intercept Ivy, putting myself in the line of fire.

The blaster going off and hitting me in the chest—again.

A second blast going off as the Borsk fell backward, his arm dropping away from BJ's neck. And then a blinding pain that pulled me into darkness just as a green shadow fell over me.

The pain comes back with a force that has me gritting my teeth, but I am still unwilling to relinquish my hold on my lehti.

"Hold still. This will ease the discomfort until the healers can see to you." Someone grabs my arm, and I follow the line of the large green hand to the familiar face of a Hosa.

"Qlai?"

He grunts then nods, his expression stoic. "I came on board to request transport to the nearest departure port since my ship left spans ago, only to find pirates had taken over this vessel. Your son apprised me of the situation and, along with the Fein, came up with the plan to distract the Borsk so I could disarm him."

"Where is Ylt'r?"

"They have been taken to a safe location. They asked that

I wish you well." He's holding a medi-pen. He moves to inject my arm, but I shy away.

"Give it to my son."

"Dad," BJ's eyes shift back as he shakes his head. "I have a black eye. Your arm is literally hanging off your body."

My smile hurts; it's so wide. BJ looks away, his cheeks pulsing again, before meeting my gaze. The hurt I noticed before is gone, and his eyes shine with youthful optimism.

Ivy looks between us with a small smile of her own.

"Please, *Dad*, let the man give you the shot. I promise, I'll let him fix me up right after."

Ivy sniffles, her eyes damp. I take a moment to compose myself as well before offering my arm to Qlai. He administers the nanites, and I hiss as the damaged tissue and bone begin to reconstruct themselves. When I'm able to rotate my arm again, I move to stand.

"Hey, take it easy." Ivy takes my arm, and I allow her assistance, although I don't need it.

Our son smiles fondly at our clasped hands as we approach. Qlai has prepared another medi-pen, but when he moves to inject BJ, I take his arm, stopping him.

"Let me. I haven't," my cheeks pulse as I hold my hand out for the pen. "I have not tended to his wounds before. I know he is an adult, but—"

"He's still your son. That means he is never too old for you to show your care for him. Here." Qlai gives me the pen, and when I turn to BJ, he's waiting with an indulgent crinkle to his unswollen eye.

"Wait," Ivy holds out a hand just before I can administer the pen. She smiles at our son, who watches her in confusion. Suddenly, her hand strikes out, the palm hitting BJ along the side of his head. The sharp *smack* stuns us all, and our son winces, hunching his shoulders against the assault.

"Mom!"

"Out here running around with pirates when you're supposed to be doing college work! Is this what you were doing when I found you sneaking into the house? Is this why you haven't answered any of my calls?" She rains a volley of strikes over his head and shoulders, making him chuckle and shy away. Aside from the first strike, she isn't using any true force, and the look on her face speaks more to worry than anger. "If I ever!"

"You won't. I promise, Ma! *Ap'ha!*"

I shrug. "I'm pretty sure you deserve this."

Halting her assault, Ivy humphs and plants her hands at her hips, her eyes narrowed. "I better not. Now let your father fix you up."

She stomps away, mumbling about "kids stressing her out," and BJ meets my gaze with a sheepish one of his own.

I wink and press the pen to his arm, releasing the nanites and waiting as they do their work until his face is a true reflection of mine again.

"Thanks, Dad."

The sigh that frees itself from my chest is the only catharsis I need. I pull him into a hug, which he immediately returns. "I'll never tire of hearing you say that."

"I won't stop saying it." He releases me and claps me on the shoulder. "I mean, until you're a grandpa."

He laughs, a deep rolling chuckle, when my eyes widen.

Epilogue

BA'IR

"On this Kal Sai, let us honor our reunited kin, Ba'ir. We waited many rotations for you to join us again, and we look forward to celebrating many more with you here."

My ap'ha's father raises his cup, and the other members of my extended family do the same.

"As do I." With a nod of acknowledgment, I take a sip of the traditional Lyqa spirit, catching Ivy's gaze over the rim of my cup.

I wink, and she smirks. Her lips touch the rim of her glass, and I'm reminded of the time we spent in our cabin before tonight's dinner.

She got to her knees for me, doing things with her tongue that made me, for a moment, believe I had ascended to a new realm of existence.

Ivy and I have enjoyed making up for lost time. After the dramatic turn to our Qiton trip, we arranged another vacation, this one thankfully free of pirates or revenge schemes. Since then, it has been one night after another of careful exploration of each other's desires.

"Dahni, I believe there was something you wanted to do as well?"

I glance at my Ap'hati, who watches me with a knowing expression, and take a moment to calm the rush of heat that flooded me as I thought of my lehti.

Clearing my throat, I rise and meet Ivy's gaze. "There is something I would like to do if my *lehti* will join me."

Ivy frowns but stands to come around the table. When she passes BJ, who is bouncing his little sa'aih on his lap, he reaches out and squeezes her hand.

As a true older brother, our son is what Ivy calls a "baby hog." He is rarely found without his sister and has spent the entire Kal Sai entertaining his young cousins. Even now, as little Nisi babbles happily on his lap, her hand fisted tightly in his newly short hair, BJ doesn't make a move to dislodge her.

Ivy pauses to lean down and kiss his head, then our daughter's, before continuing to me.

I take her hands, bringing them to my lips, and she draws sounds of approval from those watching when she returns the gesture.

"I love you." Hearing her say this, I wonder, as I have often over the past rotations, how I ever thought she didn't mean everything to me.

Still, nerves make my voice catch when I speak. "*Lehti,* being here with those I love would not be complete without those I love the most—our son, our daughter, and you. On this day, when my family welcomes me back into the warmth of its embrace, I would pledge my commitment to you," I drop to a knee, and Ivy's eyes widen, "in hopes that you will say yes."

Her smile is brilliant as she nods. "Of course, I say yes."

Reaching into my pocket, I pull out the box hidden there. Ivy gasps when I open it, and I take the ring out to slip it onto her finger. She raises her hand, peering closely at the ring, her smile slowly shifting into a frown. "Ba'ir, this looks like..."

FEIN COLONY TWENTY-ONE ROTATIONS AGO

She made it.

The last thing I remember is the pod ascending into the atmosphere, taking Ivy away to safety.

I smile with the thought, tasting blood in my mouth and feeling it sticky on my skin. It clouds my eyes when I peel them open.

Shifting to my side, I groan as my ribs protest, but grit my teeth and push onto my bottom in what turns out to be a small cage. There is barely enough room to sit, so I keep my head ducked to remain fully upright. In this position, instead of being uncomfortable, the compression relieves some of the ache from my injuries.

Inhaling a lungful of fire and grit, I attempt to assess what has been damaged, but there is too much pain in too many places. There's also pressure building in my head. It's concentrated at the base of my skull, which cannot mean anything good. I raise a hand to feel for a wound, only to realize my fist is clenched around something hard.

There isn't much light, but I bring my hand beneath my face and open it to find the glittering stone I chose for Ivy nestle inside. I must have gripped it in panic as we fled from the cave.

The stone casts colorful prisms along the walls of my cell, and in them I see the beauty of my lehti's metal-encased smile and her kind brown eyes. I feel the joy she brought to my life, if only for a short while.

My shirt is torn on the side. Feeling with my other hand, I find the gash beneath; it's deep. I can recall the burn of the claw slicing through my flesh as I screamed for the pod to take Ivy away.

Sinking my teeth into my arm to muffle my whimpers, I brace myself and push the stone beneath my skin, using my finger to wedge it below my First heart, accepting the agony as different than the rest of the pain I feel.

This pain is worth it.

This pain is for Ivy.

When it's done, I settle back onto my side, focusing on the feel of it and letting everything else drift away.

I don't know what fate awaits me, but I know that whatever it is, eventually, it will lead me back to her.

THE END